A Dying Echo

A Yorkshire Murder Mystery

DCI Tom Raven Crime Thrillers
Book 9

M S MORRIS

This book is a work of fiction and, except in the case of historical fact, any resemblance to actual persons, living or dead, is purely coincidental.

Margarita Morris and Steve Morris have asserted their right under the Copyright, Designs and Patents Act 1988 to be identified as the authors of this work.

Published by Landmark Media, a division of Landmark Internet Ltd.

M S Morris® and Tom Raven® are registered trademarks of Landmark Internet Ltd.

Copyright © 2025 Margarita Morris & Steve Morris

msmorrisbooks.com

All rights reserved.
ISBN-13: 978-1-914537-43-1

CHAPTER 1

'You said you were going to give me the name of a murderer.'

Detective Chief Inspector Tom Raven was sitting opposite the journalist and broadcaster Liz Larkin in the restaurant bar at Scarborough Spa. Liz sipped elegantly from a glass of white wine, while he cradled a sparkling mineral water with ice and lemon. The blackness of the window next to them reflected their contrasting images – hers pale, with long blonde hair tumbling over her shoulders; his dark, with coal tar hair and black woollen coat, the collar turned up. Outside, the autumn wind gave a low howl. A storm was on its way.

To an observer, they might look like any other couple on a night out. But this wasn't pleasure for Raven. Strictly speaking, neither was it work. If this had been an official inquiry, he would have brought his sergeant, DS Becca Shawcross with him. As it was, he hadn't mentioned he was going to meet Liz Larkin.

Becca would have raised her eyebrows at the very idea. He could picture her look of indignation and hear her acerbic voice in his head. 'What does *she* want? You know you can't trust her. She's an attention seeker. She always has an agenda.'

Becca was right, of course. Her voice was the voice of reason. Just recently, she had stepped in and saved him from making a career-ending error of judgement when his anger had threatened to get the better of him. She was more than just his sergeant, she was his guiding light and, he hoped, his friend. But he had kept this meeting a secret from her.

He'd been wary about accepting Liz's invitation. He suspected it was just a ruse to drag him out on a cold October night. Liz had been shamelessly flirting with him ever since he'd first encountered her during a tricky murder investigation. She had hindered his efforts on that occasion, and had been a longstanding thorn in his side, but there had been a spark of attraction between them too, he couldn't deny it. He supposed he ought to feel flattered, as she was undeniably a beautiful woman and some fifteen years his junior. But if that was her true motive, he should definitely have refused to play along. Liz Larkin was a dangerous woman, the type not to be trusted. The type he so often seemed to find himself drawn to.

'What murderer?' he prompted.

Liz gave him an enigmatic smile. 'We'll come to that in a moment. First, a bit of background.'

Maybe it was the chance to revisit a long-lost part of his youth that had finally persuaded him to agree. Echoes of Mercury were playing at Scarborough Spa, the final night of their sellout UK comeback tour. And Liz had two tickets. How could he refuse?

She leaned across the table towards him. 'How much do you know about what happened to Echoes of Mercury back in the day?'

'I know all about it,' said Raven. 'The big mystery. Who doesn't?'

Liz's face broke into a grin. 'I bet you were a fan. Go on, admit it.'

'A huge fan,' admitted Raven with a smile. 'Still am, in

fact.'

He'd first heard the band play live at the spa decades ago, as a teenager, with his then-girlfriend Donna Craven. A vision of Donna flashed unbidden into his mind now, aged sweet sixteen. Strawberry blonde hair, red parted lips. The face of an angel and the figure of a goddess.

They'd lost their virginity to each other listening to *Let's Go To Bed* by The Cure. Echoes of Mercury had been another of the goth bands they'd played while having sex.

And there had been a lot of sex.

Whenever his dad was out on the fishing boat and his mum was at work they would retreat to his top-floor bedroom, crank up the stereo and jump under the covers. When he was alone, he had played their music to remind himself of Donna. The sound had blasted out of his stereo on a near-continuous loop. He'd driven his father mad with the racket. His mother had suffered in silence. Those were the days when no one listened to music on headphones. The heavy bass guitars, thudding drums, and melancholy lyrics had been the soundtrack to his formative years. He still loved their music, and now he had the chance to hear them once again.

'So I hardly need to tell you that the band's original frontman went missing and was never seen again,' said Liz.

Raven regarded her as she casually sipped her wine. Tonight, Liz seemed different. For once, they were alone, with no film crew to record his every word for a breaking news story. Off-air, she seemed softer and more relaxed. She wasn't dressed in one of her primary-coloured power suits; instead, she wore a pair of skintight black jeans and a leather biker's jacket. Her hair fell in soft waves and her eyes sparkled like emeralds.

'Mickey Flint,' said Raven.

The news had hit him badly as a teenager. Mickey, the moody lead singer of Echoes of Mercury, whose gravelly vocals Raven could still hear in his head, had simply vanished off the face of the earth, leaving his fans distraught. It had been front-page news for a short period and then the band had fallen into oblivion, overtaken by newer, younger groups whose music sounded manufactured to Raven's ears.

Liz leaned closer, her perfume firing up his emotions with a deep-seated memory. He'd know that scent anywhere.

Obsession by Calvin Klein. Donna's Saturday job behind the perfume counter at Boots had given her access to the sample bottles and she had liberally doused herself in the stuff each week. The smell had lingered on his bedsheets.

'Mickey disappeared in 1990,' said Liz, 'the night before the band was due to embark on their debut tour of America. In the days leading up to his disappearance, Mickey's behaviour became very odd. He gave a TV interview in which he appeared to be answering different questions to the ones the interviewer was asking him. He was admitted to hospital with a suspected drug overdose, although the hospital lost the blood samples and the reason for his illness was never officially confirmed. He got into a fight with a fan who came to his home. He also withdrew large sums of cash from his bank account but left all the cash behind, as well as his car keys. And although there was still money left in his account, it was never touched.'

Ever the journalist – she always had the facts at her fingertips.

'I was sixteen at the time,' Raven told her. 'And since we're trading facts, I can tell you that the band had been going for four years. Their first record was released in 1987. I can also tell you that Mickey's body was never found, and in fact his manager received a letter purporting to be from Mickey saying that he was alive and well and not to worry. In fact, a witness claimed to have spoken to him in the grounds of Whitby Abbey a week after his last confirmed sighting, and a month later he was spotted in Brazil. But there were no records of him ever getting on a plane, and he left his passport behind with his wallet.'

Liz nodded, impressed. 'Mickey was twenty-two years

old when he vanished. Possible explanations include' – she started to tick them off on her manicured fingers – 'one: suicide, although as you say, no body was ever found; two: he ran away because of the pressure he was under and is still out there somewhere, possibly under an assumed identity; three: abduction, or four: murder.'

Raven sat up straighter. 'Are you saying you have evidence that Mickey Flint was murdered?'

A bell rang, indicating that the show was about to start, and the other audience members began making their way towards the concert hall.

Liz finished her wine and stood up. 'I'll tell you afterwards. Come on, I'm sure you don't want to miss this gig.'

Raven got to his feet with a sigh and followed her into the auditorium. Really, this woman was impossible. But she was right – he didn't want to miss the music.

CHAPTER 2

Becca Shawcross shivered and hugged her mug of steaming tea to keep her hands warm. The wind was picking up and soon she would be forced back indoors. But she wanted to savour the moment for as long as possible.

From the tiny balcony of her loft apartment, she surveyed the sparkling lights illuminating the broad sweep of the South Bay. The incredible view was the reason she had chosen to live in this poky, one-bedroom flat. It certainly didn't have much else to recommend it. When her parents had visited, they had been visibly dismayed by the lack of facilities in the kitchen, and the black mould festering in the poorly ventilated bathroom. Her mother had suggested she'd be better off moving back home.

'You can come back whenever you like, Becca, love,' Sue had insisted. 'We haven't turned your old bedroom into a guest room. We've kept it just like you left it, haven't we, David?'

But Becca wasn't going back to live at her parents' B&B. Especially now that her annoying brother, Liam, had returned to live there. She loved her parents, her grandparents too, and even her brother, but she needed her independence. 'I'm fine here, Mum,' she said. 'The flat's plenty big enough for me. And I'll put some bleach on the mould tomorrow. That will fix it.'

Her hilltop eyrie gave her a grand view of the harbour and lighthouse beneath the headland, the Grand Hotel standing proud in the centre of the bay, and the Victorian spa buildings on the far shore against the backdrop of Oliver's Mount. And almost directly below her flat, in the narrow old street at the bottom of the hill, was Raven's house.

Becca had only been inside the house on Quay Street once, when she had assisted Raven with an "off-the-record" investigation – an episode that had given her a terrifying glimpse into her boss's inner darkness. Although he was outwardly calm, an anger burned deep inside him, a dark rage that could boil over into violence if provoked. A fury that frightened her to the core.

She wondered what Raven was doing now. He didn't have a social life. On a night like this, he was probably drinking strong black coffee in his front room and listening to terrible music from his ancient CD collection. The image brought a smile to her face. He'd helped her move into her new flat, but even though they were practically neighbours, he'd never asked her round for a cup of tea. Becca's mother, Sue, was always nagging her to invite Raven to the family guest house on North Marine Road for Sunday lunch, but Becca couldn't picture her grumpy boss making small talk with her parents. He was a very private person.

And yet, he'd briefly let her into his life. They'd worked together to find the person who had killed his own mother. Then, standing on this very balcony, squashed side-by-side, he had told her that now she was living up the hill she'd be able to keep an eye on him. She had laughed it off, but he sounded as if he really meant it. As if he needed her to watch over him. As if he didn't trust himself to make the right choices without her by his side. The thought warmed her, but she didn't know how to reach out to him.

Invite herself round for tea, perhaps? No, that wasn't going to happen.

She thought of his house – the polished wooden floors, the white-painted walls, the modern, minimalist furniture. Everything tidy and in its place. Raven's Black Labrador, Quincey, would be snoozing contentedly in front of the fireplace, or perhaps laying his head in Raven's lap.

Music and laughter drifted up from the fairground and bars on the foreshore. It was Saturday night and it seemed that half of Scarborough's residents were out enjoying themselves despite the weather. Becca had no one to go out with that evening. Liam was probably out with mates, but Becca had no desire to tag along with him. She wondered what her former flatmate, Ellie Earnshaw, was up to now. Ellie always knew how to have a good time. On a Saturday night, she was usually drinking wine or cocktails somewhere with friends before going on to a nightclub. Living with Ellie had been exhausting, but now Becca missed her. She should message her and suggest they catch up. She didn't want to lose contact.

The wind blew the first cold drops of rain against her face and Becca retreated reluctantly into the warmth of her flat. A storm was forecast for this weekend and it seemed to have begun. She pulled the roof window shut but left the blinds open, allowing the harbour lights to cast their shimmering glow into the room.

She sat on the sofa and picked up the file outlining the exams she would need to pass for promotion to detective inspector. Now that she lived alone, she had peace and quiet to focus on her career. Raven had suggested she should be looking for promotion in the next six to twelve months, having – in the words of the National Police Promotion Framework – demonstrated competence in her present rank of detective sergeant. Now there was just the matter of studying for and passing the exams. Well, she had nothing better to do this evening so she might as well get started.

She turned to the first page and started scanning the alphabetical list of subjects that might come up in the exam. Child protection; criminal damage; firearms and gun crime; homicide. The list went on for pages. She yawned. She should have started earlier in the day when she wasn't so tired. But was she really expected to give up her weekends after a hard week at work?

Her phone rang, a welcome distraction. She checked the caller ID before answering. *Sue.* Her mum's calls were rarely short, and Becca was glad she had made that mug of tea.

'Hi, Mum. How are things?'

'Oh, Becca, love.' Sue sounded out of breath and close to tears. 'I'm calling from the hospital.'

'The hospital? What's wrong?'

'It's your grandmother.'

The study file slid from Becca's lap to the floor, forgotten.

*

'Under here!' said Ellie, grabbing Hannah's arm.

They ran, laughing, under the bus shelter as the first big drops of rain began pelting against the glass. Quincey, Raven's Black Labrador, shook himself dry, spraying them in yet more water. They collapsed, laughing, onto the bench. Even getting soaked on a Saturday night was funny after a few glasses of wine.

They were on a girls' night out, Quincey their only male escort. Ellie had sworn off men after her breakup with Liam Shawcross, and Hannah's job had been to listen and console. She hadn't needed to do much consoling, however. Her friend was never down for long and had perked up considerably after a few glasses, toasting Quincey and declaring that dogs were far more reliable than men and a solid bet all round.

Ellie gave the dog's head a good rub. 'How come you're looking after Quincey on a Saturday night anyway? Isn't your dad at home?'

'He's gone to hear some ageing rockers playing at the spa,' Hannah giggled. 'He asked me if I wanted to go with him, but I declined. I bet half the audience are collecting their pensions.' The truth was she didn't want to be dependent on her dad for her social life. How sad would that be?

'Hmm,' said Ellie, suddenly serious for a moment, 'talking of pensions, have you given any thought to your future?'

Hannah looked at her friend in surprise. 'I'm not planning to retire yet. I'm only twenty-two.'

Yet Hannah knew that retirement wasn't what Ellie was referring to. Even after half a bottle of wine, Ellie was still the astute businesswoman who managed a brewery. Whereas Hannah had no idea what she was going to do for a career. After a law degree from Exeter University, she'd walked into an internship with a firm of defence lawyers in Scarborough, and a week later had walked straight out again, unable to stomach the idea of spending the rest of her life defending crooks. Since then she'd been waitressing at Ellie's dad's restaurant while she "sorted herself out". It was money to tide her over, and she enjoyed working at the bistro. But she knew she was in danger of drifting.

'You can't spend the rest of your life as a waitress,' said Ellie, 'not a high-flyer like you.'

'I don't intend to,' said Hannah.

'Good. So what is it that you really want to do?'

'Well, I mean, I...' The problem was, Hannah didn't have a clue what she wanted. There were so many options, and she didn't seem to be qualified for any of them, apart from the one she had already rejected.

'Let me ask you a different question, then,' said Ellie. 'What are you passionate about?'

Hannah thought about it for a moment. She liked a lot of things – books, music, art – but she wasn't creative or musical at all. She would need to find something more practical. But what?

'Okay,' said Ellie, 'here's another question. What makes you angry?'

This was a much easier question to answer. Hannah launched into a long list. 'Injustice. Racism. Child abuse. Poverty.' She could feel her pulse starting to race as she listed the big issues that got her riled up whenever she heard about them on the news.

'Now we're getting somewhere,' said Ellie. 'We need to dig deeper and see if we can come up with an action plan.'

'What, now?' said Hannah, startled.

'Totally,' said Ellie, seizing her hand. 'And for that I think we need another bottle of wine. Come on.'

CHAPTER 3

Raven followed Liz through to the Grand Hall, a spacious auditorium with an ornate gallery running around the sides and back. Music was pumping out of the loudspeakers, but it wasn't Echoes of Mercury, just something to warm the audience up. They made their way almost to the front of the stalls and along the narrow row to the centre, Raven struggling as usual with his bad leg, stepping on toes as he went.

'This is us,' said Liz brightly, taking a seat. 'I got the best seats in the house. We'll have a great view.'

Raven nodded. They *were* good seats, much better than the time he'd come with Donna and they had skulked at the back behind a pillar.

Liz slipped out of her leather jacket, revealing a black sleeveless top that showed off her toned arms. Raven kept his coat on. He hadn't dressed for the concert, preferring to stick with his usual white shirt and charcoal trousers. Other concertgoers were sporting varying degrees of goth wear – military-style jackets, Dr Martens boots, black eyeliner and lipstick – even though many of them were as old as Raven, or even older. Like him, they had clearly discovered their love of music as teenagers and had not grown out of it. He wondered why Liz was so interested in the band, and what had drawn her here tonight. She was fifteen years his junior, just a baby when Mickey Flint had given his final performance here at the spa and then vanished into the night, leaving nothing behind but a perplexing trail of clues and an enduring enigma.

The supporting act took to the stage – a band Raven had never heard of. As his eardrums endured the blast of bass guitar and frenetic drumbeats he wondered seriously if he was getting too old for this sort of thing. He was relieved when the band wrapped up and stagehands started to prepare the stage for the main act.

The background music returned but at a much lower volume than the supporting act. In the relative quiet, Liz leaned closer to Raven, her perfume enveloping him. 'So, do you want to hear my theory?'

'That's the reason I agreed to come here tonight,' he said. Liz had promised to reveal to him the name of a murderer, and although he still suspected a trick, he was willing to play along. After all, if she really had found out what had happened to Mickey, it would solve one of the most perplexing mysteries in the history of rock music.

She spoke directly into his ear, her breath as soft as a whisper against the side of his face. 'I believe Mickey Flint was killed by Robbie Kershaw, the Echoes' lead guitarist. Robbie always wanted to be lead singer of the band. He also wanted Mickey's girlfriend, Skye, who played bass guitar. With Mickey out of the way, he got both of his wishes. Robbie and Skye are now married.'

'Is that it?' Raven was almost speechless with annoyance. Had Liz really dragged him here on one of the most miserable nights of the year to trot out one of the standard conspiracy theories that had grown up around the band over the years? *Robbie killed Mickey.* You only had to type the phrase into Google to find dozens of online forums chewing over the facts to support flimsy hypotheses. While the motive was clear, the evidence was non-existent. Which was why it had been impossible to put an end to the speculation.

'I have evidence that's never been seen before,' said Liz, laying a hand on his arm. 'I'll show you later. It's in my hotel room.'

Raven opened his mouth to respond, but before he could utter a word, the hall was plunged into darkness and the audience roared in applause as Echoes of Mercury took to the stage amid a blaze of flashing lights.

Raven's brain was in turmoil after Liz's revelation. What evidence could she possibly have dredged up after all these years? To support a charge of murder, you ideally needed a dead body as a starting point, and whatever Liz had in her hotel room, he was pretty sure it wasn't a corpse. He was more certain than ever that this was all just an elaborate trick to lure him out on some kind of bizarre date. Now, it seemed, he was going to have to accompany her back to her hotel room after the concert on the pretence of seeing some so-called evidence.

Whatever.

He resolved to forget about Liz's promise and just enjoy the performance. He settled back into his seat as the opening number began with a familiar guitar chord and a blast of synths, and the band launched into one of his favourite songs, *Twin Track*, transporting him instantly back to his teenage years.

Me on my track; you on yours.
Strangers on trains; closing doors.
These twin track lives of shattering shards,
They slice through your flesh,
And mine is scarred.

God, he'd almost forgotten how good the band was. Their dark, melancholy lyrics were one of the things he'd liked best about them. They had spoken directly to his teenage angst in metaphors he could grasp, especially after Donna, since the songs were mainly about broken relationships and shattered love. Here was poetry he could get his head around, not like the stuff they were taught at school. He found himself tapping his foot and singing along silently to the familiar words and tune.

Your shadow flickers in the pane,
Fading fast, blurred by rain.
I reach, but the glass won't break,
Your eyes, cold as fate,
Hold secrets I'll never take.

The band members had aged considerably since he'd last seen them – Stu on the keyboard, Pete on drums, Skye on bass guitar, and Robbie now on lead vocals as well as lead guitar. The men had more wrinkles and less hair, and Raven guessed that he did too. But in the darkness of the hall with lights flashing on stage and that well-known beat making every bone in his body vibrate, he could almost believe he was sixteen again and that the woman sitting beside him was Donna. As the music soared to its ear-splitting climax with a virtuoso display on the drums from Pete, Raven nearly put his arm around Liz, but pulled back at the last moment. He shook his head. What had come over him?

After another song, Robbie waited for the applause to settle, before holding up his hand to indicate he had something to say.

He leaned in close to the microphone. 'It's great to be back here in Scarborough!'

The crowd erupted in cheers and whistles.

'Best fish and chips we've had on the whole tour!'

Even louder cheers went up. Scarborians were rightly proud of their battered fish and thick, juicy chips liberally coated in salt and vinegar. Raven joined in the applause.

'Seriously, though,' continued Robbie, adopting a more sombre tone, 'this is where it all began a long, long time ago. And it's been many years since we lost our beloved friend, Mickey.' A hush fell over the hall. 'Mickey was a genius and without him the band wouldn't have existed at all. I know you all loved Mickey as much as we did and wish he was still here. It's a privilege for me to be standing here tonight, stepping into Mickey's shoes.' Respectful applause rippled across the hall. Beside him, Raven caught Liz raising a sceptical eyebrow. 'I'll have some big news for you at the end of the concert so don't go anywhere, but this next song is in memory of our departed friend. Wherever you are Mickey, this one is for you!'

Robbie bent down, picked up a water bottle, unscrewed the lid, and took a long swig. He put the bottle back on the floor and grasped hold of the microphone. A spot bathed him in cold white light. Wreaths of dry ice swirled around him, an echo of those black-and-white music videos from the 80s and 90s. Plaintive chords sounded from the keyboard, accompanied by a slow, rhythmic beat from the bass guitar and drums. Raven's heart swelled inside him. *Doctrine.* It was one of the band's great anthems, Mickey's tormented lyrics reaching across the years.

Raven closed his eyes, waiting for the familiar words.

No light without shadow; no truth without lies.
No life without you. Now bid your goodbyes.
The creed we wrote in blood and despair,
A gospel of ruin, whispered in air.

Each vow was a tether, a link to decay,
Each promise a spectre that won't go away.
We built cathedrals from ash and bone,
But the echoes remain, and I'm left alone.

Something was wrong.

Robbie had missed his entry to the third verse. Had he forgotten the words? Surely not. Even Raven could have sung this song, although no one would have paid to listen to him. He opened his eyes as the audience shifted in disquiet.

Robbie released the microphone with a groan. He clutched at his throat as if gasping for air. Then he swayed on his feet and keeled over forwards, his guitar crashing onto the stage. The microphone went flying.

The music stopped. In the stunned silence, Skye, the bass player and now Robbie's wife, screamed.

*

Becca jumped into her car and put her foot to the floor, pushing the Honda Jazz as hard as it could go around Scarborough's narrow streets and tight bends until she reached the hospital. Saturday night was peak time in the emergency unit as she knew only too well from her time as a uniformed officer. On top of the usual medical emergencies, the staff had to deal with a fair few alcohol-fuelled injuries, the result of late-night brawls or general idiocy. The reception desk was jammed and Becca looked around for someone to help her who didn't already have their hands full.

'Becs!' She turned at the sound of her brother, Liam, calling her name. He strode over to her.

She threw her arms around him and hugged him close. She had never been so relieved to see him. 'Tell me what happened.'

'Calm down. Everything's under control,' said Liam, disentangling himself from her embrace. 'They're doing tests.'

'Where is she?'

'Follow me.'

She hurried alongside him as he led the way along a corridor. The hospital's emergency unit was modern and spacious, but it still had the chaotic and frenzied atmosphere of any emergency department. She turned a corner and the sharp smell of disinfectant rushed up to meet her.

She was reminded instantly of the year she'd spent at the bedside of her former boyfriend, Sam Earnshaw, while he'd been in a coma following a hit-and-run incident. It had been the hardest year of her life. Sam had survived his ordeal, but their relationship hadn't. In different circumstances, they might have married and settled down together, but the situation had been too fraught. He'd asked her to go with him to Australia, but she'd chosen to remain in Scarborough with her family. For a while she'd regretted that decision, but now she was glad she had stayed. She would have hated to be on the other side of the world with her grandmother rushed into hospital.

Liam stopped at the end of the corridor and turned back to her, lowering his voice. 'Grandad phoned to say that Nana had collapsed and that an ambulance was on its way,' he explained. 'I drove Mum and Dad straight here. Grandad came with her in the ambulance.'

'What was it?' asked Becca. 'A heart attack?' She was aware that her grandmother took tablets for her blood pressure.

'We'll know soon enough.' Liam seemed to have matured during the short period since he'd moved back in with their parents. His recent run-in with Scarborough's criminal underworld seemed to have pulled him up short and perhaps given him the shock he needed.

Becca wished now that she'd gone to see her grandparents during the week when she'd had some free time. Instead, she'd spent her evenings enjoying the peace and quiet of her new flat. But it was too late for regrets.

In the visitors' room a doctor was talking to Becca's mum and dad who were seated either side of her grandfather. Her parents appeared to be in a state of shock and her grandfather looked frail and badly shaken. The doctor welcomed Liam and Becca to the conversation. His name badge read *Dr Clarkson*. He was in his forties, tall and spindly with greying hair that stood on end.

'I was just explaining that the CT scan indicates that your grandmother has suffered from a stroke. It appears to be quite serious but before we decide how to proceed we need to run more tests to establish whether it's a blood clot or a haemorrhagic stroke.'

Becca wasn't sure if her parents or grandfather were in a fit state to take in what the doctor was saying. 'And what will happen now?' She was aware that she had slipped into professional question-asking mode. It was a way of helping her cope with the situation. She wasn't going to be fobbed off with soothing words. She wanted the truth.

Dr Clarkson seemed to sense a fellow professional and responded in kind. 'We've transferred her to an intensive care unit where we've taken measures to stabilise her vital signs. We've put her on intravenous antihypertensives to control her blood pressure and reduce the risk of further strokes, and we're also giving her oxygen to help her breathing. In elderly patients there is always a risk of secondary complications such as pneumonia. There is also a risk of seizures which would be very serious indeed. We'll need to run further tests – an MRI and an ultrasound scan, as well as an ECG and blood tests – and then we'll know more about the situation and how best to proceed. But I have to warn you that, given the patient's age and general health, the prognosis is...' He hesitated before continuing. 'Uncertain.'

'I see,' said Becca. 'Thank you.' As soon as she had a chance, she would google everything the doctor had said to get a better understanding.

'Can we see her?' asked Sue.

'Of course,' said the doctor. 'But she's unconscious at the moment.'

Becca took her grandfather's arm and helped him to his feet. The doctor led them into a dimly lit room where machines hummed and beeped, keeping the patient alive.

The figure in the bed was small and frail, the oxygen mask obscuring most of her face. Becca barely recognised her grandmother. It broke her heart to see her lying there, so helpless, like a child. She reached out to touch the bony fingers lying on top of the blanket and finally burst into tears.

CHAPTER 4

The stunned silence following Robbie's collapse on stage was more overwhelming than the loudest music. But it only lasted for a fraction of a second before people were on their feet, craning their necks, pointing and speculating. Mobile phones were whipped out, the glare of screens reflecting the morbid fascination of the audience as they held their devices up to record the unexpected turn of events. It wasn't what people had come to see, but they were going to get their money's worth, music or no music.

The lights in the hall went up and the spotlights on the stage stopped moving. But the dry ice continued to rise and swirl, obscuring the scene in a white mist that made Raven think of a cemetery at night. Robbie lay unmoving where he had fallen. Skye dropped her bass guitar and ran to Robbie's side, screaming for help. The other two band members looked too shocked to move. One of the stage crew rushed to Robbie's aid and began performing CPR.

The spa staff began clearing the hall, asking the audience to leave in an orderly manner so that the emergency services could do their job. But Raven didn't wait for the people in his row to move. He pushed past them and headed towards the stage.

A security guard intercepted him, obviously mistaking him for a fan wanting to get close to his hero, or worse, a lunatic intent on doing harm.

'Not this way, mate!' The security guy held out a meaty hand to block Raven's path, his stance tense as if preparing for confrontation.

Raven reached into his coat pocket for his warrant card, aware that the movement could easily be misconstrued as reaching for a weapon, and thrust the card into the guy's face. 'Detective Chief Inspector Tom Raven. Scarborough CID. Please let me through.'

The security guy hesitated for a moment. 'And who's she?'

Liz had appeared behind Raven, having also ignored the calls to exit the hall.

'Liz Larkin, reporter with BBC Look North,' she said, answering for herself.

The security guard frowned. 'I'm not authorised to allow news reporters or journalists through.'

Liz stepped forward, her tone calm but persuasive. 'I'm not here in a professional role and I don't have a camera crew with me, but this news will be all over social media in a matter of minutes and you'll want someone who can give an accurate account of what has occurred. Someone you can trust.' She gave the guy a disarming smile. 'I work for the BBC.'

The guy's walkie-talkie crackled into life as someone in another part of the building called for assistance. Apparently there was a disturbance at the entrance with some people refusing to leave, even though it was obvious that, for once, the show really could not go on.

'All right,' grumbled the guard. He nodded them through and hurried off in the direction of the main entrance.

Raven turned to Liz. 'All right, you may have hoodwinked your way past that guy, but that's not going to work with me. I want you to keep out of the way and stay off the stage.'

Liz raised an eyebrow playfully at him. 'Whatever you say, Chief Inspector.'

Feeling a stab of pain in his bad leg, Raven clambered up onto the stage, flashing his warrant card at the stage crew before they could object to his presence. But everyone was too occupied by the fallen singer to pay him much attention. He pushed his way to the front.

Up close, he could see that Robbie was unconscious. A stagehand was still performing CPR but without any obvious success. There was a rosy flush to Robbie's skin, and his lips were cherry red, but his eyes were closed and his jaw slack. A line of drool trailed from his open mouth.

Skye was kneeling beside him, distraught. She was dressed in black leather trousers and matching jacket. Her jet black hair had fallen over her eyes as she wept.

A blonde woman stood beside her, filming the scene on a high-tech digital video camera.

Stu, the keyboard player, stepped in front of the camera, holding out a hand. He was dressed casually in ripped jeans and a long-sleeved shirt. His head was completely bald. 'Stop filming, can't you? Show some bloody respect.'

The woman complied and turned away.

'Has anyone called for an ambulance?' asked Raven.

'Yeah,' said another of the stage crew. 'They're on their way. Ten minutes, they reckoned.'

Raven watched as the stagehand continued to administer CPR, but it was rapidly becoming apparent that Robbie was dead. Raven's mind raced through the possibilities. Death by natural causes was the most obvious explanation by a country mile. The singer was getting on in years and a heart attack might well be to blame.

He turned to Stu. 'Did Robbie have any medical conditions that you were aware of?'

Stu shook his head. 'Not as far as I know.'

'Then did he take anything before the show?'

Stu's expression turned frosty. 'What do you mean, mate? And who are you, anyway?'

'I'm DCI Raven from Scarborough CID. And I think you know what I'm talking about. I'm asking if he might have suffered from a drugs overdose.' They were dealing with a rock band, after all. Who knew what the singer may have taken before going on stage? A puff of marijuana, an amphetamine pill, a quick snort of coke to help him relax and boost his confidence.

But Stu gave a decisive shake of his head. 'Robbie? Nah. He never touched drugs.'

Pete, the drummer, joined them. He had a thick grey beard and his outfit was even scruffier than Stu's. He waved an arm to dismiss Raven's suggestion. 'Stu's right. Robbie wasn't into anything like that.'

Raven could hardly believe that he was here, questioning his teenage idols. At one time they had seemed like gods to him, but their grief stripped them of any mystique. They were just people, stunned and powerless in the face of loss.

Raven's mind was already shifting gears. Natural causes might still be the most likely explanation for what had happened, but he couldn't dismiss the fact that Robbie had taken a drink of bottled water just moments before his sudden collapse. A member of the stage crew was just about to pick up the bottle and remove it.

'Don't touch that!' shouted Raven. He marched over to the bewildered stagehand. 'This is a potential crime scene, and no one is going to touch anything until I've had an opportunity to examine it.'

He glanced up at a sound of fresh activity at the back of the hall. An ambulance crew was arriving, their footsteps echoing across the polished floor as they covered the length of the hall, weaving past stunned onlookers and making their way up onto the stage. The assembled members of the band and stage crew stepped back. Stu took Skye by the hand and gently led her aside so that the paramedics could get to work. They quickly assessed the situation, removed Robbie's shirt and attached a defibrillator to his chest.

'Stand clear!' commanded the lead paramedic.

Everyone waited in breathless silence.

Robbie's torso and limbs jerked suddenly as the machine sent an electric shock through his body. It was almost as if he had returned to life. Yet a moment later, he lay as motionless as before.

The paramedics tried again, with the same result.

They gave it one last go before pronouncing him dead.

A sombre silence fell over the stage. A moment of respect to mark the passing of a much-loved musician. Skye's sobbing filled the silence.

And then a stocky, ginger-haired man with a wild tangle of a beard blundered onto the stage from the wings. 'Jeez, guys, what the fuck's going on?' He was Scottish. Glaswegian, judging by his accent, and older than the band members – probably in his mid- to late sixties. The man's ruddy complexion and the tangle of broken capillaries on his nose suggested a lifelong fondness for the bottle.

He was followed by another man of a similar age, who in contrast to the Scot cut a refined figure, his silver hair impeccably combed back and his Roman nose lending him an air of distinction. He wore a tailored suit and a shirt with silver cufflinks. He stood to one side, assessing the scene with detachment. The curve of his nose resembled the beak of an eagle.

The ginger-haired man stopped short of Robbie's dead body. 'Bloody hell,' he cried in anguish. 'Aw naw, man, not Robbie!'

Raven stepped up to the newcomer. 'And you are?'

'Chaz. Chaz McDonald.' The big man studied Raven from head to foot, before leaning closer to inspect his warrant card. '*Polis*, is it?' he asked, using the colloquial Scottish term.

'Police,' confirmed Raven. 'What's your role here?'

'I'm the band's manager,' Chaz declared proudly. 'Been with them since the beginning.'

'And where were you during the performance?'

'Having a drink with wee Rupert here.' He indicated the man in the suit. 'We came as quick as we could when we heard the news. Couldnae believe it.' He turned to Skye, embracing her in a bear hug. 'Come here, hen. Ah'm so sorry!'

Raven addressed himself to the man in the suit. 'And how are you involved with the band?'

The man extended a cool hand. When he spoke it was with an upper-class accent in marked contrast to Chaz and the band members. 'My name is Rupert Devizes. I own the band's record label.'

'And you were with Chaz while the band were on stage?'

'Absolutely. As Chaz said, we were celebrating the end of a successful tour with a finger or two of single malt.'

Raven's gaze returned to the dead man lying centre stage. The paramedics were preparing to move the body and the hall was now clear of spectators. 'This wasn't exactly the kind of tour ending you were hoping for, I expect.'

'Not quite.' Rupert's face betrayed no emotion. 'But they say there's no such thing as bad publicity.'

Chaz pulled an anguished face. 'Rupert, man, show some respect!' He gestured expansively at the other band members – Skye, Stu and Pete. 'I cannae believe it. First Mickey, and now Robbie. I loved them like my own wee lads.' A tear ran down his ruddy cheek. 'Come on, I cannae handle this right now.'

Chaz set off, taking Rupert with him. Stu and Pete began consoling Skye. The filmmaker stood to one side, her camera still in her hand but switched off.

'What's your name?' Raven asked her.

'Frankie.' She was about fifty, with blonde hair, darker at the roots, and large, dark-framed glasses.

'And what's your business here?'

The woman held up her video camera. 'I'm recording the tour for a documentary about the band.'

'You've been filming today?'

'Sure. I film everything. You never know when you might capture some unexpected gem.' Her glance shifted to the prone body, as if Robbie's death was just one of those moments she treasured.

'Hold on to the footage,' said Raven. 'We might need it.'

The woman smiled. 'I never throw anything away.'

The stage was rapidly clearing and Raven turned his attention back to the water bottle that Robbie had drunk from shortly before he collapsed. The metal bottle stood where he had left it, one of the few items that hadn't been knocked over when the singer crashed to the floor. Raven reached deep into the pockets of his coat, pulled out a pair of gloves and snapped them on. He picked up the bottle with care, unscrewed the lid, and sniffed its contents.

His nose wrinkled immediately at the sharp smell. Not everyone had the ability to detect this particular odour, but Raven belonged to the twenty to forty per cent of people who could.

Bitter almonds.

His stomach tightened as he realised that his instincts had been correct. Robbie Kershaw hadn't died from a heart attack or any other natural cause. He had drunk water laced with cyanide.

CHAPTER 5

'So, where does this leave your theory that Robbie murdered Mickey?' Raven asked Liz Larkin. To Raven's surprise, she had obeyed his instructions to keep off the stage while the paramedics tried in vain to resuscitate Robbie. Following confirmation of the singer's death, Raven had declared the area a crime scene and called in uniformed backup to clear everyone away from the stage. A funeral director had arrived to take the body to the mortuary, and Raven had arranged for the family liaison officer, PC Sharon Jarvis, to take care of Skye.

Then he had phoned Becca. She was the person he wanted at his side now. He knew he'd have to explain to her what he was doing in the company of Liz Larkin – and why Liz was still there – but he would worry about that later. The important thing was to get hold of Becca. But she wasn't picking up, and her mobile went to voicemail. He tried a second time but the same thing happened. He supposed she was out enjoying herself. It was a Saturday night after all. He couldn't expect her to be always at his beck and call.

Instead he tried DC Jess Barraclough who answered

immediately. She willingly agreed to come to the spa, sounding almost glad to be called to a crime scene. Didn't Jess have anything better to do on a Saturday night? Perhaps not. If it hadn't been for Liz Larkin's unexpected invitation, he would have been relaxing at home with Quincey, his feet up on a stool.

Liz ran a hand through her long hair, seeming put out by Raven's question. 'I still think it's possible that Robbie may have murdered Mickey,' she declared. 'His motive was clear, he had the opportunity, and the evidence I have in my possession...' She trailed off uncertainly.

Whatever this mysterious evidence was – and she still hadn't given Raven a hint of what it might be – even Liz was beginning to have doubts about it. Because if Robbie really had murdered Mickey some thirty-odd years ago, then who had just murdered Robbie? One murder in a rock band was believable, but two was stretching credibility.

Raven resisted the temptation to pour fuel on the fire and press her further on the matter. After all, he was grateful now that she had called him out of the blue with her cryptic promise and the offer of free tickets to what had surely been the Echoes' final performance. Not only had he been able to watch the concert, but he had been perfectly positioned to witness the tragedy that unfolded.

He was already thinking about what came next. Though he was convinced Robbie had died from cyanide poisoning, a full post-mortem examination was necessary, and he would need to fast-track it. Interviews with witnesses would be his next priority, and since he was here at the scene, he might as well crack on. With Skye gone, and Stu and Pete looking too upset to say much, he decided to begin with Chaz McDonald.

The band's manager was sitting alone with his head in his hands. Although he had until recently been in the company of Rupert Devizes, Rupert was now nowhere to be seen.

Raven approached respectfully. 'Mr McDonald? Can we speak?'

Chaz lifted his bearded face, giving Raven a mournful look. 'Aye. And you can call me Chaz. I'm not one for airs and graces.'

Raven pulled up a chair and sat down, while Liz lingered at his side. Raven knew she shouldn't really be there, but she was already involved and with her detailed knowledge of the band and its history, she might be able to help.

Chaz cast an admiring glance over her shapely figure. 'The *polis* get better looking every day.'

'She's not–' began Raven, but Liz jumped in before he could finish, demonstrating her well-honed ability to empathise with an interviewee.

'This must have come as a real shock to you, Chaz.'

Chaz's expression turned grave. 'Aye, right. Echoes of Mercury have been dogged by more than their fair share of tragedy over the years. First Mickey, disappearing just as the band was about to hit the big time. And now poor Robbie, right at the end of such a smashing comeback tour. I cannae believe it, man. It's like a curse.'

'Hmm,' said Liz. 'Two members of the same band murdered. What are the odds?'

'Murder?' Chaz's mouth fell open in surprise. 'You cannae believe this is murder! Who'd want to kill Robbie? Everybody loved Robbie.'

'Then what's your explanation for his death?' asked Raven.

'Well, I don't know,' said Chaz. 'That'll be for the doctors to decide, surely?'

'The post-mortem will determine the cause of death, certainly.' Raven had no intention of sharing his suspicions about the water bottle laced with cyanide with Chaz at this point in the investigation. He would have to wait for the PM results and a toxicology report before he could be one hundred per cent certain about the poison. 'But did everyone really love Robbie?'

'Well, sure, aye.'

'Were there any tensions in the band?' pressed Raven.

'Well...' Chaz pulled a chequered handkerchief from his pocket and mopped his brow. 'I cannae go into details, but when you've got a bunch of creative types working together, they don't always see eye to eye. That's a normal part of the creative process. It's where the magic happens. But I'm sure you can picture what it's like when you've got four highly strung folk and two of them are married. People take sides.'

'What sides?' Raven glanced up towards the back of the stage where Stu the keyboard player and Pete the drummer were watching over their instruments. They weren't talking, and Raven detected a certain coolness in their body language. It might simply be shock, or it could be that the two guys hated each other.

Chaz squirmed in his seat, manoeuvring his well-padded behind into a more comfortable position. 'I'm just saying there's gonnae be creative differences in any band.'

It wasn't the most satisfying answer, but it confirmed that tensions within the band were real. Raven would have to pursue this matter with the other band members.

'You've been with the band since the beginning, haven't you?' asked Liz.

Chaz brightened at her question, perhaps because he preferred a pretty face to Raven's grouchy features, or because the topic was more to his liking. 'Och, aye. They were just wee kids starting out when I discovered them. They were playing in a bar in Whitby on a Friday night, maybe twenty people in the audience and only half of them listening. But I can spot star quality a mile off.' He tapped his bulbous nose and gave Liz a conspiratorial wink. 'I offered them my services and the rest, as they say, is history.'

'So you know them all well?'

'Oh, aye. As well as anyone.'

'What were the dynamics like when Mickey was still alive?' asked Liz.

Chaz shifted again in his chair. 'How d'you mean?'

Liz lowered her voice. 'I mean that Skye was originally

Mickey's girlfriend, instead of Robbie's wife. And obviously Mickey was the lead singer, as well as writing all of the band's songs. Robbie must have been jealous of him.'

Chaz frowned. 'Let me tell you something, hen. In my world, everyone's jealous of other folk's success. What you need to grasp is that the confidence that singers, actors and other performers display onstage is very often skin deep. Beneath the bravura, these people are fragile. They crave affection, recognition and the adoration of their fans. That's what drives them.'

'So is that why Robbie killed Mickey?' asked Liz.

Her bombshell left Chaz floundering. He gaped at her and his accent grew even stronger. 'Ah dinnae ken what ye mean.'

'What I mean,' explained Liz patiently, 'is that everything points to Mickey being murdered. And Robbie was the most likely suspect.'

Chaz scratched his head. 'I don't know anything about murder, hen. Hell, I don't even believe that Mickey is dead.'

'Why do you think that, Chaz?' asked Raven before Liz could steer the conversation even further away from present day events.

The Glaswegian looked relieved to have Raven back in control. Perhaps it was dawning on him that Liz might not be a police officer after all. 'Because that's the only explanation that makes any sense to me. Robbie would never have killed his best mate, not in a million years. And Mickey wasn't the suicidal type. He just couldnae handle the pressure of fame, so he disappeared and went under the radar. It's my firm belief he's out there somewhere, alive and well.' He rose to his feet. 'Is that it for now?'

'One final question,' said Raven before Liz could intervene. 'What was Robbie going to announce at the end of the show? Just before he began the last song, he said he had some big news to reveal at the end of the concert.'

'Oh that.' Chaz shrugged. 'Probably nothing. You'll

have to ask Skye. She might know.'

'I will,' said Raven. 'And thanks for your time. Just one thing – how long are you planning to stay in Scarborough?'

'A few days, at least. There's always work to be done at the end of a tour. But then I need to head back to London.'

'Just be sure to check with me before you go,' said Raven.

After Chaz had gone he drew Liz aside. 'It's time for you to show me this so-called evidence that Robbie killed Mickey. I need to know if it's relevant to the current investigation.'

'Willingly,' she said. 'Like I said, it's in my hotel room.'

*

The rain had begun as DC Jess Barraclough was leaving her house and was torrential now, but Jess was an outdoor girl and wasn't fazed by weather. More of a problem was the unbroken river of people and vehicles all trying to leave the spa just as she was arriving. After a few minutes waiting in vain for a break in the flow, she abandoned her car and walked the last few hundred yards on foot.

She'd set off for the spa as soon as Raven called. A real crime scene was more appealing to her than another night watching police dramas on Netflix. Her social life was in the doldrums at the moment, although she hoped to remedy that soon. Arriving in the spa's Grand Hall, she slung her wet coat over the back of a chair and took a moment to assess the scene.

The hall had been cleared apart from a few members of staff who lingered at the back, whispering to each other. The stage was still set up for a concert, but the musical instruments – a set of drums, keyboards, microphones and guitars – now lay silent and abandoned. Police crime scene tape encircled the whole area. Her gaze alighted on Raven, who was conducting an interview with a large, ginger-haired man. Jess couldn't make out everything the man was saying, but his Glaswegian intonation carried well even at this distance.

Who was that woman standing next to Raven? Was it the TV presenter, Liz Larkin? Blimey, she hadn't wasted any time getting here. But what was Raven doing, allowing Liz to listen in to a police interview? It was well known that Raven couldn't stand the woman. Jess had to admit, though, she did look quite stunning in figure-hugging jeans and a sexy sleeveless top.

Jess continued to look around, certain that Becca must be here somewhere. Raven would have been sure to call Becca before he phoned her, but she was nowhere to be seen. Jess set off towards the stage just as Raven concluded his conversation with the Glaswegian. She stopped mid-stride as Raven pulled Liz aside and said something to her. His voice was too low to catch, but from the way Liz smiled at him, Jess felt sure that she was witnessing some kind of intimate encounter between the pair. The idea disturbed her in a way she couldn't articulate. She approached them warily.

Raven still hadn't noticed her arrival so she cleared her throat noisily to interrupt their little tête-à-tête. 'Boss?'

Raven moved away from Liz as if he'd been scalded. 'Ah, Jess, thanks for coming over at such short notice.'

'No problem. Where would you like me to start, sir?'

He handed her a metal water bottle sealed inside a plastic evidence bag. 'I'd like you to make sure this goes to the lab for a full toxicology analysis. Fingerprinting too.'

'Righto. Anything else?'

'That woman over there' – he pointed to a middle-aged woman in the wings who was speaking to a younger woman whose attention was fixed on her phone – 'Frankie, has been filming the tour. Speak to her and ask her to hand over all the video footage she has from today.'

'Okay. Is that it?'

'Speak to everyone who was behind stage this evening. I want to know who was where, at what time, and especially if they saw anyone touch this bottle of water that Robbie drank from.'

'Robbie – he's the victim, right?'

'That's right.' Raven turned away from her and began heading towards the exit, Liz Larkin at his side.

'Boss?' said Jess.

He stopped and turned back to her. 'Yes?'

'Are you leaving now?'

'I am. But you can call me at any time.'

'Very good.' Jess watched in bemusement as Raven and Liz made their way down the hall and left together through the main exit. Very odd. Very odd indeed. But not Jess's problem.

Instead, she introduced herself to the filmmaker that Raven had pointed out. The woman was middle-aged but carried herself with youthful energy. She had dyed blonde hair and was dressed casually in relaxed black jeans, combat boots and a bandana around her golden hair. 'Hello. Frankie, is it? I'm DC Jess Barraclough from North Yorkshire Police. DCI Raven said you've been filming here today.'

The woman held up her video camera as if to confirm what Raven had said. 'That's right. I've been on the road with the band for weeks. I'm making a documentary about their tour. I recorded hours of footage, just from today.'

'What kind of footage?' asked Jess.

'Mostly behind the scenes. Getting ready for the concert, conversations between band members, the work of the stage crew, last-minute preparations off stage. And then the concert itself, of course. I stopped filming just after Robbie collapsed.'

'So, are you the official filmmaker for the tour?'

'Not exactly,' said Frankie. 'I work independently. But when I heard that the band was planning a comeback tour, I contacted their manager and suggested filming a behind-the-scenes video. It's more a fly-on-the-wall thing than an actual documentary. I've been granted access to everything that goes on.'

'I see,' said Jess. 'Well, that sounds like it could be really valuable to us.'

'Happy to help,' said Frankie.

The younger woman that Frankie had been talking to glanced up briefly from her iPhone. She was about Jess's age – early twenties – and was avidly scrolling through her social media feeds, thumbs nimbly swiping and tapping away. 'There's loads of stuff online,' she muttered. 'Robbie's collapse is trending on all the socials. It's crazy out there.'

Jess couldn't tell whether the woman was happy about the situation or horrified. 'And you are?'

'Taylor Reed,' said the woman, barely looking up from her scrolling. 'OMG, look at this!'

'Can I see?' asked Jess.

'Um, sure.' Taylor reluctantly passed her phone to Jess. It was the latest model, worth hundreds more than Jess's own smartphone.

Jess studied the online exchange that Taylor had found. Three Echoes of Mercury fans had got into a heated debate.

@EchoesAndLies: History repeating itself all over again. First Mickey. Now Robbie's dead too. RIP

@FanFuryTheory replying to @EchoesAndLies: Don't believe shit, man. Mickey's not dead. He's still out there

@HiddenTracks replying to @FanFuryTheory: WTF? Prove he's alive!

@FanFuryTheory replying to @HiddenTracks: No, you prove he's dead!

@EchoesAndLies replying to @FanFuryTheory: LOL. Where is Mickey now then?

@FanFuryTheory replying to @EchoesAndLies: They don't want us to know. He could be anywhere, man

'Okay, thanks. I get the picture.' Jess returned the phone to Taylor, who took it back with trembling hands, clutching it tightly as if it were a lifeline. She immediately resumed her scrolling and tapping.

'Are you with the band too?' asked Jess.

'I work for the record label,' said Taylor without looking up. She flicked her long hair over her shoulder. 'I handle the band's social media accounts. But I wasn't ready for anything like this. It's just blowing up.'

'So, did either of you see what happened?' asked Jess. 'When Robbie died, I mean? Did you notice anything suspicious beforehand?'

'I was too busy sharing photos and replying to comments,' said Taylor.

'And I was filming,' said Frankie. 'I can't say I noticed anything suspicious, but in any case it's all on here.' She handed Jess a flash drive. 'That's everything I recorded today. Let me know if you need more. Like I said, I've been with the band since the beginning of the tour.'

'Thank you,' said Jess. 'Will do.' She pocketed the memory stick and headed back out into the rain. Never mind Netflix, she was going to have a lot of real-life video to watch.

CHAPTER 6

Raven and Liz were drenched by the time they reached her hotel up on the Esplanade. The storm was raging at full blast now, gale-force winds lashing biblical quantities of water in horizontal directions. Raven's coat hung heavy on his shoulders, rain streaming from its hem, while Liz's hair clung to her face in damp, windswept tendrils. They staggered inside like storm-beaten travellers from another world, the warmth of the hotel foyer a sudden, inviting welcome.

They rode the lift in silence, the air between them charged, broken only by the low hum and rattle of the machinery. Liz stood next to him, close enough that her wet hair brushed his damp sleeve. He didn't step away.

The doors parted at the top floor and Liz led the way along the deserted corridor to room 503. The sound of the storm outside seemed to follow them, the howl of the wind reverberating faintly through the walls. She unlocked the door and flicked on the lights. The room, a spacious double, came to life in a glow of subdued lighting.

Raven followed her inside, letting the door close softly behind him. He leaned against it, watching her.

'Look at the state of us!' said Liz, laughing as she shook water droplets from her hair. The wind had whipped it into a wild mess, wet strands framing her face like a mermaid. Droplets of water sparkled on her skin like diamonds. She looked younger and freer, as if the storm's disarray had added something raw and unguarded to her usual composure. 'Here, let me take your coat.' Her fingers brushed his shoulders as she eased the sodden fabric off him, folding it over the arm of a chair. Her eyes held his as she removed her leather jacket and draped it over his coat.

Raven's breathing quickened. He knew what was going to happen next and had no desire to stop it. He had known all along. This was the reason he'd agreed to come back to the hotel with her. Not for the case, not to examine evidence pertaining to the supposed murder of Mickey Flint by Robbie Kershaw, who was now himself dead, but for this, for her. To allow himself to be seduced by this woman whose perfume reminded him so intensely of Donna. It had been an emotional rollercoaster of an evening – the sounds of his youth, memories of his first love, a suspicious death right before his eyes – and Raven needed the physical release of sex. It had been too long since he'd slept with a woman.

Liz stepped closer, her eyes never leaving his, and he knew that he was powerless to change course. Her fingers brushed lightly across his jaw, tracing the stubble there. 'You're soaked,' she murmured. Her lips parted slightly as she tilted her head up towards him.

When her mouth met his, he responded to her touch. The storm outside felt like a distant memory as he sank into her soft kiss. Then they moved together towards the bed, leaving a trail of discarded clothes in their wake.

*

'Go home, love. Get some rest. You need to take care of yourself too.' David Shawcross pulled Becca into a hug. His arms were warm and steady, but his voice was heavy with weariness. It had been a long night. The ward was now wreathed in shadows, the dim glow of a nightlight casting long, soft shapes across the walls. The machines at the bedside flickered and beeped quietly. Her grandmother's chest rose hesitantly and then fell again, its rhythm faint and almost imperceptible.

'What about you and Mum?'

Sue Shawcross sat by the bed, holding her mother's limp hand as though sheer willpower might tether her to the world a little longer. Becca's grandfather sat on the other side of the bed, hunched over as if in prayer. His broad shoulders were slumped, and in the dim light he looked impossibly smaller than she remembered. Liam was sprawled in a chair in the corner, his chin on his chest, snoring softly. Becca had brought her father a cup of tea from the vending machine in the corridor, but it sat untouched on the small table beside him.

'I'll get Liam to drive us back soon,' her dad said, his tone firm but his eyes betraying his exhaustion. 'Your grandfather can stay with us for the night. We've got plenty of spare rooms at this time of year.'

Becca nodded. It made sense to go home and get some sleep. The next day was a Sunday and she would be able to return and spend more time at the hospital without work weighing on her mind. But knowing that didn't ease the knot of worry in her stomach or the tension thrumming through her every muscle. Leaving felt wrong, like walking away from a vigil. 'Call me first thing,' she told her father, giving him a kiss on the cheek. 'Let me know how Nana is doing. I can drop in at any time.'

'Of course, love. Drive safely.'

She said goodbye to her mother and grandfather, and kissed her grandmother's cool forehead, lingering for just a moment. She murmured another gentle goodbye, then made her way to the hospital exit.

The corridors were eerily quiet, the echoes of her footsteps ringing hollowly as she walked. Her chest felt tight, her head aching from so many hours of worry. She reached into her pocket, pulling out her phone more out of habit than expectation.

Her stomach twisted when she saw the screen. Two missed calls. From Raven.

He'd phoned just as she'd arrived at the hospital. Nearly two hours ago. Her heart sank. She hadn't deliberately ignored him, but with everything going on, she hadn't even noticed the phone ringing. And, of course, in typical Raven fashion, he hadn't left a message.

What could he possibly want on a Saturday night? Knowing him, it wasn't likely to be a social call. Something must have come up.

She paused in the hospital lobby, glancing at the rain hammering against the glass doors. She hit the call button, pressing the phone to her ear. It rang. Once, twice. Then it went to voicemail. She listened to his familiar deep voice.

'Raven here. Leave a message after the tone.'

She didn't trust herself to speak. Not now. Her grandmother's pale, fragile face was still etched in her mind, the hum of the machines echoing faintly in her ears. She hung up without leaving a message. He'd see her missed call. If it mattered, he'd phone again.

The knot in her chest tightened further as she pushed through the hospital doors into the storm. The rain was relentless, pounding against her skin, soaking her hair and clothes in seconds, but she didn't care. Her pulse raced as her steps quickened, the wind whipping around her. By the time she reached her car, she was drenched, shivering, and barely aware of anything except the gnawing uncertainty following her into the night.

*

Raven must have dozed off because the next thing he knew, Liz was stepping out of the bathroom wrapped in a fluffy white towel, her wet hair tumbling over her bare shoulders.

She switched on the bedside light and perched on the

edge of the bed, the towel slipping slightly to reveal a tantalising glimpse of what lay underneath before she tugged it neatly back into place. Her eyes locked onto his with a playful glint. 'Time for work, DCI Raven. That's why you're here, isn't it?' Her lips curved into a knowing smile. 'Coffee?'

'Please.' He pushed himself up in the oversized bed, pulling the duvet over his bare chest. He had no idea what time it was or how long he had been asleep, but he felt more refreshed than he had done in weeks. The wind had finally calmed, although the darkness outside told him it was still night.

'How do you like it?'

'Black, no sugar.'

Her smile deepened. 'Same as me.' She handed him a steaming cup of coffee, the aroma sharp and rich, before pouring another for herself. Then she retrieved a battered, leather-bound notebook from her briefcase and handed it to him, climbing into bed. 'I think this is what you came here to see.'

Raven handled the old notebook gingerly, its worn cover dry against his fingers. 'What is it?'

'Mickey's journal. He kept it until just before he disappeared.'

'His journal?' In all the years of speculation surrounding Echoes of Mercury, there had never been any mention of a journal belonging to the missing singer. 'Where did you get it?'

'From his parents' house – a ramshackle place out in Broxa. Ever heard of it?'

The name stirred faint memories. 'Six miles west of Scarborough. Just a farm and a few cottages. That's it, isn't it?'

'That's the place. I visited years ago. Mickey's parents were still alive then, though I'm not sure what's happened to the house now.'

'And what? You blagged your way inside, and Mickey's parents just let you take his journal away with you? Did you tell them you were a journalist?'

'Of course I did. What do you take me for?' She gave him a playful swat on the arm, but her expression turned more serious. 'Anyway, they hadn't read it. I think they were too afraid of what they might find inside.' She opened the journal to a bookmarked page and handed it back to him. 'Start here.'

Raven adjusted his position against the headboard, the duvet slipping lower as he held the notebook. The paper was old, slightly yellowed, the ink faded. The entry was dated four days before Mickey's disappearance. The handwriting was untidy, almost a scrawl, and smudged in places – the sign of a left-hander. He squinted at the words, piecing them together.

Off to the States in five days. Chaz says he's sorted out a string of gigs. If he has, it'll be the first time he's ever done anything useful. Guy's a waste of space. We should ditch him when we get back...

Beneath the text was a sketch of Chaz stepping onto a cartoonish landmine, the cartoon perfectly capturing Chaz's facial features and hair – he'd had even more of it in those days. Mickey had been a talented artist, his bitterness laced with dark humour.

...If we get back. Shit scared that Robbie's gonna kill me. He wants to be lead singer and he wants Skye. Stu and Pete reckon I'm paranoid, but I've seen the way Robbie looks at me. Maybe they'll find my body in a ditch somewhere. Maybe I'll disappear and never be seen again.

Raven's chest tightened as he absorbed the words. Another sketch followed: Robbie, eyes dark with malice, devil's horns sprouting from his head, surrounded by crucifixes, guns, and daggers. One image showed Robbie digging a grave in a forest, Mickey's lifeless body lying beside it, waiting to be rolled in. A woman who could only be Skye hovered in the background, watching with wide eyes.

A chill ran down Raven's spine despite the warmth of the bed. Mickey had sketched this image and written those prophetic words just days before he had vanished.

He turned the page. More sketches, more entries. Page after page of ramblings and accusations. Fear and paranoia woven through every word.

'This proves nothing,' he said, closing the notebook. 'All it shows is that Mickey had a vivid imagination, and he was a good artist too.'

Liz's eyes sparkled with challenge. 'It also proves he wasn't suicidal at the time of his disappearance. And it shows he was terrified of Robbie. That's worth something.'

'Paranoid delusions,' Raven countered. 'That doesn't make Robbie a murderer.'

'Maybe not. But the police should have investigated the possibility at the time.'

Raven nodded grimly. They both knew that the police hadn't really been interested in finding the missing singer. They had regarded his disappearance as a publicity stunt, not worth dedicating significant resources to. By the time they eventually realised it was serious, the trail had gone cold.

'Let's say you're right,' Raven said, 'and that Robbie murdered Mickey and disposed of his body. Where does that leave us now?'

Liz's face fell. 'I don't know. Perhaps someone killed Robbie for revenge? Or could he have poisoned himself because of guilt?'

Raven shook his head. 'Or it could all be unrelated. Just a tragic coincidence.'

'Maybe.' Liz took the journal out of Raven's hands and set it aside, her movements slow and deliberate. She turned to him, her expression softening, her smile returning – not the one she wore for the camera, but something more private, more genuine. 'Which is why we need you, DCI Raven, to investigate this case thoroughly.'

She untucked the towel from around her breasts and let it fall away, her bare skin bathed in the soft glow of the bedside light.

Raven met her gaze, his hand reaching to her waist. 'I will investigate it,' he murmured, taking her in his arms. 'Most thoroughly. But later.'

*

Sometime later, he woke from a deep, dreamless sleep to a pale glimmer of streetlight reaching between the curtains. The storm was gone, leaving a hushed stillness in its wake. For a moment, he lay there, disoriented, unsure of where he was. Then memories of the night before came flooding back.

He'd slept with Liz Larkin. Twice.

The first time, frenzied and urgent. The second slower, more deliberate, but no less intense. He rolled over and gazed tenderly at her sleeping form beside him. Her soft, golden hair fanned out across the pillow, catching the glow from the streetlight. Her breathing was slow and steady, her features relaxed in sleep. For a fleeting moment, he wished he could freeze time and stay here forever.

But duty called.

A man had died on stage last night. He didn't yet know if it was murder or suicide, but it hadn't been a natural death. That much was clear.

He slipped silently from the bed, alert and ready for the day ahead. Liz stirred in her sleep, her hand twitching against the duvet, but she didn't wake. He allowed himself one last glance at her before gathering his scattered clothes from the bedroom floor. Dressing quickly, he slipped out into the corridor, carrying his shoes in one hand.

CHAPTER 7

'All right, let's get started,' called Raven. He glanced at the clock on the wall of the incident room. Nine o'clock on a Sunday morning, and his team sat bleary-eyed around the table clutching steaming mugs of tea like lifelines and nibbling at biscuits to inject a little sugar into their blood and some energy into their day.

Raven had skipped breakfast but was already three coffees in and riding the caffeine buzz. He needed to concentrate, yet even as he rose to his feet to begin outlining the events of the previous evening, his attention succumbed to the steady stream of memories fighting to break through the surface and knock him off course. He opened his notebook, feigning focus, yet the images kept coming.

Him and Liz locked in a fevered embrace; the heat of her touch lingering long after he had slipped out of room 503. Him, sitting alone in the hotel lobby, pulling his shoes on and tying his laces, grateful that the place was deserted.

It was still dark as he left the hotel. Birdcage Walk lay in murky gloom. The McBean Steps beside the Grand

Hotel were so dark that he'd had to use the light on his phone to see where he was going. That was the moment he'd noticed the missed call from Becca. The timestamp couldn't have been more damning – precisely the moment he'd been "otherwise engaged" with Liz. A knot of guilt tightened around his stomach, although – he told himself – he'd done nothing wrong and owed Becca nothing.

Nevertheless, he scurried along the Foreshore like a thief.

When he crept into his house on Quay Street, Quincey stirred from his basket with a soft whine and Raven hurried to calm him down, afraid he would bark and wake Hannah. He had no desire to explain to his daughter why he was coming home at such an unearthly hour.

'Good dog,' said Raven, patting the dog's head. 'We'll keep this between ourselves, shall we?' He crouched low to scratch behind Quincey's ears and waited until he settled back in his basket.

His secret was safe with his dog.

Now, showered and dressed, he felt wide awake and ready for the day ahead. Which was more than could be said of his team.

DC Tony Bairstow sat at his usual spot, neither especially energised nor sleepy, but Jess looked like she'd had a late night. No surprise, given Raven had sent her to interview witnesses at the spa.

Becca looked positively rough, as if she hadn't had much sleep. Neither she nor Raven had acknowledged their missed calls. Instead, Raven had texted her first thing, asking her to come into work. Her tired eyes darted to her phone every couple of minutes. Perhaps, as Raven had conjectured, she'd been out with a boyfriend the previous night and was waiting for a follow-up call.

The thought eased the peculiar sense of guilt he was feeling about his own romantic encounter. Although why Becca's love life should have any bearing on his relationship with Liz was anyone's guess.

He shrugged off the thought and returned to his

briefing. 'Echoes of Mercury were playing at Scarborough Spa on the last night of their UK-wide comeback tour. Does everyone know them? Late 80s, early 90s goth band.' He was met with blank faces as if no one else in the room had heard of them. He carried on, regardless. 'They split after their original lead singer and songwriter, Mickey Flint, disappeared. He was presumed dead, although that's never been confirmed. Last night, their new lead singer, Robbie Kershaw, collapsed on stage straight after drinking from a bottle of water. Efforts to revive him failed and paramedics pronounced him dead at the scene.'

Raven turned to Jess. 'Did you get the water bottle sent off to the lab?'

'Yes, boss. It's there now, but they won't process it until Monday.'

'Right. I had a quick sniff myself. Bitter almonds. My hunch is that cyanide was added to the water but we'll have to wait for the post-mortem and toxicology results to confirm.'

'So you think he was murdered?' said Tony, his tone even.

'We can't rule out suicide,' Raven replied. 'But Robbie didn't sound like someone planning to kill himself. Moments before he drank the water, he said he would be making a big announcement at the end of the concert. Why would he say that if he intended to die?'

'Maybe someone didn't want him to make that announcement?' Jess suggested, her pen poised over her notebook.

'It's possible,' Raven conceded. 'For now, we're going to work on the assumption that foul play may have been involved, and that someone deliberately contaminated Robbie's drinking water.'

Jess nodded, jotting down notes, but Raven's attention shifted to Becca, who was checking her phone again. The repeated action was beginning to irritate him. Whatever – or whoever – she was waiting for, it was distracting her from the case.

'Jess,' he continued, 'did you get the video footage from Frankie?'

'I did. There's hours of it, though. It'll take time.'

'Fine. Just keep at it. Look for anything suspicious – tampering with the water bottle, anything unusual on stage.'

'Yes, boss. I also spoke to Taylor from the record label. She handles the band's social media. Robbie's death is already all over the internet. Conspiracy theories are flying. Mind you, with Liz Larkin at the concert, it'll probably be on breakfast news too.'

Becca's head jerked up. 'Liz Larkin? What was she doing there?'

Raven felt Becca's searching gaze on him and found that he was unable to return it. Jess blushed pink, as if she realised she'd said too much. A faint smirk tugged at Tony's mouth. Was it really that obvious to everyone what had happened?

The silence extended and started to become awkward. Raven was going to have to say something.

'She invited me to the concert,' he said, his voice as level as he could make it. 'She had a theory about Mickey's disappearance. She believes Robbie killed him. Personally, I think that's unlikely. Anyway, enough about Liz Larkin. Tony, can I ask you to run the usual background checks on all the band members, their manager Chaz McDonald, and their record label executive, Rupert Devizes?'

'I'm on it, sir.'

'Jess, keep watching the video footage. I'm going to visit Skye, the bass player. She was married to Robbie, so the interview will need to be handled with tact and sensitivity. Becca, you'd better come with me.'

CHAPTER 8

Becca was barely holding herself together, her worries about her grandmother compounded by a broken night's sleep. Sue had called first thing to say that her grandmother was stable and that Dr Clarkson was waiting for the results of further tests before deciding whether or not to operate. Becca had wanted to rush straight back to the hospital but Sue had told her – practically ordered her! – to go into work. 'It'll take your mind off everything, love. Go and do your job, you'll feel better for it.'

Becca seriously doubted that, but she'd reluctantly agreed. 'Promise me you'll call as soon as there's any news,' she had insisted.

Jess's revelation that Liz Larkin had been at the concert, and Raven's sheepish admission that they had gone there together had almost tipped her over the edge. If she hadn't felt so emotionally numb in the wake of her grandmother's hospital admission, it would have cut her to the quick. As it was, she felt betrayed and angry.

She knew, of course, that Raven's personal life was none of her business and that it was up to him who he chose to spend his evenings with. But Liz Larkin? On screen, the TV news reporter might project a polished and professional look, but Becca had seen through that in an instant. At close quarters, Liz Larkin was an opportunistic and self-serving woman who thrived on attention and never missed a chance to get it. Her moral compass, if it even existed, pointed in whatever direction suited her ambitions. It hadn't escaped Becca's notice that Liz always made a beeline for Raven, fluttering her lashes and pointedly ignoring Becca's existence. Every question, every comment, was directed at him. Couldn't Raven see beyond her smooth skin and glossy hair to the ruthless operator beneath?

Well, he was a man. Maybe he couldn't.

Becca clenched her jaw, heat rising in her cheeks as she accompanied Raven out of the police station. She understood that by asking her to join him for the interview with Skye, he was attempting some kind of reconciliation, but her emotions were in such a tight knot she wasn't sure how she could untangle them. She followed him to the car park, the crisp breezy air doing little to clear her head.

He stopped next to his BMW M6 and turned towards her, his brow furrowed as though weighing up whether to say something to her. For a moment, Becca thought he might actually speak – might offer an explanation, an apology, *something*. But then his expression shifted, hardening into his usual stoicism. He shrugged, pulled out his key fob, and unlocked the car with a click.

Fine. If he had nothing to say, she wasn't going to help him out.

She slid into the passenger seat without a word, folding her arms as the tension grew thick and stifling. Yet if Raven noticed or cared, he didn't show it. The silence stretched as he started the engine and pulled out of the car park, the rumble of the tyres the only sound between them.

After a short drive, they pulled up outside an end-of-terrace house on Ramsey Street, nestled in the Victorian heart of the town. Becca regarded the unassuming building with faint surprise. It wasn't the kind of place she imagined a rock star living, but then again, she'd never met anyone from a real rock band before.

Raven cut the engine but didn't immediately move. He sat staring through the windscreen, hands resting on the steering wheel.

Becca waited.

'You know,' he said finally, his voice quiet, 'I owe you an explanation about last night. About Liz Larkin. About why I was there with her at the concert. She–'

'–You don't need to explain,' said Becca, cutting him off, her tone sharper than intended. She suddenly found she had no wish to hear Raven justifying being there with Liz. His reason was clear enough already. 'It's good you were there to witness the death,' she concluded in a softer tone.

Raven turned to face her, his dark eyes giving nothing away. 'Right,' he said at last. He opened the car door. 'Come on, let's go and speak to the widow.'

At the front door, Raven rang the bell and stood back to wait. Becca let her gaze wander over the front of the property. It wasn't a badly kept house but had the air of being unoccupied. A dripping gutter left a green streak down the wall. The front garden was scruffy where dirt and dead leaves had blown in from the street. No doubt the house had lain empty while the band was on the road.

The door was opened by PC Sharon Jarvis, the family liaison officer Becca had worked with before. Sharon was always dependable with a quiet competence that made her a natural at dealing with bereaved families.

'DS Shawcross, DCI Raven,' Sharon greeted them.

'How is she?' asked Raven, keeping his voice low.

'Much as you'd expect,' said Sharon, 'for a woman who saw her husband die in front of her. Come on through. She's in the sitting room.'

She showed them into a room that had been knocked through and looked out over both front and rear gardens. The room felt dank even though the radiators were hot to the touch. No doubt the heating had been turned off for months and was struggling to feed warmth back into the bricks and mortar of the old house. Skye was sitting at a table by the rear window, a full ashtray and a mug of untouched coffee in front of her. The garden beyond was unkempt, with bare branches and piles of rotting leaves pushed against the fences. At the far end of the long, narrow strip of overgrown lawn, Becca saw a modern garden pod, the sort of place people used as home offices or gyms.

Skye looked up as they entered. She was a mess, there was no kind way to say it. Her shaggy black bob hung limp, with strands of hair falling into red-rimmed eyes smudged with the previous day's makeup. Her thin arms were wrapped around her torso against the cold, though all she wore was a *Joy Division* T-shirt and a short black skirt. Her legs were bare, save for a pair of scuffed ankle boots.

'DCI Raven and DS Shawcross are here,' Sharon said gently. 'Is it all right if they ask you a few questions?'

Skye gave a silent nod and reached for a vape, taking a long pull and filling the air around her with a pungent haze.

'I'll put the kettle on,' said Sharon. 'Coffee?'

'Tea, please,' said Becca, automatically.

Sharon headed into the kitchen.

Skye studied Raven's face. 'You were at the gig last night, weren't you?'

'Yes,' said Raven, his usual composure faltering. 'We're very sorry for your loss.'

'Thank you.' Skye managed a faint nod, cradling the vape in her hand. 'It was a huge shock, you know. But... I've been thinking, and I know Robbie died doing what he loved. That's got to be the best way to go, right?'

Raven appeared unable to answer the question, so Becca stepped in for him. 'It's some comfort, at least, Mrs–'

'Call me Skye. I know that Robbie and I were married, but I always hated being called *Mrs*. I'm not – you know – defined by my relationships to men.'

'Skye, then,' said Becca levelly. She appeared to have touched on a sensitive topic for Skye. Not surprisingly perhaps, since her first boyfriend had disappeared off the face of the earth after she left him, and now her husband had potentially also died by suicide. Under those circumstances, no woman would want to be defined by her relationships to men.

Raven remained silent, so Becca continued. 'So, Skye, if it's all right with you, we'd like to ask you a few questions about Robbie and the band, and about yesterday in particular. Is that okay?'

'Sure. I guess. But... can I ask something first?'

'Of course,' Becca said.

'Why are the police so involved? I know there will have to be a post-mortem and all the official stuff. But... it feels like you're treating Robbie's death as suspicious.'

Raven finally found his voice. 'We're keeping an open mind,' he said, his tone firm. 'The post-mortem will determine the cause of death. Until then, we're gathering information.'

Sharon returned, bearing a tray laden with four steaming mugs and a plate of biscuits. Becca gratefully took a chocolate digestive, hoping she didn't appear rude. She hadn't had time for breakfast that morning and couldn't even remember if she'd eaten the evening before.

'Did Robbie have any life-threatening medical conditions?' she asked, leaning forward slightly.

'No,' Skye replied. 'Not that I know of.'

'And you discussed that kind of thing, did you? He would have told you if he'd been diagnosed with a serious illness?'

'Of course he would. But Robbie hardly ever needed to go to the doctor.'

'Okay.' Becca shot a glance at Raven. He really was making her do all the heavy lifting in this interview. She pressed on. 'And forgive me for asking this, but did Robbie have any reason to want to take his own life?'

'No!' Skye flinched, her eyes narrowing. 'That's

ridiculous.' She took another drag from her vape, her hand trembling slightly. Suicide was definitely a sensitive subject for her.

'What about money problems?' persisted Becca.

Skye folded her arms defensively. 'We got by. As you can see from this place, Echoes of Mercury never made us rich. But we were doing all right. In fact, things were starting to look up with the band coming back together.'

Raven perked up at that. 'How was the tour going?'

'It was good,' Skye said, a faint smile touching her lips before it disappeared. 'Until last night.'

'Can you talk us through yesterday?' Raven asked.

Skye shrugged. 'I don't know what to say. There was a lot of excitement because it was the final night of the tour. And it was Scarborough, so we were coming home. But that didn't really change anything. We had a rehearsal and sound check in the afternoon.'

'What time was that?'

'From two till four. Then we had a break of three hours before the concert.'

'What did you all do in those three hours?'

'I went for a walk then back to the bus for a nap. One of the sound crew brought me fish and chips.'

'The bus?'

'We've been travelling round the country on a tour bus hired by the record company. Bands don't normally stay in hotels when they're touring. It's far more private to sleep on the bus.'

Becca had often wondered how famous people managed to travel around the country without needing to stop at motorway services for a loo break and a sandwich like everyone else. A luxury sleeper bus was obviously the explanation.

'What about Robbie?' asked Raven. 'What did he do during those three hours?'

'Robbie preferred to spend time on his own before a gig. It's a lot of pressure being the frontman in a band. I didn't see him again until we were backstage at the venue, just before seven. And before you ask, I don't know what Stu or Pete did.'

Raven thought for a moment, then said, 'Just before he died, Robbie said he was going to make a big announcement at the end of the concert. What was he going to say?'

A shadow passed briefly across Skye's face, but it may just have been that she was getting tired. 'I don't know what Robbie was going to announce. He could be a dark horse sometimes.'

'I see,' said Raven. 'Before we go, I'd like to ask you about Mickey. You were a couple once, is that correct?'

The shadow that had played across Skye's features returned in earnest. 'That was a long time ago. Mickey and I broke up and then he disappeared. I don't know why you're bringing that up now.'

'Why did you split up, if you don't mind me asking?'

Skye set her vape aside and reached for a packet of cigarettes. She lit up and inhaled, holding the smoke in her mouth before sending a circle towards the ceiling. 'I just couldn't handle him anymore. The band had achieved such amazing success, we had a record deal and we were about to go on a tour of the States, but Mickey was a mess. Maybe he put too much pressure on himself, I don't know, but he couldn't write any more lyrics. He was convinced that nothing he ever wrote would be as good as his early songs.'

'He was blocked,' said Becca.

'Worse,' said Skye miserably. 'He was totally depressed. Maybe I should have stuck with him, but I just couldn't stand any more of his negativity. Robbie was always the positive one. I needed positivity in my life. I didn't need Mickey.'

'We understand this is difficult, Skye,' said Becca, 'but what do you think happened to Mickey?'

Skye looked out of the window before turning back. When she spoke, tears streamed down her cheeks. 'I think he killed himself. I left him for Robbie when he was already depressed, and it pushed him over the edge. I blame myself for Mickey's death.'

CHAPTER 9

'There's a sombre mood outside Scarborough Spa this morning where, as you can see, fans have been paying tribute to Robbie Kershaw, lead singer of Echoes of Mercury, who tragically died on stage during last night's concert.'

The camera swung to capture a shot of the bouquets of flowers that had been laid in front of the spa, then back to Liz, who was broadcasting live from the scene of the drama. She continued confidently in her best TV voice, injecting just the right amount of compassion and solemnity into her tone. 'It was the final night of the band's successful UK comeback tour and should have been a time for celebration. Instead, fans have been plunged into a state of shock and grief. I'm joined now by two people who were in the audience last night, Roy and Janet.' She turned towards the middle-aged couple. 'What do you remember from last night?'

The pair blinked like deer caught in the headlights as Liz waited for them to respond. Really, members of the public could be hopeless in front of a camera, but their raw, unscripted responses to shocking stories helped to bring the events to life. Anyway, with the band members and their manager unavailable for comment, Liz had to work with the material available. She gave Roy and Janet an encouraging smile, hoping that one of them would say something soon.

'It were dreadful,' said Roy eventually. 'One minute he were standing there, right as rain, the next minute, he'd keeled over. Just like that.'

'For dedicated fans like you,' said Liz, 'Robbie Kershaw was an icon. How did you feel, watching your hero die on stage?'

Janet began to tremble, her head shaking from side to side. Roy gripped her hand. 'It was simply the worst thing ever,' she blurted, dissolving into tears.

'Thank you so much for sharing your feelings with us,' said Liz. 'I'm sure that other fans will agree one hundred per cent.' The camera moved subtly to the side so that Roy and Janet were no longer in the shot. 'The cause of death is not yet known, but we understand that police are investigating.' She paused, just long enough for the viewers to form their own conclusion about that, before wrapping up. 'We'll bring you more news as soon as we hear it. This is Liz Larkin, reporting for BBC Look North.'

The red light on the camera blinked off and Liz relaxed her smile. She had called the studio as soon as the incident had taken place and arranged for a cameraman and sound engineer to meet her that morning outside the spa. This was her story and she was determined to be the first to broadcast it on breakfast TV, before Sky News or any of the other scavengers arrived.

She'd already persuaded her producer to foot the bill for her accommodation at the Crown Spa Hotel. 'This is hot news,' she'd told him. 'I was there. I can bring real insight.' She'd had to remind him that this was the band's second lead singer to hit the news, and that there would be revived interest in the disappearance of Mickey Flint so many years earlier.

But the breaking story wasn't the only reason Liz

wanted to stay in Scarborough. She smiled to herself as she remembered the previous evening in her hotel room.

She'd been attracted to Tom Raven from the day she'd first interviewed him following the murder of a young man whose body had been found in Scarborough harbour. The next time she encountered him was during the Whitby Goth Weekend. Windswept and wearing his trademark black coat, he made her think of Heathcliff standing against the backdrop of the ruined abbey.

It wasn't just his brooding good looks – although there was that, of course. She'd sensed immediately that they were kindred spirits. Beneath Raven's reserve, he was lonely. And in her more honest moments, she had to admit that she was lonely too, although she hid it well behind the glamour of her career.

She knew he found her intrusive when she was doing her job as a reporter. That was why she'd wanted to show him a different side to her personality last night. She hadn't been surprised to wake up and find him gone. It was rather romantic, the thought of him creeping out in the middle of the night after making love to her. She had little doubt he would come back. The chemistry between them had been explosive.

There was just enough time before her next scheduled broadcast for Liz to return to the hotel for a coffee and a freshen-up. As she made her way back up the winding cliff road, her mind switched seamlessly from Raven to the day ahead. Although she had more interviews lined up, she was itching to speak to the band members or someone close to them. Someone who might actually give her something useful.

As she entered the hotel lobby, Chaz McDonald was sitting in the lounge, speaking on his phone. He looked up briefly, his thick brows furrowed as if trying to place her, then his expression brightened.

An opportunity too good to miss.

Chaz rose to his feet as she approached, ended his call and put the phone away. He was unshaven, his suit crumpled. He looked like he'd slept in it. But he seemed to have recovered his sunny disposition.

'May I join you?' She flashed him her most disarming smile.

He grinned and offered her a chair. 'My pleasure. Sit yourself down, lass. Would you like a coffee? Or are you in the mood for something a wee bit stronger?'

Liz treated him to an indulgent chuckle. 'It's not even ten o'clock, Chaz.'

'That's never stopped me before,' he said, sinking into the armchair opposite hers, though when he flagged down a passing waiter, it was to ask for two coffees. 'Now then,' he continued, more seriously, 'I think you owe me an explanation.'

'Oh?' Liz tilted her head, her smile unwavering.

'You led me on a dance last night. You were with that Raven fella, so I thought you were *polis*. But you're far too bonnie to be a detective.'

'You're right, Chaz. I'm not a police detective. I'm a reporter for BBC Look North.'

Chaz chuckled, settling back in his chair and making himself comfortable. 'I knew it. A face like yours was made for the camera.'

'I bet you say that to all the women,' said Liz, smiling graciously.

'Only the bonny ones,' he replied, winking. 'Now, I didnae catch your name?'

She extended a hand. 'Liz Larkin.'

'Pleased to meet you, Liz,' said Chaz, holding onto her hand just a little too long. 'Now, would that be Miss Larkin?'

The arrival of the waiter bringing their coffees spared her from answering. She extracted her hand with a polite smile, ignoring Chaz's question. 'Now, Chaz,' she asked once they were alone again, 'have you spoken to any of the band members about what happened last night?'

He sighed, leaning back in his chair. 'I had a wee blather with poor Skye this morning but I've not had the chance to see either of the lads yet.'

'She must be taking it very hard.'

'The poor wee lass. She's had her heart broken, just as her luck seemed to be taking a turn for the better.'

'You mean because of the success of the tour?' prompted Liz.

Chaz's mood brightened again. 'Aye. A complete sellout. It was even better than I hoped for.'

'What prompted the band to reform and start touring again after such a long time?'

'That's a cracking question,' said Chaz, stirring cream into his coffee with a silver spoon. 'But the real question is, why didn't they do it before? I've been trying to get them back on the road for years.'

'What finally changed their minds?'

He gave her a sly grin. 'You could say it's my charm and powers of persuasion. Which are renowned between here and Drumchapel, by the way. But it's really no great mystery. Everyone needs to earn a crust.'

'You're saying they needed the money?'

He took a sip of coffee, leaving a smear of cream on his red beard. 'That's what makes the world go round.'

Liz raised an eyebrow. 'I thought they would have made enough money from their record sales. After Mickey's disappearance, the band achieved cult status. Even now they must still earn an income from streaming?'

Chaz shifted awkwardly, the armchair creaking under his weight. He scratched at his beard. 'Well, not every band earns royalties from their recordings, you know.'

Liz set down her cup, leaning forward. 'You mean they were paid nothing?'

Chaz hesitated, his gaze dropping to the table. 'They were paid for their time in the studio, and when they played gigs.' He dropped his voice. 'The truth of the matter is, hen, the record label stitched them up back in the day.'

'But you were their manager, Chaz. Wasn't it your job to negotiate the best deal for them?'

Chaz's face darkened, his shoulders stiffening. 'I did the best I could, but we were all just bairns back then. No experience, see? Whereas a shark like Rupert... he was born with a nose for the kill. That's one of the reasons I wanted to get the band back on the road. I knew I could do better for them this time.'

'You renegotiated their contract?'

Chaz wrinkled his nose at his coffee, as though regretting not ordering something stronger. 'I shouldnae be talking about this, especially with a journalist. Let's keep this confidential for the moment, just between you and me. All I can say is... there's something in the pipeline.'

Liz blinked, incredulous. 'In the pipeline? That's going to be a bit late for Robbie, don't you think?'

CHAPTER 10

Jess pulled her headphones on and settled down with a mug of tea to watch the video footage that Frankie had given her the night before. The flash drive contained almost ten hours of unedited footage in total, from the start of the day until Robbie's death. Jess didn't really know what she was meant to be looking for, but she would know if she saw it, she supposed. Of course, there might be nothing on camera and his death could be entirely due to natural causes. But there was also a faint chance she would see someone adding cyanide to his water bottle.

That would make up for putting her foot in it at the morning's team meeting.

She could have kicked herself for revealing that Liz Larkin had been at the concert with Raven. She hadn't meant any harm by it, in fact she hadn't meant anything at all. It simply hadn't occurred to her that it was an illicit rendezvous to be kept under wraps. But as soon as she'd spoken she knew she had made a terrible faux-pas. Raven appeared mortified and Becca looked shellshocked.

Jess considered Becca a friend, yet even she hadn't picked up on how Becca felt about Raven. Had Raven known? And did he feel the same way? Presumably not, since he was going to concerts in Liz's company.

Raven was so much older than Becca, but did that matter? Jess didn't know. She wasn't the best person to consult when it came to matters of the heart. Her first serious boyfriend had been found dead in the harbour, the victim of a vicious stabbing. And she had briefly suspected another guy who liked her of cold-blooded murder, which had rather soured the relationship.

Dead boyfriends and almost-boyfriends: dating was a minefield, and life was far simpler on her own.

She clicked her keyboard and watched as Frankie's video began to play and Scarborough Spa appeared on her screen shrouded in the half-light of early morning. The footage was shot with a hand-held camera that gave it an authentic, fly-on-the wall feel. Frankie, behind the camera, approached a sleek, black double-decker bus and went inside. This must be the tour bus that Jess had noticed parked outside the spa the previous evening.

The interior was like no bus Jess had ever travelled on. This was luxury on six wheels. Sofas, televisions, a dining area. Robbie was making coffee in the tiny but high-spec kitchen. He grinned at the camera.

'Here we are,' he said, unprompted, 'back where it all started thirty-seven years ago. Glorious Scarborough. We weren't playing the spa back then, mind you. In that first year, we played anywhere we could – in pubs, clubs and backrooms. Now, we return in glory! After my morning coffee, I'm off for a brisk walk along the sands.' He pointed to the top deck. 'Go and give those lazy bastards a prod! Tell them it's time to get out of bed.'

Robbie had certainly been in high spirits and good health on the morning of his final day. He didn't look as if the tour had worn him out. There was no hint in his behaviour that he intended to take his own life later that evening. He looked as if he was enjoying himself.

Frankie said nothing, but she obviously took Robbie's suggestion to heart because the next few seconds consisted of shaky shots of the staircase before she emerged onto the top deck. Here, bunk beds ran lengthwise down both sides of the bus, each bunk screened from the central walkway by a curtain. Jess enjoyed camping, but she could picture tensions running high when you were living cheek by jowl for an extended period in such an enclosed space. Annoying little habits could become major sources of discord.

A curtain twitched and Jess caught a glimpse of Stu, the keyboard player, unshaven and ashen grey. In contrast to Robbie, Stu looked like he'd had a terrible night. 'Hey, turn that bloody thing off,' he growled angrily before retreating behind his curtain with a rude hand gesture aimed at the camera.

Frankie said nothing in reply, but the camera advanced slowly along the bus.

Skye appeared from a bunk wearing a baggy T-shirt and not much else. She had authentic bed hair, sticking out at all angles. Spotting the camera, she put a hand out to shield herself from the prying eye of the lens. 'Shit, I look a fright in the mornings,' she grumbled. But she also laughed to show she didn't take herself too seriously.

Pete was nowhere to be seen but the camera lingered near the next bunk long enough to pick up the sounds of loud male snoring. Going on tour was not as glamorous as Jess had imagined.

The next clip was filmed inside the spa itself. A whole team of roadies was busy setting up the stage. They must have been well practised at it by now, but to Jess the operation looked chaotic and stressful. Cables weren't long enough, the lighting wasn't right, the sound checks were ear-splittingly loud. Stu and Robbie got into a blazing row over the location of the keyboard. Stu wanted it moved forward but Robbie said it would get in the way of his microphone cable.

'You just want all the fucking limelight,' said Stu. 'It's not all about you.'

'I just want the best for the band,' retorted Robbie.

Chaz wandered in front of the stage and attempted to mediate. 'Guys, guys, cool it, will yer? We're meant to be a team.'

Robbie took a swig from his water-bottle. 'You don't need to tell me that! Tell this arsehole.' He jabbed his thumb in Stu's direction.

'You're the arsehole!' said Stu. 'You don't know when to step back, that's your trouble!'

A pained expression crossed Chaz's face. 'Guys, let's all step back for a minute, shall we?'

In response, Stu stormed off the stage, leaving Robbie alone with the stage crew.

In the foreground, Chaz swung round to face the camera. 'Cut that bit!' But the camera continued to roll, panning right to reveal Rupert Devizes, quietly observing the row between the band members, his expression unreadable.

It seemed to Jess that Frankie was deliberately portraying the band in an unflattering light. First, the early morning shots on the bus. Then, the tensions prior to the concert. No doubt that made for a more interesting documentary. One thing was certain, though. There had been nothing wrong with Robbie's water bottle on the morning of the gig.

*

With a tip-off from the road crew, Raven tracked Stu down to a rough-looking pub on Eastborough. The kind of place where daylight barely penetrated, and the smell of stale beer clung to the walls. The Echoes' keyboard player sat hunched in a dark booth at the very back, washing down a plate of egg and chips with a pint of lager. Raven didn't know if this was Stu's breakfast or lunch, but from the collection of empties littering the table, it clearly wasn't his first drink of the day.

'Mind if we join you?' Raven didn't give Stu a chance to refuse the company, but slipped onto the bench opposite. Becca dragged up a chair and placed herself at the end of the table, angling her body away from the sticky residue of the table surface.

'So whassup?' Stu's eyes were bloodshot and glassy. He looked as if he'd crawled straight out of bed and into an old pair of jeans and T-shirt. He wore a two-day stubble on his chin and no doubt his hair would have been dishevelled too if he hadn't already been as bald as a snooker ball. Even the greasy aroma of fried egg couldn't disguise the wafts of stale body odour in his vicinity.

Raven sat upright on the bench, keeping a healthy distance. Yet if Stu noticed his discomfort, he didn't show it. 'We need to talk to you about Robbie.'

'Can't I eat my breakfast in peace?' grumbled Stu, cutting his way through the middle of one of his eggs and allowing a glistening pool of yellow yolk to soak into the surrounding circle of chips. He speared a chip with his fork, dipped it in the yolk and shoved it into his mouth. 'What's there to talk about? Robbie's dead. It's all over.'

'How do you think he died?' Raven asked.

Stu chewed his food, a bright sliver of yellow on his chin. 'Dunno. I'm no doctor, am I? Heart attack or summat?' He turned his attention to the football match playing on the pub's big screen.

Raven watched the man before him with a growing sense of dismay. Echoes of Mercury had been teenage heroes for him. He'd listened to their tracks, hanging on every word of Mickey's lyrics, relishing Robbie's guitar chords, Stu's synth melodies, Skye's fingers on the bass and Pete's drumbeats. Stu Lomas was a genius, the way his hands could conjure magic from the keyboard.

Look at him now.

It wasn't only Robbie who was dead. Raven's icons were dying before his eyes.

'We're waiting for the post-mortem,' he said flatly, 'but we're treating the death as suspicious.'

'Suspicious?' Stu ran a hand over his bald pate.

'You don't seem too fussed that Robbie's dead.'

Stu dropped his knife and fork with a clatter and wiped his chin with the back of his hand. 'You know what, mate? I don't think I am. Robbie was a pain in the arse, and I can't claim I'm too cut up about him kicking the bucket. Sorry for Skye, mind you. But Robbie? Nah.'

Becca leaned forward, her tone sharp. 'And what about the future of the band? You've lost two lead singers. What happens now?'

Stu gave a brief and bitter laugh. 'I've already worked that one out, love. We're done. But I managed to keep my head above water before the reunion. I reckon I'll survive.'

'How?' asked Raven. 'What were you doing before the band got back together?'

'Freelance stuff. Gigs with other bands. Studio recording here and there. Played on a cruise ship for a while – until Covid shut that down. Hell, I've even delivered pizzas to make ends meet. Life of a rock star, eh?'

It was a far cry from the lifestyle Raven had imagined for the band members in his younger days.

'But you must have been pleased when Echoes of Mercury got back together? Surely that was better than delivering pizzas.'

'At first, yeah,' said Stu. 'It seemed like a great idea. But you know what? This band is cursed. First Mickey disappears. Then Robbie drops dead. I'll be glad to see the back of it. So it's all over for me, mate. Guess it's time to start stacking shelves.' He returned to his breakfast of eggy chips, chasing them lazily around the greasy plate with his fork.

Raven exchanged a glance with Becca. He wasn't sure what he'd expected from this interview, but it wasn't this – cynicism drowning in lager and self-pity. The bitterness in Stu's tone was palpable, almost contagious. He couldn't say what shocked him more – Robbie's dramatic onstage death, or Stu's cynical display of indifference at the back of this seedy pub.

Becca broke the silence. 'So Stu, what do you think happened to Mickey?'

Stu swallowed the last chip and downed the remains of his lager, setting the empty glass down with a thud. 'What does anyone think? He killed himself.'

'Why do you say that?'

'You have to ask?' Stu's voice dropped, tinged with something between annoyance and regret. 'His lyrics said it all, didn't they? The guy was in a dark place.' He looked past Raven, his glassy eyes unfocused. '"What is a prayer but a desperate cry? A hymn to the void, to the absent sky,"' he recited quietly. '"I sang it for you, a dirge for the damned, but silence replied, cold as your hand."'

Raven recognised the words immediately. *Doctrine,* the anthem Robbie had been singing when he collapsed on stage. One of the band's darkest tracks – and one of Raven's teenage favourites. He could hear the melody in his mind, could still feel the weight those words had carried for him back then.

No solace in shadow; no peace in the light.
No end to the darkness; no end to the fight.

A hymn to hopelessness. A lament for Mickey.

'We should have seen it coming,' said Stu, a hint of compassion creeping into his voice for the first time. 'We just thought, yeah, awesome lyrics, man. But we should've known better. We should have reached out to him.'

'What was Robbie's relationship with Mickey like?' Raven asked after a pause.

Stu grimaced. 'What do you think? Fireworks, mate. Always fireworks. There's only room in a band for one frontman, and Robbie wanted that role bad. That's why me and Pete stayed in the background. It's safer there.'

'And Skye?' asked Becca. 'Where did she fit in?'

'She always went for the dominant male,' Stu said, his tone bitter. 'She started out with Mickey, but he was dragging her down. When she couldn't handle his depression anymore, she moved on to Robbie.'

Raven nodded slowly. 'And when the band reformed?

Were there rivalries then?'

'Not like before.' Stu's gaze dropped to his hands, which were trembling slightly. He quickly tucked them under the table. 'Robbie was the frontman. End of story. No one else wanted the job.'

'Are you all right, Stu?' asked Becca, noticing the tremor.

'Just need another drink,' Stu muttered. 'Can I get a pint?'

'In a minute,' promised Raven. His tone hardened. 'Just before he died, Robbie mentioned Mickey and then said he was going to make an announcement at the end of the concert. What was he going to say?'

'No idea, mate.' Stu rubbed his bald head. 'But I'll tell you what. Robbie was obsessed with Mickey. Maybe he wanted to dredge up the past again. I kept telling him to leave it alone. There was no point digging it all up.'

'What did he think happened to Mickey?'

Stu hesitated, his elbows on the table and his head in his hands. 'I don't know for sure, but he wouldn't stop going on about it. Did we think Mickey was still alive? Crap like that. Now, is there anything else you want to ask, 'cause I really do need another drink.' He made to rise to his feet.

'One last question,' said Raven. 'What did you do in the hours before the concert?'

'Why are you asking me that?' Stu's hand trembled as he reached for his empty pint glass.

'Just answer the question,' said Raven evenly.

'I don't know,' snapped Stu. 'Hung out with the road crew. Had a nap on the bus. What does it matter?'

'Did you touch Robbie's water bottle?'

Stu blinked, confusion flickering across his face. 'What? No. Robbie always sorted that himself – wait.' He paused, scratching his head.

'What, Stu?'

'I remember now. Pete offered to fill it up for him.'

CHAPTER 11

'I just need to make a quick call,' said Becca as they left the pub. Without waiting for a response from Raven, she walked a few steps away, turning her back for more privacy. She had promised to call her mother, and this was the first opportunity she'd had.

Sue picked up right away. 'Becca, I was just about to call you.'

Becca's breath caught. 'Is there news? Are the test results back?'

'Yes…' A pause. Just long enough for dread to curl in Becca's stomach. 'They've confirmed a clot in a blood vessel.'

Becca felt her heart quicken. She pressed her fingers to her forehead, bracing herself. 'Is Dr Clarkson going to operate?'

'Yes. He wants to remove the clot. The nurses are prepping Nana to go into surgery now.' Sue's voice wavered, and Becca could hear the effort she was making to stay calm. 'It's the best chance she has, but the operation itself is risky…'

That was all Becca needed to hear. 'I'm coming to the

hospital right now.'

'Are you sure, love? Don't you have to work?'

Becca glanced over at Raven. He was on his phone too, speaking in low tones, his back half-turned to her. He was probably talking to Liz Larkin.

Her resolve hardened. 'I'll make time.'

She ended the call before her mother could insist otherwise. A tightness gripped her chest as she went over to Raven. He was just ending his call. He looked up, expectant.

'There's something I have to do,' she told him. 'I'll be back later.'

His brows pulled together. 'You're leaving now?'

'Yeah.'

For a second, she thought he might argue. Instead, he studied her face and said, 'Okay, can I give you a lift?'

The offer caught her off guard. Now she felt bad for letting him down in the middle of a case. 'Thanks, but no need. My car's just up the road.'

He nodded, but something unreadable flickered in his expression. 'All right. Drive safely.'

She turned towards Castle Terrace, pushing down the wave of guilt. Work would have to wait.

For once.

*

As Raven watched Becca walk away, he wondered what was up. She'd been quieter than usual all day, seemingly absorbed in her own thoughts. Had he said or done something to upset her? She hadn't taken the news about Liz Larkin being at the concert well, but he had an inkling something else was going on – something she wasn't sharing with him.

He headed back to his car to contemplate his next move. Having spoken to Skye and Stu, he urgently needed to speak to Pete, the drummer. Especially now Stu had revealed that Pete filled Robbie's water bottle before the concert. He dialled Pete's number but it went straight to voicemail. 'Mr Hollis, this is DCI Raven from Scarborough CID. I'd be grateful if you could return my call at your earliest convenience.'

His conscience was pricking him, telling him he should really have called Liz Larkin by now, but he didn't know what to say to her. What did she expect from him? Was last night a one-off, or would she want to see him again? He knew he wanted to see her again. But she would distract him from his work if he called her now. Instead, he returned to the station to find out how Tony was getting on with his background checks.

The place was almost deserted on a Sunday afternoon, with most offices dark and empty. Tony sat at his desk, quietly engaged with his tasks. He looked up as Raven entered the incident room. 'Hello, sir. I've put in a request to the phone company to release Robbie's phone records. Same with the bank. Just waiting to hear back. In the meantime, I've run background checks on the other band members. Nothing noteworthy on Stu or Skye, but Pete has a previous conviction for possession of drugs.'

'What kind?'

'Heroin. This was about fifteen years ago.'

'Really? Did he do time?'

'No, it was a first offence, so he was sent on a rehabilitation programme instead.'

'He got off lightly.' Heroin was a class A drug, the maximum penalty for possession being seven years in prison.

'I've also been reading the file from the investigation into Mickey's disappearance,' said Tony. 'Skye was the one who reported him missing. The police interviewed his parents, but they didn't know what had happened to him. He wasn't living at home then, and the first his family knew he'd disappeared was when the police came to speak to them.'

'Who else did the police interview?'

'There's a witness statement from a taxi driver who says

he saw Mickey with a man the night he disappeared. It's an obvious lead, but that man was never identified. Frankly, the police don't seem to have tried very hard to find him.'

Raven wasn't too surprised to hear it. In some of these historic cases, the investigations weren't what they should have been.

'Did Mickey get into this taxi? Where was he going?'

'I'm not sure, sir.'

'Well, see if you can find out.'

He tried Pete's phone again but it was still switched off. 'Tony,' he said. 'I need to get hold of Pete Hollis ASAP. Can you get me an address?'

*

Becca found Sue sitting with her grandfather in the main visitors' lounge of the hospital. Empty Styrofoam cups and out-of-date celebrity lifestyle magazines littered the table. Did the NHS really think that tabloid gossip and glossy photos of the royal family could distract people from the fact that their loved ones were critically ill?

She bent to kiss her grandfather's cheek, then wrapped her arms around her mother. Sue clung to her for a moment longer than usual, gripping her tightly.

'Thanks for coming, love,' she murmured.

Becca had expected to see the whole family there. She glanced around. 'Where's Dad? And Liam?'

Sue sighed, rubbing at her temples. 'Your dad had to stay at the B&B to see to things. We've got new guests arriving this afternoon.'

Becca frowned. 'Can't Liam deal with them?'

Liam had been getting free bed and board since moving back home – surely the least he could do was be there to greet new arrivals.

'He had to check on his building project,' said Sue with resignation. 'It's at a critical stage.'

Becca let out a sharp breath. Liam's projects were

always at a "critical stage." This one, in particular, had nearly ruined him, dragging him into debt so deep it had cost him his relationship with Ellie. And now, at thirty, he was back under their parents' roof, with no real sign of leaving anytime soon.

'He ought to be here,' she muttered.

'He'll come later,' Sue said, though there was little conviction in her voice.

'Would you like a cup of tea?' asked her grandfather, rising from his seat with some difficulty.

Becca quickly placed a hand on his arm. 'I'll get them. You sit down.'

'No, no, love,' he said, shaking his head. 'I need to stretch my legs.' His voice was firm, but there was something else in it – a quiet insistence, the need to feel useful.

Becca hesitated, but Sue leaned in, whispering, 'Let him go, love. He needs to keep busy.'

She nodded, watching as her grandfather slowly made his way down the corridor, his steps deliberate but careful. He had always been a proud, fiercely independent man, never one for sitting still. She recognised that trait in her mother too. Maybe stubbornness ran in the family.

She sat beside Sue and took her hand. 'Any news?'

Sue exhaled, her fingers tightening briefly around Becca's. 'She's in surgery now. The doctor will update us when there's anything more to tell.'

'I'll stay until we hear from him,' Becca said without hesitation. 'Raven won't miss me. I've put in enough extra hours for him in recent months.'

Sue gave a small, weary smile and patted Becca's hand. 'You're a good girl.' She glanced in the direction Becca's grandfather had gone. 'He's putting a brave face on it, but even if the surgery is successful... things won't be the same. Your grandmother might need residential care. And your grandfather...' She swallowed, her voice faltering. 'He might have to move into the guest house with us.'

Becca opened her mouth to respond, but movement at

the doorway caught her attention.

Her grandfather reappeared, carefully balancing three steaming cups, his focus on not spilling a drop. Becca jumped up to help, taking one from him before he could protest.

'Ah, brilliant, Grandad,' she said with a warm smile. 'Just what I need. A proper cuppa.'

He gave a satisfied nod, settling himself back into his chair with a soft grunt of effort. 'Can't go wrong with a strong brew, eh?'

Becca wrapped her hands around the cup, letting the warmth seep into her fingers. No, you couldn't go wrong with a cup of tea. But even the strongest, sweetest brew couldn't fix everything.

CHAPTER 12

Rupert Devizes sank into the deep leather armchair, stretching out his legs with a satisfied ease. He had chosen a quiet corner of the hotel lounge in which to contemplate his next move, enjoying the company of a generous finger of fifty-year-old single malt. He raised his glass, tilting the whisky to catch the light. Dark copper with a reddish glow like polished antique coins. He swirled it slowly, inhaling its aroma: sweet and smoky, with notes of polished mahogany and aged leather. A drink like this deserved to be savoured.

He took a slow sip. Liquid heat unfolded down his throat, spreading warmth through his chest.

Heaven.

The prospects for Echoes of Mercury looked bleak after Robbie's demise, but that didn't mean that everyone associated with the band – and by that Rupert primarily meant himself – had to go down with the sinking ship. He had no doubt that if he'd been on the Titanic, he would have been safely seated in a lifeboat, watching from a comfortable distance as the remaining passengers and crew scrambled in vain for survival. He would have heard their cries, seen their hands grasp at nothing, but he would not have jumped in after them. Instead, he would have watched impassively as their desperate cries rose into the frigid night, the sound swallowed by the vast, indifferent ocean. Survival wasn't luck. It belonged to those who understood the game – who knew when to step forward, when to step back, and, most importantly, when to let others sink so they themselves could stay afloat.

He set the whisky down and unlocked his iPad, swiping effortlessly to the spreadsheet that detailed the band's financial situation. Bleak, from their perspective. The deal Chaz McDonald had struck back in the '80s had been lucrative for the record label but a disaster for the musicians. Chaz liked to think he was a canny businessman, but Rupert knew better. The industry had never been kind, and now – with giants like Spotify and Apple swallowing the lion's share of profits – it was a bloodbath.

But Rupert had ridden the waves and come out on top. Vinyl, CDs, streaming – whatever the format, he had milked it dry.

Mickey's disappearance had, ironically, been good for business, propelling the band to cult status and boosting sales to new highs, even while the surviving members scraped by on session work and pub gigs. But the long "wilderness years" that followed had left Rupert wondering what might have been if Mickey was still around. He'd been delighted when Chaz announced that the band was reforming and going on tour, with Robbie as the new frontman. The band's reunion had been a gift – one last golden goose.

But now Robbie was dead.

The tour had gone well, although the band wouldn't see much of the money. Rupert's cut came first. Then came the road crew, the venues, publicity, coach hire, Chaz's commission.

Speak of the devil.

He was just closing the iPad when Chaz McDonald

stumbled into view, drink in hand. Windblown and ruddy-cheeked, the Scot looked like he'd braved a storm. More likely a whisky-fuelled tour of Scarborough's drinking establishments.

'I thought I'd find you here, Rupert.'

Rupert smiled thinly. 'And gosh, you were right.'

His sarcasm was lost on the Glaswegian. He didn't wait for an invitation before dropping onto the sofa opposite, his glass sloshing dangerously. 'Mind if I join you? We need to talk.'

Rupert lifted an eyebrow. 'Do we?'

'Aye, we do.' Chaz leaned in, his breath a pungent mix of alcohol and stale cigarette smoke. 'This carry-on with Robbie – it's like Mickey all over again. Except this time, there's a body lying stone cold in the morgue.'

Rupert swirled his whisky, letting the silence stretch. For once, Chaz wasn't wrong.

'What are you suggesting?' he asked smoothly.

'The *polis* think it's murder.'

Rupert didn't blink. 'Murder, you say?' He took another slow sip of whisky. 'What makes them think that?'

Chaz's gaze flicked over his shoulder. Paranoia, or just the drink making him jittery?

'You can tell by the questions they're asking. They spoke to me last night. Then Skye, then Stu today. And there's a reporter snooping about, a bonny lass called Liz Larkin. She came to speak to me this morning. Tricked me into saying more than I meant to. She was at the gig with that DCI Raven. I reckon those two are a couple.'

Rupert sighed. Chaz was a liability on his best day, a walking disaster on his worst. A journalist with a nose for scandal was the last thing they needed.

'Watch what you say,' Rupert cautioned. 'To the police, to the press. There are a lot of vested interests at play here.'

'You mean yours,' Chaz said, narrowing his eyes.

Rupert didn't rise to the bait. Chaz liked to think he had some measure of power, but they both knew who held the reins. He set down his glass and met Chaz's gaze coolly. 'If you play your cards right, there's money here for everyone. And when I say everyone, I mean you and me. Remember how record sales went through the roof after Mickey disappeared? Echoes of Mercury are already a cult band. This could be the opportunity of a lifetime for us.'

Chaz frowned. 'And Skye? The poor lass has been left high and dry. What's she supposed to do now her husband's dead? And what about Stu and Pete? Don't they deserve something too?'

Rupert's lip curled in irritation. 'If you want to split your share with them, that's your business. But the contract is clear. You negotiated it yourself, remember?'

Chaz's mouth twisted. 'Aye, I remember. I remember you bled us dry.'

Rupert rolled his wrist in a lazy, dismissive gesture. 'Let's not dredge up the past. We have other things to deal with. Like that filmmaker you so kindly let tag along on tour. Did you even think to put an NDA in place?'

Chaz squinted. 'NDA?'

'Non-disclosure agreement. A legally binding contract that would have stopped her from including whatever she likes in this documentary of hers. If you'd told me, I'd have sorted it. Then she would have been an asset. Instead, we now have a wildcard.' He waved a hand. 'I've already asked Taylor to monitor anything that goes online. You can't take chances these days – the internet's the Wild West.'

Chaz didn't seem to be listening. His fingers twitched around his glass. 'The *polis* asked about Mickey, too. They're linking his disappearance to Robbie's death.'

Rupert stilled. His gaze sharpened. 'Now why would they do that? You didn't put that idea into their heads, did you?'

Chaz swallowed, beads of sweat forming at his temple. 'No, of course I didn't.'

Rupert leaned forwards slightly, voice soft but dangerously precise. 'Now, listen, Chaz. Here's what you have to do. Keep cool and be careful what you say and to whom. Even better, say nothing to anyone. Best of all, stay off the booze until this has all blown over.' He plucked the whisky glass from Chaz's hand and placed it out of reach.

Rupert smiled, just a little, as the Scotsman pushed himself unsteadily to his feet and headed off back the way he had come. Some people were so easy to handle.

He returned his attention to his own whisky, lifting the glass slowly. There were storms ahead. But Rupert Devizes had never been one to go down with the ship.

CHAPTER 13

The days were growing short, and darkness had already swallowed the line of the coast by the time Raven turned off the Filey Road, following signs for the caravan park at Cayton Bay. Becca still wasn't back from wherever she'd gone, but Raven couldn't wait any longer before speaking to Pete.

The xenon headlamps of the BMW sliced through the gloom as he eased onto the rough gravel path leading down towards the cliff edge. The steel coil springs of the M6's suspension took the worst of the bumps, but Raven still drove slowly – the last thing he wanted was to misjudge the terrain and find himself suddenly too close to the edge. Beyond the bright arc of the headlights, the world fell away into nothingness – sea and sky merging into a black abyss.

It was well out of season now, and the park was deserted. Rows of static homes stood in eerie silence, their windows dark, no sign of life. Raven inched the car along the track until he picked out a faint glow behind a curtained window. He scrunched to a halt in front of one of the units.

The moment he stepped out, the unmistakable scent of

cannabis hit him, thick and pungent in the cooling air.

Someone was definitely home.

He rapped his knuckles on the side of the caravan. No answer.

He knocked again, harder this time.

A few seconds passed before the door creaked open, revealing Pete slouched in the doorway. The joint hanging from his lips glowed faintly, the tip smouldering as he exhaled a slow ribbon of smoke. His eyes were unfocused and bloodshot, the lids heavy.

'Yeah?' His voice was languid, slow, like he was wading through treacle to form a thought. Then his eyes focused as recognition flickered through the haze. 'Oh, wait. You're that detective from the gig.' He plucked the joint from his mouth and held it awkwardly between thumb and forefinger, as if trying to work out how to hide it.

'DCI Raven.' Raven wasn't much interested in cannabis, or whatever else Pete might have stashed for his own recreational uses. He was just relieved to find that the drummer wasn't too stoned to recognise him. 'Can I come in? I'd like a word.'

Pete hesitated for the briefest moment, before beckoning him inside. 'Yeah, sure.'

Raven coughed as soon as he entered the fuggy atmosphere of the caravan. The air in the confined space was thicker than a coffee house in Amsterdam. 'Can we open a window?'

'Oh yeah, no problem.'

Pete fumbled with a latch, pushing open one of the small caravan windows. Cold night air rushed in, battling against the stink of smoke. He stubbed out his joint and led Raven through to the cramped living area of the caravan, taking a seat on a narrow bench covered in a threadbare tartan blanket. A fold-out dining table took up most of the remaining space. The kitchenette was no more than a microwave, a kettle, and a two-ring hob. There was barely room for the flatscreen TV that was fixed to the wall, and certainly nowhere to keep a drumkit. Yet according to

Tony's records, this was Pete's permanent address when he wasn't on tour with the band.

'You live here alone, Pete?' asked Raven, perching on the seat opposite. It was little wider than a padded shelf.

Pete's eyes took on a dreamy look. 'Aye. I have company now and then, but I'm a loner at heart. This little place suits me just fine.'

'Where do you keep your drumkit?'

'Robbie and Skye have a studio at the end of their garden. I go there to–' He stopped as he realised what he'd just said. *Robbie and Skye.* 'I guess it's just Skye's place now.'

Raven let him regain his composure before asking, 'You and Robbie were close?'

'Like brothers. Me, Stu and Robbie. And Skye too – like a sister.' Pete's fingers twitched against the tabletop. 'Robbie's death hasn't really sunk in yet. It's all too heavy, man. I don't know how I'm gonna face it.'

His voice caught slightly, and Raven thought he might stop. But Pete wasn't looking to hold back.

'You know, after Mickey disappeared and the Echoes broke up, I went to pieces. The band was the only good thing I had in my life, and it was gone. I didn't know what to do. I mean, what do you do when everything is suddenly taken away from you? Truth is, I went off the rails. Got into the hard stuff – cocaine, heroin, whatever came my way, I wasn't fussy. It was like I was on some kind of death wish. The worst thing that I could imagine had already happened, so I figured life couldn't get worse.' He gave Raven a rueful grin. 'I was wrong though. Life can always get worse. I became homeless for a while, but eventually I got back on my feet. I'm clean now.' He lifted a sleeve to prove he was no longer an addict. Sure enough, his skin was free of needle marks.

Raven took another breath. The skunky haze of cannabis was slowly clearing, but Raven didn't think it would ever quite leave. A thick earthy residue would linger on in the fabric and furniture of the caravan.

Pete caught his look and acknowledged it with a shrug. 'Apart from the weed, I mean, but that doesn't count.'

An uneasy melancholy gripped Raven as he regarded the man he had once considered a genius on the drums. There was no denying Pete's skill as a musician, but beyond that? He was a wreck, just like Stu. Even now, in his supposedly "clean" state he could hardly be held up as a role model. He was more like an object lesson in how badly a life could go off the rails.

Yet Pete wasn't just a faded rockstar. He was a suspect.

'You say that you and the other guys were like brothers,' said Raven, 'but I've heard reports of tension between band members.'

Pete blinked slowly. 'We weren't any worse than any other band. I mean, I'm easy-going. Drummers keep things steady, you know? We're the ones sitting at the back and holding it all together. Songs would fall apart pretty soon without a solid beat to keep the tempo.'

Raven could believe that Pete had never craved the limelight for himself. He was too laid back. 'What about Robbie?'

Pete sighed. 'Robbie was... highly strung. Insecure, I reckon. I suppose he felt he had to prove himself, stepping into Mickey's shoes as the frontman. Skye always backed him up, even when he was wrong. And Stu? A few beers, and he can turn nasty.'

'I've spoken to Stu.'

Pete gave a wry smile. 'Then you'll know he likes his beers.'

'And Chaz?'

Pete pulled a face. 'Thinks he's everyone's best mate. He's not. Taylor's okay, I suppose, although she's a bit of a snitch, reporting everything back to Rupert. And Frankie's always poking her nose – and her camera – into every situation, trying to stir things up.'

'So,' Raven said, watching him carefully, 'there was a great deal of friction between almost everyone on the coach.'

Pete hesitated. 'Well... yeah. I guess there was.'

Raven let the silence hang before speaking. 'A witness reported seeing you fill Robbie's water bottle just before the concert.'

Pete froze, his pupils contracting slightly. 'Well, yeah, now you mention it, I guess I did.'

'With what?'

'Tap water. Why? What's the deal with the bottle?'

Raven studied him. Pete appeared to be genuinely puzzled. 'What happened to it after you filled it? Did anyone else touch it?'

Pete shrugged. 'Backstage is chaos right before a concert. Everyone's moving around. Stuff gets shifted about all the time. Anyone could have picked it up or moved it.'

Raven couldn't argue with that. They would have to rely on other witnesses, or fingerprint analysis to say who else might have handled the bottle.

Pete's brow furrowed as he pieced things together. 'Wait... are you saying there was something in Robbie's water?'

'We have to consider all options.'

'Shit,' said Pete, staring at the tabletop. 'The Echoes are finished for real this time. It's time to head off into the sunset like Mickey.'

'Into the sunset?'

'Yeah. I know most people think he's dead, but I never believed it.'

'Why not?'

'I just don't feel it, you know? I reckon he's still out there, watching over us, keeping an eye out for his old mates.'

Raven frowned. 'Why do you say that he's watching you?'

Pete chuckled. 'Maybe I'm just an old romantic, holding out hope. But there's this poet online and some people say it could be Mickey.'

'What poet?'

'Someone calling themself *Frost and Fury*. They post stuff online. Poems, songs... now I could be wrong, but hell, those words sound like Mickey's to me.' He reached into a pocket and absentmindedly pulled out another joint. 'Do you mind if I smoke another of these?'

Raven rose to his feet. It was time for him to go. 'We're done for now, Pete. But don't go anywhere. I might need to speak to you again.'

Pete lit the joint as Raven left. 'Where else would I go?' he said mournfully.

CHAPTER 14

'Cheers!' murmured Hannah as the familiar clink of glass against glass rang out, her nightly ritual in the plush surroundings of Ellie's apartment. She raised the wine to her lips and took a slow sip, the chilled white sliding down easily at the end of the day. 'What's this one?' she asked, rolling the glass between her fingers.

'An Italian Pinot Grigio,' said Ellie lazily. 'Light and zesty.' She tucked her legs beneath her on the opposite end of the sofa, mirroring Hannah's relaxed sprawl.

'I like it.'

Ellie laughed. 'Come on, I want more than that. Let's see how much you've learned these past few weeks.'

Hannah's wine education was progressing apace. Despite running a brewery, Ellie's real passion was for wine, probably due to having a bistro owner for a father. Keith could talk grapes for hours, and Ellie had taken it upon herself to instruct Hannah in all the major grape varieties.

Hannah swirled her glass, watching the pale gold liquid catch the light before taking another sip, this time savouring the crisp flavours before swallowing. 'I'm getting grapefruit and lemon hints. Is that right?'

Ellie eyed her playfully. 'Anything else?'

'Mineral undertones and a refreshing acidity?' Hannah ventured.

'Did you read that off the label?' mocked Ellie.

'No! I can really taste it!'

They both laughed, and Hannah took another mouthful, for pleasure this time, not so she could prove herself as a wine critic. She felt the weight of another day ease as the alcohol did its work. Although she enjoyed waiting tables, she knew it could only be a stopgap. Sooner or later she would have to make some difficult decisions about her future. But for the time being, she was content to push hard choices down the road. Here, in Ellie's gorgeous apartment, life was simple. Two glasses, one bottle, and the soft murmur of waves against the North Sands.

Except it was never just one bottle.

Most nights, it was several, although in fairness, Ellie generally polished off at least two glasses for every one of Hannah's.

On the rug by the sofa, Quincey stirred at the sound of their laughter, opening one sleepy eye before settling back down. Hannah had walked him here across the North Bay after finishing her shift. With her dad out all hours, she was spending more time than ever in the company of the Black Labrador. Her arm ached from throwing soggy tennis balls across the sand, and she worried she was beginning to smell permanently of wet dog.

She absently scratched his head, still damp from the sea air. At least Quincey wouldn't tell tales about how much she was drinking.

She could picture her dad's disapproving expression if he knew how much wine she got through on these nights. But what he didn't know couldn't hurt him. And anyway, he was never around. Besides, she was doing fine – more than fine – keeping a friendly eye on Ellie and making sure she wasn't drinking alone now that she had split with Liam and Becca had moved out of the flat. If she wasn't here, Ellie would probably be knocking back even more.

Hannah's phone buzzed and she scooped it off the coffee table. She was surprised to see her dad's name on the display.

'Hi, Dad, everything okay?'

His voice came through steady but distant. 'Yes. Just wanted to let you know I'll be late back. No need to worry.'

'Working late again?' she teased. 'Thought you were supposed to be trying harder at this work-life balance thing.'

Not that she actually believed he was working. Late was normal for him, but five o'clock in the morning? That was stretching things. She'd heard him creeping back into the house in the early hours, trying not to wake her, but he couldn't cover his tracks that easily. Nor had she imagined the scent of perfume on his clothes.

There was definitely a woman involved.

'I'm busy on this new investigation,' he said. 'The suspicious death at the spa.'

'Sure thing,' said Hannah. Now wasn't the time to press him for answers. He would tell her when he was ready.

'How's Quincey?'

The Black Lab opened one eye at the sound of his name, his tail giving the faintest of thumps.

'He's fine. We're both fine, Dad. We're at Ellie's.' She almost said, *Go and enjoy yourself*, but caught herself just in time. 'Don't work too late.'

A pause. Then, softer than before, 'I won't.'

He rang off.

Ellie raised her glass again, clinking it against hers with a knowing smile. 'To another late one?'

Hannah hesitated – just for a second. Then she smiled back. 'To another late one.'

★

Raven ended the call and slipped his phone back into his pocket, exhaling slowly. His fingers tightened into a fist before he forced himself to relax.

He hated lying to his daughter, but he couldn't bring himself to tell her the truth. Not yet. Was he worried what Hannah would think of Liz Larkin? Well, yes, he was.

But she wasn't being entirely frank with him either. He had caught the echo of Ellie's laughter in the background, the tell-tale clink of glasses. Hannah had been drinking. Again.

She thought he hadn't noticed. But he had spent his childhood watching his father drink himself into oblivion – he knew the signs. The way people hid it in plain sight, masked it as social, as fun, as just one more. First they hid their habit from others. Then they hid it from themselves.

Raven stared at his reflection in the darkened window of his car. He ought to confront her. Ask her what the hell was going on. But Hannah was stubborn, so much like her mother. If he pushed too hard, she might shut him out completely – or worse, leave Scarborough altogether.

And he couldn't lose her again.

Not after all they'd been through.

With a grunt of frustration, he wrenched the car door open and stepped out onto the slick pavement, inhaling the sharp salt air. He crossed the road and entered Liz's hotel, shaking the tension from his shoulders.

Visiting Liz was work, of a kind.

At least that's what he told himself.

Liz was a journalist, someone with access to different sources, people who wouldn't talk to the police but might let something slip in casual conversation. If she had learned anything useful about Robbie's death, it would be stupid not to take advantage of it.

Or so he reasoned as he stepped into the lift and watched the numbers blink upward.

The fifth floor was silent, the plush carpet muffling his footsteps as he made his way to her room. He knocked.

The door swung open almost immediately, as if she'd been expecting him.

Liz leaned against the doorframe, hair shining, lips curved in a rosy invitation. 'Well, hello, Tom.'

Without a word, he reached for her, and she pulled him inside. The door swung shut, and for a while, Raven let everything else fade – Hannah, Becca, the case. The only thing that mattered was the warmth of Liz's skin, the weight of her body against his.

For a blessed time, nothing else existed.

When it was over, she wrapped herself in a bathrobe, made them each a coffee, and slid back into bed beside him. 'How was your day?' she asked, businesslike again.

He liked that she hadn't called him or pushed for updates, but had simply waited for him to come to her. He hated being put under pressure in a romantic relationship. He had spent too long with Lisa nagging him to do more, be more, always be somewhere else.

In Liz's company, he could simply be.

'Busy,' he said, stretching out his legs. 'I spoke to all the surviving band members.'

'I'm jealous,' said Liz. 'You get to go wherever you like, speak to whoever you want. Being a police detective is easier than being a journalist.'

He regarded her with wry amusement. 'Really? You should try it one day. You'd find that the people you most want to talk to either won't say a word or they lie through their teeth.'

'So who lied to you today?' she asked, eyes gleaming.

'Not sure yet. But someone did.'

Liz snuggled closer to him. 'So what did they tell you?'

'It wouldn't be very professional of me to discuss an ongoing inquiry.'

She nudged him playfully. 'Well, if you want to hear what I found out, you'd better give me something in return.'

Raven shook his head, amused. Even in bed, Liz Larkin remained a journalist, hungry for a story.

'Fine,' he said, sipping his coffee. 'Do you want to hear their theories about Mickey?'

She perked up immediately. 'Go on.'

'Skye is convinced he killed himself. It seems he was suffering from writer's block and couldn't write any new songs. Skye couldn't handle his depression and left him for Robbie just when he was at his lowest. She blames herself for his death.'

Liz scoffed. 'Self-indulgent. She's twisted Mickey's story to make it all about her.'

'Maybe,' said Raven. 'But Stu agrees. He thinks Mickey took his own life, and he regrets not seeing the warning signs.'

Liz made a face, clearly disappointed. 'So none of them think it was murder?'

'No, but Pete has a completely different theory.' Raven set his mug on the bedside table and leaned back against the headboard. 'He thinks Mickey is still alive.'

Liz blinked. 'Seriously?'

'Yep. And that he's been writing poetry online.'

Liz let out a short laugh. 'That's ridiculous. What's the poet's name?'

'*Frost and Fury*.'

Liz reached for her phone, tapped out a search and scrolled briefly before stopping. 'Found them. Listen to this. It's called *Your love is a poison*.' She read the poem aloud, the light from the screen casting a soft glow over her face.

Your love is a poison. A deadly perfume.
Forbidden pleasures. Tainted dreams.
Hot bodies. Cold sweat.
Moving together as one in the night.

Undress me. Strip me bare.
Look at me now. Your hands on my skin.
Your love is a poison. My lust is a beast.
I kiss you tonight. Your blood on my tongue.

It wasn't what Raven would have called a poem. The rhythm was too irregular and there was no clear rhyming. Yet he wasn't going to air his opinions about modern poetry to Liz. What did he know? He was only a policeman. 'You think Mickey wrote this?'

'It's a possibility. It's reminiscent of the band's lyrics.'

The notion that Mickey had staged his own disappearance and lived under a new identity for thirty years seemed far-fetched to Raven. He was surprised that Liz was willing to entertain the idea. 'So, have you given up on your theory that Robbie murdered Mickey?' he asked, teasingly.

'Not yet, but I'm prepared to be open-minded.' She set the phone aside and stretched out beside him. 'Anyway, I had an off-the-record chat with the band's manager today.'

'Chaz McDonald? And?'

'Well, when he wasn't flirting with me, he let slip some details about the band's contract with their record label. Rupert ripped them off. He still owns all the rights to their songs and keeps a hundred per cent of their royalties.'

'Is that normal in the music business?' asked Raven.

'It's not unheard of, but even back in the 80s, bands usually got something. Chaz must have been completely useless as a manager to sign off on that deal. He's been trying to renegotiate, but Rupert isn't budging.'

Liz's discovery explained a lot – why, despite their early success, the band had barely made a living from their recordings and had turned instead to live performances to earn some money.

Raven exhaled and glanced at the bedside clock. It was late. He had an early start.

'Enough about Echoes of Mercury,' he said, sitting up. 'I should be going.'

'There's no need,' murmured Liz, flashing him a sweet smile. She let her robe slip from her shoulder.

Raven hesitated.

For a brief moment, Hannah flashed in his mind again

– the clink of her glass, the too-bright tone.

Then Liz ran a finger down his arm.

And just for tonight, he let everything else fade away.

*

Jess was already twenty minutes late when she pushed through the doors of the pub, the warmth and buzz of conversation hitting her immediately. After a long, monotonous day chained to her desk, her eyes glazing over from watching hours of unedited footage of roadies hauling equipment and band members bickering backstage, she was desperate for real conversation – and something stronger than office coffee.

More than that, she was eager to talk about her favourite subject – walking.

She had already conquered the Lyke Wake Walk, a gruelling forty-mile trek across the North York Moors from Osmotherley to Ravenscar, but that had only whetted her appetite for a grander route, a walk that would truly test her endurance. The Yorkshire Three Peaks had been a tempting challenge, with its rugged twenty-six-mile route spanning Whernside, Ingleborough, and Pen-y-Ghent, but in the end, she had set her sights even higher.

Wainwright's legendary Coast to Coast Walk, from the windswept shores of St Bees in Cumbria, through the towering peaks of the Lake District, across the rolling valleys of the Yorkshire Dales, and finally onto the wild, heather-clad expanse of the North York Moors, stretched a staggering 190 miles. It demanded endurance, planning, and more than a little stubbornness – all qualities Jess had in spades. It wasn't something to be tackled lightly, and Jess had sensibly chosen to join an organised group rather than attempt it alone.

She had never met the other members before tonight, but spotting a table strewn with Ordnance Survey maps and a group of five deep in discussion over route plans, she knew instantly she had found her tribe. She smoothed her jacket, stepped forwards, and flashed a bright smile.

'Hi, I'm Jess. Sorry I'm late – long day at work.'

As soon as the words left her mouth, she regretted them.

She didn't want the inevitable follow-up – *What do you do for a living?* The last thing she needed was to explain that she was a police detective, especially not when her current case involved a suspicious death at the spa. Worse still, her first attempt at the Lyke Wake Walk had ended in the discovery of a dead body at a Bronze Age burial mound. Not exactly the kind of anecdote that would reassure new hiking friends.

'No worries,' came a warm, easy reply.

Jess turned to the speaker – a tall, broad-shouldered man around her age. His dark hair was windswept and slightly tousled, as if he'd spent the day out on the fells rather than stuck behind a desk like her. His chunky knitted sweater looked like it had seen plenty of miles in the great outdoors.

'We're just getting started,' he said, flashing a grin. 'What can I get you to drink?'

Jess hesitated for a moment, catching the twinkle of amusement in his eyes as he registered her uncertainty.

'A beer,' she said at last, mirroring his easy tone.

His grin widened. 'You got it.'

Jess took a seat at the table as he set off to the bar.

The others introduced themselves. They were a friendly mix of men and women, all buzzing with the same pre-adventure excitement. Their voices overlapped as they compared routes and debated the best stop-off points.

By the time the dark-haired guy returned, setting her beer in front of her with a casual 'Here you go', Jess was already settling in, feeling at home.

'Thanks,' she said as he took the seat next to hers.

'You're welcome.' He held out his hand. 'Jess, wasn't it? Nice to meet you. I'm Gavin.'

Jess shook his hand, his grip firm and warm, and took a sip of her beer, the frothy head coating her lips. A comfortable glow settled over her as the group began to swap tales of epic treks and disastrous weather, and she knew that for the next hour or two, she wouldn't have to think about goth bands, crime scenes, or police reports – just open footpaths, fresh air, and the kind of people who understood the thrill of putting one foot in front of the other for miles on end.

CHAPTER 15

Raven awoke with a jolt. Six o'clock in the morning. Liz's hotel room.

Shit.

His stomach lurched as reality crashed in. He hadn't meant to stay the whole night. He'd planned to slip away hours ago – before dawn, before this could feel like more than it was. Yet here he was, tangled in the warm sheets, Liz's bare arm draped possessively across his chest.

What kind of man was he becoming? The kind who met his secret lover for clandestine assignations in hotel rooms? The kind who lied to his daughter? He wasn't in the mood to examine the answer.

Carefully, he lifted Liz's arm and swung his legs over the side of the bed. The air was cool against his skin, but his guilt burned hot.

He dressed in the same rumpled shirt and stale-smelling jacket, suppressing a grimace at the lingering scent of Pete's cannabis clinging to the fabric. He needed to go home. Shower. Change. Erase the evidence before Hannah realised what he'd done. Pretend that none of this had happened.

Liz stirred but didn't wake as he moved towards the door.

Good.

If he caught another glimpse of her bare shoulder, the curve of her hip beneath the sheets, he wasn't sure he'd be able to walk away.

Without a backward glance, he slipped out, closing the door behind him.

As soon as he let himself back into his house on Quay Street, Quincey came bounding out of the front room, tail wagging, claws skittering on the wooden floor. The dog's boundless joy was pure, unconditional. Raven swallowed hard. He didn't deserve it.

The Black Labrador cocked his head, nose twitching, giving Raven's rumpled suit a thorough sniff before pulling back and sneezing.

'Yeah, yeah, I get it, I stink,' muttered Raven, rubbing a hand over the dog's sleek fur.

Quincey whined softly, tail thumping against Raven's leg. It was more than just a greeting. It was an accusation.

'I know, mate.' Raven crouched down, stroking his ears. 'I'm neglecting you. And Hannah too.'

But judging by Quincey's glossy coat and well-fed frame, they were managing just fine without him. Maybe he was the dispensable one.

'Shh, boy.' He scratched behind the dog's ears. 'Remember our secret? You won't tell Hannah where I've been, will you?'

Quincey cocked his head to the side and looked at him with doleful eyes. Raven didn't need his dog's disapproval.

Raven sighed and straightened. 'Listen, if you get out of my way, I'll take a shower and put on some clean clothes. Go back to bed, there's a good boy.'

The dog padded back to his basket and Raven climbed the stairs as quietly as he could, dreading the thought of his daughter finding him in the previous day's clothes smelling like a pothead.

Thirty minutes later, fresh and dressed in clean clothes,

he was back at the door, leaving a hastily scrawled note for Hannah to drop Quincey off at the dog minder's. As he pulled the front door shut behind him, he caught the dog's mournful gaze from across the room.

Christ. He really needed to get his act together.

★

The alarm went off and Becca rolled over with a groan, her eyes squeezed shut. How could it be morning already? It felt as though she'd only just drifted off.

All night she'd tossed and turned, her mind spinning with worry. She had stayed late at the hospital the previous evening until her grandmother had come out of surgery. Then Sue had insisted she go back to the guest house for something to eat. The meal had been a tense, joyless affair, the kind where even the clink of cutlery sounded too loud. Liam had droned on about his never-ending house renovations, and Becca had finally snapped, telling him there were bigger things to worry about than his bloody apartment conversion. All in all, it had been a difficult evening.

And now it was time to get up. Dragging herself upright, she flung back the duvet and stomped into the bathroom, too groggy to function without a blisteringly hot shower. Fifteen minutes later, she emerged, slightly less of a zombie but still far from human.

She was torn between going into work and being with her family, although part of her wanted to crawl straight back into bed, pull the covers over her head, and block out the world entirely.

In the end, she decided to head into work so she could leave early if need be.

She arrived at the incident room just before eight, her shoulders stiff with fatigue. She wasn't surprised to see Raven already there, his back to her as he studied the photos pinned to the whiteboard.

He turned as she entered, cradling a mug of black

coffee. 'Morning, Becca.'

'Morning.'

That was it. No further conversation. No easy camaraderie. She wasn't about to unburden herself to him, and he looked just as preoccupied.

She dropped her bag onto her desk, grabbed her empty mug, and disappeared into the kitchen in search of tea. A reason to escape, even for a moment.

By the time she returned, Detective Superintendent Gillian Ellis had arrived. Another early starter, she stood with her arms folded, listening intently as Raven updated her.

'We've started interviewing the key players,' Raven told her. 'The band members, their manager. But we still don't have a cause of death. The post-mortem is scheduled for later today.'

'I see.' Gillian nodded thoughtfully. 'Early days, then. What about resourcing? Do you need Derek Dinsdale to lend a hand?'

Becca glanced at Raven, waiting for his reaction. She already knew what it would be. DI Derek Dinsdale was the last person Raven would want sniffing around this case – hell, the last person either of them wanted sniffing around anything.

Dinsdale had grudgingly done Raven a favour during his recent undercover investigation into his mother's death. But Dinsdale was no altruist and his assistance didn't come free. Sooner or later he would demand a favour in return, and who knew what form that would take?

'I think we're fine for the moment,' said Raven, his voice carefully neutral.

'Very well,' said Gillian. 'But I'll make him available, if necessary.'

'Thank you, ma'am.'

As soon as Gillian left, Becca met Raven's gaze. 'You dodged a bullet there.'

Her remark drew a grin from his stony face. 'Next time I might not be so lucky.'

The moment felt like a watershed, a reminder of how close they had been just a few weeks earlier.

No one else knew what they'd done together. The late-night meetings, the secret conversations, the lines they'd crossed to uncover the driver who had killed Raven's mother in a hit-and-run. An intimacy that had drawn them closer than ever before.

But things were different now. Liz Larkin was on the scene.

'I—' Raven began, but the door to the incident room swung open again, and Tony entered.

'Morning, sir,' he mumbled. 'Becca?'

'Morning, Tony,' she replied, glancing back at Raven. 'You were going to say?'

He hesitated, then shook his head. 'It was nothing. Forget it.'

The door opened again, and this time Jess strode in.

'Team meeting in five,' Raven called.

He turned away, and just like that, whatever had passed between them was gone.

CHAPTER 16

Raven glanced around the incident room, his gaze settling on each member of his small team. By rights he should have welcomed Gillian's offer to make DI Dinsdale available to him. The addition of a senior detective would have significantly bolstered his meagre resources. But Raven had good reason to keep out of Dinsdale's way. On previous cases, the irritating detective inspector had continually proved to be a thorn in his side, and Raven was particularly eager to avoid him at present. He pushed Dinsdale to the back of his mind and kicked off the morning meeting by summarising what he'd learned over the weekend.

'Echoes of Mercury were trying to revive their careers with this comeback tour. The band made hardly any money from record sales, and their manager, Chaz McDonald, had apparently failed to negotiate a better deal with Rupert Devizes. And so a new business model selling concert tickets seemed to be the way to go. It seemed to be working – until Robbie died on stage.'

Becca frowned. 'Sorry, but where's that coming from? Neither Skye nor Stu mentioned the terms of the band's record deal yesterday.'

Raven tensed. He had dug a hole for himself and unless he thought quickly, he was going to fall right into it. There was no way he could admit the information had come from Liz Larkin – in bed of all places!

'I went to see Pete afterwards,' he said smoothly. 'On my own.' He could have added, *because you'd dashed off somewhere*, but there was no need to turn up the heat.

Yet if he thought that would end the matter, it seemed Becca wasn't going to be so easily fobbed off. Her expression didn't shift. 'And Pete told you this?'

Damn it. Why couldn't she just let it drop? There was a beat too long before he found his voice. 'Pete, yeah.'

Now he was lying to his team. What the hell was wrong with him?

An awkward silence followed. Jess found something fascinating to examine in her coffee mug. Tony scribbled in his notepad. Becca didn't call him out on it, but her look said enough – she knew. And if she knew Liz Larkin was giving him inside information, had she guessed he was sharing confidential information in return?

He was saved from his brooding by Tony. 'Sir, I got the bank statements from Robbie's account first thing this morning. One transaction stood out. Rupert's company made quite a substantial payment to him last month.'

'Perhaps that was related to the tour?' suggested Raven, seizing the distraction.

'Could be. No way to tell from the statement alone.'

'I was planning on speaking to Rupert today,' said Raven. 'I'll ask him about it.'

'Do we have any idea what Robbie's announcement was going to be?' asked Jess.

Raven shook his head. 'Skye said Robbie was a dark horse, so she wasn't in the loop. But Stu thought he might've been planning to say something about Mickey.'

'What kind of thing?' queried Jess.

'I don't know. The band members all have their own pet theory about what happened to Mickey. Skye and Stu both think he took his own life. Pete, meanwhile, is convinced he's still alive. In fact, he reckons Mickey's been writing poetry online under the name *Frost and Fury*.'

There was a murmur of surprise at this latest idea.

'Perhaps you could look into it, Jess?' Raven reviewed his notes. 'As for alibis, everyone claims to have spent the pre-show hours alone. Skye says Robbie went for a walk on the beach by himself. Jess, did you get anything from the video footage?'

Jess beamed, obviously keen to report her findings. 'The video's very revealing about the relationships between the band members. It's quite an eye-opener seeing what went on behind the scenes. The filmmaker, Frankie, described it as fly-on-the-wall, but I have to say, I think she was deliberately homing in on dirt. She doesn't portray the band in a flattering light.'

'Were there any examples of arguments on the film?'

'There was a bit of a shouting match between Robbie and Stu over the positioning of the keyboard onstage. Apart from that, it was all just low-level bickering. But one thing's clear – Robbie was in a great mood. He didn't look like a man about to end his own life. He was drinking from his water bottle throughout the day, with no issues.'

Raven nodded. 'Becca and I spoke to Stu. He said Robbie was fixated on Mickey's disappearance. There was rivalry between Robbie and Mickey when Mickey was lead singer. Stu didn't speak very highly of Skye either, accusing her of leaving Mickey when he was at his lowest.'

'She admitted as much herself,' remarked Becca. 'She took the blame for Mickey's suicide.'

'If it *was* suicide,' said Raven. 'Pete is convinced Mickey's still out there. I'll be honest – Pete wasn't the most reliable witness. He admitted to getting into hard drugs after the band broke up, and while he may have kicked that habit, he's still a heavy cannabis user.'

Becca leaned forward. 'Stu told us Pete was the one who filled Robbie's water bottle before the concert.'

'Pete confirmed it,' said Raven, 'but says it was just tap

water.'

'As long as it wasn't spa water,' said Tony.

A chuckle rippled around the room – a brief relief from the weight of the case. It had been many years since the acidic water from the old pump rooms was celebrated as a health tonic.

Raven waited for the mirth to die down before continuing. 'Tony, any progress looking into Mickey's disappearance?'

'I'm working through the case files. There's a lot to go through. It seems that the taxi driver picked up Mickey and drove him somewhere. Mickey's own car had an engine fault, which was why he left his car keys at home. I also found out that Mickey had a younger sister, but she was just a kid at the time he went missing.'

'Good. Keep at it. I think it's clear we need to dig deeper. I'm speaking to Rupert today. Tony, go through Robbie's phone and bank records in more detail. Jess, look into this *Frost and Fury* poet – see if there's anything to Pete's theory. And follow up with Frankie about more tour footage.'

'On it,' Jess said, making a note.

That just left Becca. She'd barely spoken since their tense exchange earlier, and Raven knew she was unhappy. He'd rubbed her up the wrong way, and he wasn't sure how to fix it.

'Becca, could you attend the post-mortem? Press Felicity Wainwright to confirm whether Robbie's death was consistent with cyanide poisoning. And chase the lab for the toxicology results. The sooner we get confirmation, the stronger our footing.'

Becca nodded, but her voice was flat. 'Of course.'

She didn't look at him as she gathered her things.

Raven exhaled slowly as his team dispersed. He might have dodged Dinsdale, but he wasn't convinced he'd escaped Becca's scrutiny.

CHAPTER 17

Becca waited as Dr Felicity Wainwright set out the tools of her trade with methodical precision. Scalpel, bone saw, rib shears, forceps. The instruments gleamed beneath the cold mortuary light, their cruel edges ready to taste flesh and bone. Felicity hummed to herself as she affectionately ran a gloved finger along the handle of a power saw before setting it down on a metal tray with a quiet clink. The mortuary was a cold, sterile place, but there was something disturbingly intimate about the way Felicity worked.

'So,' said the pathologist brightly, as though they were sharing small talk over coffee rather than standing over a corpse. 'How are you enjoying life as an independent woman?'

Becca stood stiffly across the room, her arms folded. The body of Robbie Kershaw lay between them, shrouded beneath a blue sheet, waiting for its secrets to be laid bare. 'It's fine,' she said flatly.

Felicity weighed a scalpel in her fingers, her thin lips twitching. 'Only fine? I was thrilled when I heard you'd taken my advice and got your own place at last. Life's so much simpler when you're alone. No one to answer to. No one watching what time you come and go…'

'Well, yes,' agreed Becca. She was in no mood to be interrogated about her personal life, especially by Felicity. She really hadn't wanted to attend the post-mortem at all, but at least she was at the hospital and would be able to check in on her grandmother afterwards.

'And it's close enough to Raven's house to keep an eye on him, isn't it?' Felicity lifted a pair of long-handled forceps, testing their tension with a metallic *snap*. 'I bet you can see his place from your window.' Her eyes gleamed over the rim of her mask. 'So… have you?'

Becca frowned. 'Have I what?'

Felicity leaned in slightly, lowering her voice like they were exchanging secrets. 'Been keeping an eye on him? You must be tempted. Just the occasional glance, a passing peek. I know I would.'

Becca stiffened. 'I didn't take the flat to spy on my boss.'

Felicity let out an exaggerated sigh. 'Oh, Becca, do lighten up. It was just a bit of fun. You're so prickly today.' She cocked her head in curiosity, as if Becca was no different from the corpse she was about to open up. A puzzle to be solved. 'Something's bothering you. I can tell.'

Becca sighed. There was no point trying to deflect. 'My grandmother was rushed in on Saturday night with a stroke. She had emergency surgery yesterday.'

Felicity replaced the forceps on the worktop. 'Oh, I'm so sorry to hear that. I know how much your family means to you. Let's get this over with so you can check in on her, shall we?'

'Please,' said Becca, grateful for the change in tone.

'Okay, then.' Felicity lifted the sheet that covered the corpse in one smooth motion, revealing the lifeless form beneath. Robbie's face, neck, arms and torso were a dark cherry red.

Felicity let out a small *hmm* of interest and surveyed the body, intrigued. 'Well, what have we here?'

A Dying Echo

'What do you think it is?' asked Becca.

'Hypoxia. An inability of the cells to take up oxygen from the bloodstream, leading to high oxygen saturation in the blood.' Felicity pulled back Robbie's eyelids and shone a light into his vacant eyes. 'Yes, here's another indicator of oxygen deprivation. See those tiny blood spots in the eyes? Petechial haemorrhages.'

Becca leaned in cautiously. 'What could cause it?'

'Certain chronic diseases, an acute interruption to the blood supply – a heart attack, for instance...'

'So natural causes, then?' Becca could hardly keep an edge of disappointment from her voice. If Robbie had died a natural death, then Raven's hunch was wrong and there was nothing further to investigate.

Felicity drew her faint brow into a V-shape. 'Patience, please, Becca. Let's not jump to conclusions.'

Becca stood back as Felicity concluded her external examination and began the gory procedure of cutting the body open. She allowed her mind to drift as the surgical saw buzzed into life and Felicity started to slice through the ribcage. Before she knew it, Robbie's internal organs were laid bare to the world.

Felicity leaned closer and took a sniff through her mask. 'Yes, I thought so...'

'What?' asked Becca, but Felicity was already reaching for a syringe before poking about in Robbie's innards. She extracted a quantity of blood from the heart into a glass bottle.

'Yes,' she murmured, holding it to the light, 'bright red. I'll send this off for spectrometry testing, although I'm confident the results will confirm my conclusion.'

'Which is?'

'Acute cyanide poisoning.' The pathologist's eyes glimmered with morbid delight. 'You know, it's really quite elegant the way cyanide works. It completely blocks the take-up of oxygen by the cells. The result – instant cellular shutdown. The first signs are headaches and dizziness, quickly followed by loss of consciousness and cardiac arrest. Death can occur within minutes, or even quicker.'

Becca breathed out slowly. Raven was right after all.

*

The hotel's health club was well equipped, with a range of exercise bikes, treadmills, weights and state-of-the-art fitness machines. The faint scent of hand sanitiser mingled with the sweat of overzealous businessmen trying to outrun their midlife crises. Raven found Rupert Devizes in the free weights section, lifting a heavy barbell with controlled effort, admiring his well-toned reflection in the mirror. He was turned out in discreetly branded gym gear and sported a smartwatch and wireless earbuds.

He caught sight of Raven and lowered the barbell back onto its stand with an exaggerated show of effort, the nostrils of his aquiline nose flaring. 'Care to join me, Chief Inspector?'

'No, thank you.' Raven had been able to deadlift a hundred and fifty kilograms during his army days, but he had no interest in engaging in a testosterone-fuelled contest with the man he had come to interview. 'I'd like to ask you some questions.'

Rupert wiped his hands on a towel and removed his earbuds. 'Go ahead. But if you don't mind, I'll get my cardio in while we talk.' Without waiting for an answer, he strode to an exercise bike, adjusted the seat for his long legs, and began to pedal.

Raven leaned against a treadmill, arms folded, watching as Rupert methodically increased the bike's resistance. The man was calculating in everything he did.

'I understand that you've been with Echoes of Mercury for a long time.'

'Ever since they started out,' said Rupert, barely out of breath. 'They were one of the first bands I signed. Chaz sent me a demo tape, I went to see them play in a small venue in York and decided they were worth a punt. So I signed them up, and the rest is history.'

'You did well out of them?'

Rupert flashed a dazzling grin. His teeth were white and even, his face well-tanned. 'They had some modest success early on, enough for me to back a US tour. But you know how that ended. Mickey went missing and the whole thing fell apart. Still, I can't complain. The publicity surrounding his disappearance bankrolled my record label for several years.'

Raven didn't flinch at the callousness. He'd already pegged Rupert for a man who measured tragedy in profit margins. 'So when Mickey vanished, you shed no tears?'

Rupert shot him a sidelong glance. 'I hope you're not suggesting I had anything to do with it?'

'I'm just interested in your thoughts. What do you think happened to him?'

Rupert's expression didn't shift. 'I don't think anything.' He pressed a button, increasing the resistance again. 'And more to the point, I don't want to know.'

'You don't want to know?'

Rupert smiled, slow and cold. 'An unsolved mystery feeds the myth and keeps the wheels of commerce turning. A solved one? I'm afraid that's just bad for business.' He pedalled harder, his muscular legs pumping smoothly. 'But it's hard for a band to sustain a long term career when its main singer and songwriter has done a bunk. Eventually, sales petered out.'

'Until you put Robbie out front,' Raven said.

'That's right. The tour went well and revenues are up again.'

'And who receives those revenues?'

Rupert picked up the pace again, beads of sweat beginning to form on his smooth brow. 'If you've spoken to Chaz, I'm sure he's given you his sob story about the raw deal the band got. Ticket sales were their cut but streaming and record sales? Those are all mine. Chaz never misses a chance to whine about it.'

'Was it unfair?'

Rupert didn't break his stride. 'Chaz negotiated the contract. Nobody forced the band to sign it.'

'They were probably desperate for a recording deal.'

'Just so,' said Rupert. 'And that's what they got. A chance at fame. Without me, they would have been just another sad bunch of wannabees.'

Raven regarded the music industry boss coldly. Rupert cared nothing for the band members and had taken advantage of them and their inexperienced manager when they were young, eager, and naïve. 'I understand that Chaz tried to renegotiate the terms of the deal recently.'

'And I said no to that,' said Rupert quickly. 'Why would I agree to less favourable terms?'

'Then how do you explain the payment your company made to Robbie last month?'

A flicker of amusement played across Rupert's features. 'Ah, I wondered how long it would take you to find that. I suppose the news had to come out eventually.'

'What news?'

'Robbie was about to go solo. We'd already signed the deal.'

'A solo career? Did the other band members know?'

Rupert slowed his pedalling and swung a leg off the bike, reaching for his towel. 'It was all hush-hush. The other band members knew nothing about it. Chaz, neither. After Robbie's previous experience with that idiot, he wisely cut him out of the deal and came directly to me.'

'So nobody else knows about this?' Raven's mind flicked through the possibilities. If Robbie was about to launch a solo career, could that be why he was killed? If discovered, the move would hardly have endeared him to Stu or Pete. Or Skye for that matter. 'And let me guess – this solo career was going to be his big announcement at the end of the show?'

Rupert chuckled. 'You got it. Kill the band onstage – just like Bowie killed off Ziggy Stardust. You have to admit, it would have been a fantastic PR stunt. Of course, that's not going to happen now.' He grabbed a bottle of water, took a long drink, then met Raven's gaze. 'So as you can see, DCI Raven, if you suspected me of having a motive to kill Robbie, you're very much mistaken. I'd already invested time and money into making Robbie a star. His death is a major inconvenience to me.'

'Unless,' Raven said smoothly, 'you were banking on the idea that another tragedy – like Mickey's disappearance – would boost Echoes of Mercury's sales again.'

Rupert sighed dramatically, rubbing the towel over his face before tossing it onto the bench. 'An interesting suggestion. But I have to disappoint you – even I'm not that cynical.'

'Can you think of a reason anyone else might have wanted Robbie dead?'

Rupert shrugged. 'Petty rivalries, bruised egos?'

'And did you notice anything unusual at the venue that night?'

'No. I wasn't there. As you already know, I was here in the hotel with Chaz. We came when we heard something had happened.' He picked up his gym bag and moved towards the exit.

'One last thing,' said Raven, voice level. 'You don't seem the least bit surprised that I'm investigating Robbie's death as suspicious.'

Rupert stopped at the door. A slow, crocodile smile spread across his face. 'You're a police detective, aren't you? What else might you be here for?' He strode through the door without another word, leaving Raven amid the gleaming machines, listening to the rhythmic drone of a treadmill as someone else pounded out their frustrations.

*

Jess pulled up outside the Crown Spa Hotel in her battered old Land Rover, wincing as the engine gave a final sputtering cough before cutting out. The vehicle looked embarrassingly out of place next to the sleek executive cars parked along the Esplanade. She climbed out and gave the door a firm slam, then noticed Raven's silver BMW a few spaces away. He was here for Rupert, no doubt.

She, however, had arranged to meet Frankie. Now that the tour was over and the band's coach had moved on, the filmmaker had holed up at the hotel for a few days. Jess tipped her head back to take in the hotel's elegant white façade, with its gold-topped pillars and wrought-iron balconies. This kind of grandeur was beyond her means. She was more used to staying in youth hostels, especially while on walking holidays.

The thought made her smile. The Coast to Coast Walk was still on her mind. The group she'd met at the pub seemed solid – friendly, yet serious about the challenge ahead. And Gavin... he'd been easy to talk to, the kind of guy she could imagine sharing a windswept path and a celebratory pint with at the finish line.

But she had been hurt badly this past year and wasn't ready for anything more than that. Not yet.

With a deep breath of cool, salt-tinged air, she squared her shoulders and headed inside. Time to see what Frankie had for her.

The lift carried her smoothly to the third floor. Jess knocked twice at Frankie's door, stepping back slightly as it swung open.

'Hi, Jess, come on in.' Frankie greeted her in a baggy hoodie and jeans, hair piled high in a messy bun. A few grey strands escaped at the sides. The hotel room was a cluttered mix of creative chaos and temporary living space. On the desk by the window, dozens of memory sticks were laid out in neat, methodical rows, each carefully labelled in black marker. A high-end laptop sat open, cables snaking around an empty coffee cup teetering dangerously close to the edge.

'As you can see,' said Frankie, gesturing at the memory sticks, 'there's *a lot* of footage. I've been following the band for the entire tour. You're welcome to all of it, but if you can tell me what you're after, I might be able to point you in the right direction – speed things up a bit.'

'Um... to be honest, I'm not entirely sure what I'm looking for yet,' said Jess. 'Obviously the day of the final concert is our key focus, but we also need background material – anything that might give insight into the band dynamics.'

Frankie frowned thoughtfully, tapping a finger against her chin. 'Okay... actually, there is something you should see.' She picked up one of the memory sticks, labelled with mid-tour dates, and slotted it into her laptop. A long list of video files appeared on the screen. She scrolled quickly, eyes scanning the filenames. 'Here it is,' she murmured, double-clicking. 'This was in Coventry.'

Jess leaned over Frankie's shoulder as the video played. The footage captured the usual controlled chaos of a concert setup – crew members hauling equipment, lights being tested, the echoing sound of mic checks. The camera shook slightly as Frankie moved through the backstage area, picking up snippets of conversation and the distant pulse of music through the walls. It was her trademark fly-on-the-wall style.

So far, nothing unusual.

'Wait,' Frankie said. 'It's coming up now.'

The camera panned down a narrow backstage corridor, dimly lit, with equipment cases stacked against the walls. Further along the corridor, two figures came into view. They were standing close together, perhaps too close. A man with his arm draped around a woman. The man was Robbie, but the woman wasn't Skye.

Jess leaned in, her pulse kicking up a notch. The woman had her back to the camera, but something about her posture felt unmistakably intimate. She tilted her head and whispered into Robbie's ear. He whispered something back before wrapping his arms around her and drawing her into an embrace.

Frankie paused the video.

'Is that...?' Jess began, her voice hushed.

Frankie nodded a confirmation. 'It's Taylor.'

Jess leaned in closer, confirming that the young woman

with long hair was indeed the record label's PR rep. 'Why are they standing like that?'

'Good question,' Frankie murmured. She pressed play again.

In the video, Robbie tensed as he sensed the presence of the camera. He turned abruptly, his face flashing from surprise to anger. 'Hey,' he snapped, his voice cutting through the low murmur of background noise. 'Leave us alone. You're always poking around with that bloody camera. Turn it off!'

The video cut out.

Jess straightened, folding her arms. 'Were those two having an affair?'

Frankie unplugged the memory stick, setting it aside with deliberate care. 'You'd have to ask Taylor. But…' She hesitated. 'I'd seen them together before. This was the only time I caught them on film. After this, they were a lot more careful.'

Jess exhaled slowly, running a hand through her hair.

She slipped the memory stick into her bag. 'Thanks. You've been a big help.' She glanced around at the untidy desk, at Frankie, who was watching her with that quiet, assessing gaze. 'Are you staying in Scarborough for a while?'

Frankie smiled. 'I thought I'd stick around for a few more days and see how this plays out. Then I'll be heading home to my studio for a *lot* of editing. If you need more from me, just ask.'

'Thanks,' said Jess. 'I will.' As she left the hotel, she pulled out her phone and called Raven.

He needed to hear this. Immediately.

CHAPTER 18

Becca hadn't yet returned from the post-mortem, but Jess's latest revelation about Robbie and Taylor – combined with Rupert's bombshell about Robbie's solo deal – was too important to wait. Raven needed answers, and there was one person who might have them.

He called PC Sharon Jarvis and asked her to bring Skye Kershaw into the station.

When Skye arrived in the interview room, she looked hollowed out. Dark smudges ringed her eyes, and she gathered her leather jacket around her like a protective cocoon.

Raven gestured to the seat opposite. 'Thank you for agreeing to be interviewed. You're free to leave at any time. But I need to ask you a few questions.'

Skye lowered herself into the chair, her hands trembling as she laid them flat on the table. Her voice was brittle. 'I don't suppose I can vape in here?'

'No,' Raven said gently. 'Sorry.'

'I'll fetch some tea,' said Sharon, touching Skye's shoulder as she passed. Raven caught her look as she went: *Go easy on her.*

When Sharon returned, she placed a steaming mug in front of Skye, who wrapped her fingers around it. The warmth seemed to relax her a little.

'So, Skye,' Raven began, 'you and Robbie had been married how long?'

'Thirty years.' She lifted the mug to her lips and took a tiny sip. 'We celebrated our anniversary just before the tour began.'

'Would you describe it as a happy marriage?'

Her voice wavered, but she straightened her spine. 'What marriage is happy all the time? We had our ups and downs, but we were solid. We made it through everything together. Not many couples can say that.'

'You shared confidences? Last time we spoke, you said you didn't know what Robbie intended to announce at the end of the tour. In fact, you described him as a "dark horse".'

Her fingers tightened around the mug. She knew where this was heading.

'The thing is,' said Raven, 'I spoke to Rupert Devizes this morning. He told me that Robbie had signed a new contract with the record company and was about to launch a solo career. That's what he was going to announce at the end of the show on Saturday night.'

Raven braced for an explosion – shock, fury, or some kind of heated denial. But Skye didn't flinch. She merely closed her eyes for a second before calmly responding.

'That's right.'

He leaned forwards, puzzled. 'You knew? Why didn't you tell me when I asked?'

'It was supposed to be a secret. Anyway, what does it matter now?'

Raven exhaled slowly. 'It matters, Skye, because if someone else knew, that could be a motive for murder.'

His remark drew a scornful laugh from her. 'You think Stu or Pete killed Robbie because he was going solo? That's ridiculous. They didn't know. Neither did Chaz. Rupert was the only one in on it, and he doesn't exactly

A Dying Echo

make a habit of sharing information.'

Raven could certainly believe the smarmy record executive would stay tight-lipped about his business. 'Let's assume you're right. It still seems like a strange move for Robbie – going solo when the band had just reunited and played a sell-out tour.'

Skye gave a scowl. 'It was the perfect time for him to launch a new career. The original contract the band signed left us with no other option. What use was a successful comeback if we still earned nothing from our recordings? Touring is hard work, and we're not getting any younger. Robbie and I needed to find a way to earn a living by writing and recording new material. Rupert thought that Robbie had the potential to make a go of it alone, and by cutting out the rest of the band we were able to negotiate a new deal. You may think that sounds hard-nosed, but you haven't spent the last thirty years struggling to scrape by, while that smug bastard took everything.'

There was venom in her voice when she spoke of Rupert. The bitterness of spending decades watching her own success line someone else's pockets.

'You're certain that nobody else knew about this?' pressed Raven. 'What about Taylor, Rupert's PR rep?'

Skye shifted in her seat, her shoulders tensing. Her fingers curled around the mug, as if steadying herself. 'Why are you asking about her? She's got nothing to do with this.'

Raven softened his voice. 'Skye, is there any possibility that Robbie was secretly seeing Taylor behind your back?'

She took the suggestion like a slap to her face. 'Of course he wasn't. Why would you even ask me that?'

Raven took a deep breath and exchanged a glance with Sharon. 'I'm sorry to have to reveal this to you, Skye, but one of my officers has been shown video footage from the tour. It shows Robbie and Taylor – how can I put it? – behaving rather intimately backstage. Were they having an affair?'

Skye's reaction was immediate and explosive. 'No! Of

course they weren't.'

Raven studied her expression closely. She seemed certain in her denial, confident that Robbie hadn't cheated on her. Was it possible that he had kept his relationship a secret? The cramped quarters on board the tour bus would have made that a challenge, but perhaps the very closeness of the tour environment had facilitated an illicit love affair. Robbie and Taylor had been reckless, but some people enjoyed that kind of danger.

Raven took no joy in his next move, but it had to be done. He produced a still image that Jess had printed from the video. In the frame, Robbie had his arms around Taylor, who was leaning against him, her face pressed to his chest.

Skye's jaw clenched as she regarded the incriminating image, but she shook her head with conviction. 'I don't know what's going on in this picture, but it's not what you think. Robbie would never have cheated on me.' A fiery spark lit up her face. 'Never!'

Raven regarded her with sadness. 'The problem I have, Skye, is that if you found out that Robbie planned to leave you for Taylor, just as he was about to embark on his solo career, that would give you a very strong motive to stop him by any means necessary. And as you have no alibi for the period leading up to the concert…'

He let his words trail off, the implications clear enough.

Skye's posture changed. She sat up straighter, the tension in her shoulders shifting into something more controlled. When she spoke again, there was an undercurrent of anger. 'You don't know the whole truth. What that bastard Rupert' – she spat the name with hatred – 'seems to have forgotten to tell you is that Robbie's new contract named me as his manager. The financial split was fifty-fifty between me and Robbie. So I stood to benefit from his solo career just as much as him.'

The revelation hit Raven like a wave. If Skye was telling the truth, then she had far less reason to want Robbie dead. Sure, there was the question of the extra-marital affair, which despite Skye's vehement denial was still a possibility. But if she was going to be Robbie's manager, any financial motive for murder was gone.

Raven could well believe that Rupert had failed to mention this key fact, if only to stir up trouble. He glanced at Sharon, who was taking careful notes, then leaned back in his chair, thoughtful. Even if Skye hadn't poisoned her husband, it was still possible that one of the other band members – or perhaps Chaz – had found out about Robbie's plans to wind up the band and go solo. If they had, was that strong enough reason to commit murder?

*

After leaving the post-mortem, Becca made her way through the hospital's maze of corridors to the intensive care unit, where her grandmother lay unconscious in her bed, a frail figure swallowed by crisp white sheets. Tubes and wires trailed from her body, and her fragile frame was dwarfed by the array of high-tech monitors that recorded her vital signs. The steady beeping of the machines formed a relentless backdrop, broken only by the comings and goings of doctors and nurses as they attended to their patients.

Sue sat beside the bed, hands clasped tightly in her lap, eyes distant with exhaustion. She rose to her feet as Becca entered, rubbing at her stiff shoulders. 'Becca, love, I wasn't expecting you.'

'I've just come from a...' Becca hesitated. She couldn't bring herself to say *post-mortem*, not in her grandmother's presence. 'I was here for work, so I thought I'd pop in and see how she's doing.'

Sue exhaled, glancing at the monitors. 'It's touch and go,' she admitted. 'Dr Clarkson said the next forty-eight hours are critical.'

Becca swallowed hard, her throat tightening. 'Have you been here long?'

'A couple of hours.'

She touched her mother's arm. 'You look exhausted. Why don't you get something in the café? I'll stay here for a bit.'

Sue hesitated. 'Don't you have to go back to work?'

'Not yet. Go on, get some tea and a bite to eat.'

Sue finally relented, giving Becca's arm a squeeze. 'Thanks. I won't be long.'

'Take as long as you need.'

Becca lowered herself into the chair her mother had vacated, watching the shallow rise and fall of her grandmother's chest. The sight triggered an ache of déjà vu deep in her bones. She had sat like this before – waiting, hoping, dreading – at another bedside, while someone else she loved teetered in that same no man's land between life and death.

Sam Earnshaw.

Her boyfriend had been left in a coma after a hit-and-run incident, and she had spent night after night at his bedside, talking to him, willing him to wake up. When he finally did, it had felt like a miracle.

And then, everything had fallen apart. His family had been hit with another tragedy. Sam had left for Australia.

He had asked her to go with him.

But she chose to stay.

Sometimes she allowed herself to think about what might have been. Had she made the right choice? She wondered what Sam was doing now and hoped he had found happiness.

She let out a slow breath, her fingers tightening around her grandmother's frail, paper-thin hand. The veins stood out beneath the translucent skin. Her touch felt like a lifeline and she held on tightly, unwilling to let go.

When Sam had been in a coma, talking had helped, even though he hadn't responded. Even though he had probably never even registered her words. So she did the same now.

'I'm working on another murder case, Nana,' she said softly, keeping her voice low so the nurses bustling in and out of the ward wouldn't hear. 'With Raven.'

The name caught in her throat.

'You remember when Sam asked me to go with him to Australia and I said no? I told him I couldn't leave because of family. And that was partly true. But I think' – her grip tightened – 'I think it was really because of Raven.'

The heart monitor continued to beep, steady and indifferent to her voice.

She let out a shaky breath. 'I didn't expect anything to happen between us, but I just couldn't leave while he was here. And now he's with Liz Larkin and I –' Her voice faltered. A single tear slid down her cheek and landed on the sheet.

A sudden voice behind her made her jump. 'Are you all right, love?'

Sue stood in the doorway, a cup of tea and a sandwich in her hands.

Becca hastily wiped her eyes and forced a small smile. 'Yes. I was just… having a little chat with Nana.'

She wasn't sure how much her mum had overheard, but if she had caught anything about Raven, she didn't mention it. Instead, she crossed the room and rested a gentle hand on Becca's shoulder.

'I know it's upsetting, seeing Nana like this. But you know you can always talk to me. Or your dad. That's what families are for.'

Becca nodded, swallowing the lump in her throat. 'Thanks, Mum.'

She rose to her feet, wrapping her arms around her mother in a brief but firm hug. 'I should get back to work now.'

Sue held onto her a moment longer before releasing her. 'I'll call you if anything changes.'

'Thanks.' Becca left the hospital feeling strangely lighter. Talking to her grandmother, even though she couldn't respond, had helped her get her own thoughts straight.

As she walked to her car, her grandmother's voice

echoed in her mind, warm and wise as ever.

You can't pour from an empty cup, Becca. Take care of yourself first.

She smiled faintly. Maybe it was time she listened.

CHAPTER 19

Becca *still* wasn't back from the post-mortem. What on earth was taking her so long? Raven checked his phone again. No messages. He dialled her number and listened impatiently as it rang three times before the inevitable voicemail message kicked in. He hung up.

He didn't like it when his team went dark, but he couldn't wait around all day. He had work to do.

Taylor seemed like a good place to start.

He found the young publicist sitting cross-legged on a sofa in the hotel lounge, a sleek laptop open on her lap. Her thumbs flew over her phone screen at breakneck speed, eyes flicking between devices. A pair of oversized pink headphones covered her ears, cocooning her from the low murmur of voices that filled the lounge. Raven had seen Hannah wearing similar ones. She'd explained to him that women used them as a kind of *do not disturb* sign, a subtle barrier to unwanted conversation. Raven understood the logic but had his doubts about it. Wouldn't it be safer to stay alert to your surroundings?

As if to prove his point, Taylor didn't register his presence until he was almost directly in front of her and his shadow fell across her face.

'Mind if I join you? I'm DCI Raven from North Yorkshire Police.'

Her head snapped up, eyes widening as she yanked off the headphones and draped them around her neck. 'Oh! Sorry, didn't see you there. Is this about Robbie? Rupert warned me you might have some questions for me.'

Rupert warned me. Raven wondered what exactly Rupert had warned her about.

He took a seat on a leather chair opposite her, leaned back and crossed his arms in a relaxed posture. He had only caught a passing glimpse of Taylor on the night of the concert, and he wanted to assess her properly. She was young, perhaps fresh out of uni, with long wavy hair that tumbled over her shoulders. Her skin was flawless, her eyebrows boldly pencilled, and her fashion sense was distinctly Gen Z, a vintage blazer paired with high-waisted jeans and chunky scarlet trainers. She clutched her iPhone as if it were the holy grail, her thumb unconsciously scrolling even as she spoke. A social media native.

'You're staying on in Scarborough for a while?' Raven enquired, his voice casual.

Taylor's lips curled into a faint smile. 'Yeah. Rupert asked me to stick around until he's ready to head back to London. He likes to keep his team close.' She glanced around the opulent lounge. 'Not that I'm complaining. This place is way nicer than most tour hotels, and the record label's picking up the bill.'

Her phone buzzed, and her gaze instinctively dropped to the screen. Her fingers flew across the keyboard as she typed a rapid response before glancing back at Raven with an unapologetic shrug. 'Sorry. Work never stops.'

He was used to such behaviour when talking to Hannah. 'Still,' he asked casually, as if the interruption had not occurred, 'I imagine you're keen to get back to London?'

She gave a half-hearted shrug. 'Not really. I can work easily enough while travelling. Anyway, I've been on tour with the band for so long, a few more days won't make a difference.'

Raven noted the unspoken implications behind her answer. No eagerness to return home. No mention of a partner waiting for her back in the capital. 'You've enjoyed the tour?'

She nodded eagerly, tossing her glossy hair. 'Sure. It's been good getting to know the band at close quarters. Makes it easier for me to find an authentic voice, you know, when I'm doing posts and responding to messages from fans.' This time, it was her laptop that grabbed her attention, and she quickly typed out a message on her keyboard in response. She shrugged at Raven. 'Crazy busy. I've never known anything like it. So much drama online, ever since….'

'Since Robbie died,' Raven finished. It seemed that the demise of the band's lead vocalist had only increased the need for a full-time publicist. 'So tell me, how did you get on with the band?'

'Oh really good, yeah,' said Taylor automatically. She pulled a slight face. 'I mean, some of them better than others, to be fair. You know what touring with a band is like?'

'No,' said Raven. 'Tell me.'

'Well, they're stars, aren't they? They're allowed to be – you know – temperamental.' She stopped awkwardly and checked her phone again, but for once there was nothing to distract her from the conversation.

'Temperamental?' probed Raven.

Taylor glanced anxiously around the room. 'This is off the record, yeah?'

'I won't be splashing it all over social media, if that's what you mean.'

She lowered her voice. 'Well, I mean, Skye's okay. I felt sorry for her, to be honest. She looked lost most of the time. Not really part of the band, you know? Like she was on the outside looking in. Stu can be very moody. He's always just looking for the next drink. And as for Pete, he's pretty much stoned from the moment he leaves the stage.'

'And Robbie?'

Taylor's face lit up with warmth. 'Robbie was the nicest by far. Kind, good-humoured, sweet. He was easy to work with, always polite, no ego. He always made time for people. I liked him.' She hesitated before adding, 'I know I'm probably not supposed to ask this, but... do you know what exactly happened to him?'

'Not yet. But I do need to ask you to elaborate on your relationship with Robbie.'

Taylor stiffened. Her phone buzzed again, but this time she ignored it. 'What do you mean, my relationship?'

'There's some footage from the tour,' said Raven. 'It shows you and Robbie standing very close together. He has his arm around you. So I have to ask – were the two of you romantically involved?'

He expected a flinch, or some tell-tale sign of embarrassment. But instead, Taylor gave a short, sharp burst of amusement.

'Sorry,' she said quickly, shaking her head. 'I shouldn't laugh. It's just... *romantically involved?* That's such a quaint, old-fashioned phrase. You mean, were we having sex?'

Raven raised an eyebrow. He wasn't sure he appreciated being called quaint, but perhaps she had a point. He was an old-timer for sure, well past his best-before date, but he hadn't realised he was so out of touch. His thoughts turned to Liz Larkin. Was he *romantically involved* with Liz, or were they just... *having sex*?

'Well, yes,' he said finally, 'if you want to put it like that.'

Taylor's amusement softened into a more thoughtful expression. 'The answer is no,' she said simply. 'Not that Robbie wasn't attractive – for his age – but he just wasn't my type. Anyway, he never tried anything on. I think the footage you're talking about was from Coventry. I'd just heard that my grandfather died, and I was upset. Robbie was comforting me. That's all it was. Like I say, Robbie never tried to hit on me.'

Her reaction sounded natural. Raven couldn't detect any flicker of hesitation or discomfort. Either she was telling the truth, or she was a *very* good liar.

'Okay,' he said. 'Thanks for the clarification.'

'Was there anything else?'

'Did Robbie talk about his plans for the future? After the tour, I mean?'

'Not specifically. The tour went well, so I assumed the band might want to go back into the recording studio and release some new material. I asked Rupert if I could start teasing it on social media, but he said to hold off for now.'

So it seemed that Taylor at least didn't know about Robbie's plans for a solo career. 'So what's happening online now, with all these messages you're getting?'

Taylor perked up at the change in direction, reaching for her phone. 'Loads,' she said, her fingers flying across the screen. 'Robbie's still trending. I've been trying to take control of the story, but it's just too big. There are a few tribute hashtags, but mostly it's turned into conspiracy theories.'

Raven frowned. 'What kind of theories?'

Taylor leaned forwards eagerly. 'Some people think Robbie was poisoned by an obsessive fan. Others think it was a set-up, that he was silenced because he was about to expose something – you know, the big announcement he said he was going to make at the end of the concert. The internet's a wild place. Some people are even convinced that the band was cursed.'

'Cursed?'

Taylor smirked. 'Oh yeah. There's a whole theory about the band being jinxed because of Mickey's disappearance back in the day. Some people reckon Robbie's death is some kind of delayed karma.'

Raven put no stock in online hysteria. Social media was a place to gauge public sentiment and maybe even find a lead, but he usually left it to his junior detectives. 'And what's your take on it?' he asked.

'Me?' Taylor looked surprised, then shrugged. 'I think people just need answers. And in the absence of facts, they'll make up their own stories. It's my job to give them the narrative we want them to believe.'

Raven studied her, intrigued by her candidness. 'And what narrative is that?'

She gave him a coy smile. 'That Echoes of Mercury was a legendary band, and Robbie was an icon. Tragic loss, gone too soon, the whole rock'n'roll mythology. It's what fans want, isn't it?'

He supposed that it was. 'All right,' he said. 'Thank you for your time, Taylor.'

She flashed him a bright smile. 'No problem. If you need anything else, let me know.'

He rose to his feet and made his way out of the hotel. As he stepped into the crisp evening air, his phone buzzed.

Liz: *Booked a table for seven thirty. Hope you can make it. xx*

He hesitated. The kisses. He was still getting used to that.

He considered responding with a heart emoji. Too much. A thumbs-up? Too little. A simple *See you then?* Too abrupt.

In the end, he typed: *Thanks. Will be there. Looking forward to it. R*

And pressed send.

CHAPTER 20

Jess didn't know much about poetry, and the idea that Mickey was still alive and publishing his work online seemed like a long shot. She would rather have been out interviewing band members or people involved with the tour, like Frankie or Taylor, but Raven had asked her to check out the poetry angle, so here she was at her desk again, a nice steaming mug of Yorkshire tea in front of her.

Her mind drifted briefly to the Coast to Coast Walk and the promise of healthy exercise out in the fresh air, but she steered it back to the job in hand, fixing her attention on her computer screen. She tapped out a search for *Frost and Fury* and quickly found a match on Reddit. There was an active user with that name in a Subreddit called *Original Content Poetry*. Jess clicked through to the profile.

The avatar staring back at her was a cartoon of a cloaked figure clutching a feather quill that dripped with ink. To Jess's way of thinking, it looked unsettlingly like blood. Sad, shadowed eyes peered out from beneath a black cowl, lending the image a haunting, gothic quality.

No name. No bio. No clue as to who this person was in the real world. Although, to be fair, that was common practice in the online space. Here, people were free to post anonymously and make whatever comments they wanted.

She leaned in closer to the screen. *Frost and Fury* posted infrequently but over the years had penned dozens of poems, all with melancholy or morbid titles. Jess clicked on a few at random and started to read. The poems weren't really to her taste, laced as they were with sorrow, regret, and bitterness. She had suffered enough personal tragedy in her own life recently – not least the murder of her boyfriend, and an attempt on her own life – and preferred to look on the bright side.

But one poem in particular grabbed her attention. It had been posted the day Robbie was killed. The title was *Stolen*.

You took my words; you stole my dreams,
A silent betrayal of voiceless screams.
Your empty reasons, cold and bare,
Like dying fields in poisoned air.

Could these really be the words of the band's former frontman, channelling his rage about how the band had taken his songs and performed them without him? Had something happened to Mickey all those years ago – some kind of breakdown – that made him withdraw from the pressures of fame and publicity? Was he still out there, hiding his true identity, nursing some festering grudge against his former associates?

She read on.

You begged for forgiveness, yet bore no shame,
I handed you nothing but all of my blame.
In the shadows, my hatred grew,
A garden of thorns where nothing is true.

A cold tingle ran down Jess's spine at the thought of Mickey's hatred growing as he watched the band's renewed success with envy from the sidelines.

Twisted shadows took their form,
Monsters born of a vengeful storm.
This broken world will feel my might,
A reckoning born from endless night.

She could feel the pain in the poet's words, even though she didn't understand the reason for the hurt. The talk of vengeance suggested some kind of betrayal, some injustice that had to be redressed.

The final verse was chilling:

One day, I'll rise, unbound, complete,
Your shattered remains laid at my feet.
One day, the darkness will bow to my flame,
I'll claim my dues; you'll know my name.

Could this really be Mickey? Still alive? After all these years, lurking in the shadows, nursing old wounds, threatening some kind of violent vengeance? Judging by the comments, plenty of people seemed to think so.

'Mickey's revenge on Robbie.'

'He's still out there. This proves it.'

There was no way of knowing if this was really Mickey, or just some misguided fan engaged in a twisted game. Jess wondered how *Frost and Fury* had become associated with Echoes of Mercury in the first place. Had one fan posted the theory, and the speculation spiralled into hysteria? Or was there something *real* behind the guesswork?

There was definitely a threat implied in that final verse. Not specifically aimed at Robbie, nor one that named a time or place. And yet there was a reference to poison in the first verse of the poem.

Coincidence? Jess could see how people might so easily get sucked into these conspiracy theories, analysing every nuance, every possible connection between what was written and what had taken place. The vague but vivid imagery of the poems could easily fuel that kind of speculation.

She was about to click on another link when a notification popped up.

Another poem. Published as she watched.

Frost and Fury was posting. Right now.

The new poem was called *Martyr*.

Jess clicked.

You called it devotion,
A needle's kiss.
A sacrifice offered,
To the altar of bliss.

Jess shivered at the sparse word painting of the lines.

A needle's kiss.

The phrase lingered in her mind, cold and metallic. A needle that "kissed" the skin. Was that meant literally? Poison again? Or something else? Drugs?

She drummed her fingers on the desk, thinking back to the team meeting that morning. What had Tony said about Pete?

A conviction for drug abuse. Heroin. Her gaze snapped back to the screen. *Was this poem about Pete?*

She read the final stanza.

You made me a martyr,
To pleasure and pain,
I'll open the doorway,
To hell bathed in flame.

Her stomach twisted into a tight knot.

That was surely a threat, even more explicit than the veiled warning in the poem published on the day of Robbie's poisoning.

Or was she imagining connections that weren't there?

Either way, she wasn't taking any chances.

She grabbed her phone and called Raven. 'Boss, you'll want to see this.'

★

Raven's fingers tightened around the steering wheel, his knuckles whitening as Jess's voice crackled over the car's Bluetooth. Her words were quick and halting, tumbling out in a rush as she explained what she had discovered about the online poet, particularly the latest poem that had appeared moments earlier.

Raven felt an icy tingle at the back of his neck. He had only just pulled his BMW into the car park on Quay Street, his mind on the evening ahead, when Jess had called him. Now he sat rooted in his car, listening in stony silence as she repeated the sinister words. Already he knew that his plans were evaporating.

'I might be reading too much into it,' Jess explained tentatively. 'It's just a poem published anonymously online. We have no way of knowing the true identity of *Frost and Fury*. Even if it's a real threat, it may not have anything to do with Pete. But the timing seems too much of a coincidence.'

Raven's jaw tightened. 'No harm in checking on him,' he decided. He glanced at the clock on the dashboard. Six thirty. He'd planned to shower and change before meeting Liz for dinner. Now he'd be lucky if he made it to the hotel at all. But he couldn't ignore even the slightest possibility of a genuine danger to life. 'I'll drive down to Cayton Bay now,' he told Jess. 'You head home and enjoy your evening.'

She hesitated. 'You sure?'

'Positive. I'll handle this.'

'Okay. Thanks. But be careful.'

'I will.'

He ended the call and felt the weight of silence in the car. He sat there for a moment, the engine still running, his thoughts churning. It was probably nothing. Just a cryptic post from an online crackpot. But he knew better than to ignore his instincts. And right now, they were screaming at him to move.

He reversed sharply out of the parking space, tyres skidding on the damp tarmac. The sky was bruised purple, the evening closing in fast. His headlights cut through the gloom as he pulled onto the Foreshore, straight into the slow-moving river of evening traffic.

Brake lights flared ahead, forcing him to slow. He gritted his teeth as the procession of cars crawled along the seafront, headlights reflected on the wet road. Salt water droplets spattered against his windscreen, driven by a brisk wind rolling in from the North Sea. Gulls screeched overhead, their calls sharp and discordant.

Raven drummed his fingers on the steering wheel, frustration clawing at him as he inched past the amusement arcades and chippies. He knew he shouldn't complain. The traffic in Yorkshire was nothing like in London. There, he had spent uncountable hours stuck on the roads, engine idling, the M6 like a caged lion in a zoo, yearning to be free.

Still, it felt like the traffic was conspiring against him, keeping him from moving, from getting to Pete. He checked his phone again, half-expecting another message from Jess. A follow-up, a warning, or else an assurance that Pete was safe.

Nothing. Just the screen glowing back at him, blank and cold.

He finally broke free of the seafront gridlock, the M6 surging forward as he joined the Filey Road. He put his foot down, the engine growling as he picked up speed. The road twisted and curved along the coast, flanked by dense hedgerows and plunging cliffs. His eyes flicked to the darkening sky. Heavy clouds hung low, shrouding the coastline in shadows that seemed to creep ever closer.

Raven drove fast, pushing the car through the winding turns, tyres hugging the wet road. His heartbeat matched the rhythm of the wipers, the steady thump as they swept away the raindrops. The GPS showed he was only minutes away. He silently willed the car to go faster.

The turning to Cayton Bay came into view, barely visible in the gloom. He braked hard, the car lurching as he swung onto the narrow gravel track. The potholes jolted him in his seat, slowing his pace to a crawl.

It was pitch dark now, the cliff edge invisible beyond the sweep of his headlamps. His stomach tightened as he eased the car down the pitted track, past the looming shapes of mobile homes standing silent and dark. No lights, no movement.

Then the smell hit him.

Not the pungent whiff of cannabis he associated with Pete, but something worse.

Smoke.

Thick. Acrid. Choking.

He spotted a flicker of orange in the distance. Fire.

His foot hit the brake, the car skidding to a halt. He threw open the door, the cold night air slapping his face as he jumped out.

He ran, half-stumbling across the uneven ground in the direction of the caravan. Smoke coiled through the night to greet him. It was denser now, curling through the air, stinging his eyes with a sharp, chemical smell. He stumbled forwards, his shoes slipping on loose gravel as he moved towards the glow.

He rounded the bend and stopped dead.

Pete's caravan was ablaze.

The fire roared, flames licking hungrily at windows, the thin walls buckling under the heat. The caravan's side panels were melting, blackening, collapsing inward. Sparks shot skyward, spiralling into the night.

A window shattered, the force of the explosion sending razor-sharp shards of acrylic flying. Raven threw up his arms, shielding his face as the fragments rained down around him.

The flames danced higher, fuelled by the rush of air.

He could feel the heat, fierce and suffocating, scorching his skin even from a distance. His mouth went dry.

'Pete!' he shouted, his voice raw. 'Pete! Are you in

there?'

No answer. Only the relentless crackle and roar of the fire, a ravenous beast devouring everything it touched.

Raven forced himself closer, his eyes watering as the smoke enveloped him. The air was hot, thick, heavy. He coughed, his lungs burning.

He reached the door, his hands fumbling for the handle. His fingers recoiled as pain shot through them – the metal was searing hot. He grabbed his coat sleeve, wrapped it around his hand, and tried again. The door creaked, then burst open.

A blast of heat surged out, driving him back. Raven stumbled, his right leg giving way from under him. He hit the ground hard and dragged himself away.

He scrambled clumsily back to his feet, his vision blurred, his leg a ball of agony. He wrapped one arm around his mouth to shield himself from the smoke and tried for the door a second time. But the heat spilling through the opening was unbearable.

No way in.

'Pete!' he yelled again, his voice cracking.

The only response was the crackle and howl as the inferno raged.

He was too late.

He backed away, his heart pounding, helplessness clawing at him. He fumbled for his phone, his fingers shaking as he dialled 999.

'Fire at Cayton Bay. A caravan... someone's probably inside,' he managed, his voice hoarse.

As he spoke, the caravan erupted in a fireball.

A wave of intense heat slammed into him, knocking him to the ground again as a deafening boom shattered the night. His ears rang, the world spun. Debris rained down around him. Chunks of burning plastic.

Raven pushed himself up to a seated position, his hands raw and bloody. His head throbbed, his chest felt tight. He could only watch, helpless, as the fire consumed what little remained.

Minutes stretched like hours until finally he heard the distant wail of a siren. The fire engine rumbled along the bumpy track, its headlights cutting through the smoke. A team of firefighters jumped down, unfurled their hoses and got to work. Jets of water doused the flames and the fire was quickly extinguished.

The lead firefighter approached Raven. 'Anyone inside?'

'Possibly one person,' he confirmed grimly.

The man nodded and signalled to his crew.

A man in protective gear stepped into the charred remains of the caravan. He emerged a moment later, shaking his head slowly. The universal gesture of bad news.

'One male. Deceased.'

Raven exhaled slowly. *Pete.*

Could this be a tragic accident? The result of a stray match from lighting a cannabis joint?

A careless drug user living alone could easily become the victim of his own habit.

But the coincidence seemed too unlikely.

First Robbie's death. Then Jess's discovery of the online poem and its veiled yet loaded threat.

Raven's phone vibrated in his pocket, the screen lighting up. He pulled it out with soot-streaked fingers. A message from Liz.

Are you coming?

He glanced at the time. He was already an hour late for dinner. He stared at the screen, his fingers trembling.

He typed back, barely seeing the words.

Sorry. Something's come up.

Her reply came a second later.

What?

He didn't answer. He didn't have the words. Not now. Not yet.

His hands shook as he slipped the phone back into his pocket, turned, and stared at the smouldering wreckage before him, at the glowing embers flickering in the dark.

CHAPTER 21

The charred skeleton of the caravan still smouldered in the cold morning air. The acrid scent of burnt plastic and scorched metal hung heavy, the sea breeze doing little to disperse the sharp chemical stench. The earth around the wreckage was blackened and brittle, the grass singed to nothing but cinders. Nearby, the walls of the neighbouring caravans bore streaks of soot, silent witnesses to the inferno.

Raven stepped out of his car, his shoes crunching over the damp gravel. He shoved his hands deep into his coat pockets to shield them against the morning chill. The caravan park manager was already there, pacing the perimeter of the roped-off area, muttering under his breath about insurance claims and loss of business. Raven ignored him, his attention fixed on the still-smoking ruins – Pete's home, now nothing more than twisted metal and charred fabric.

He hadn't got home until well past eleven the previous night. The house had been empty – no Hannah, no Quincey waiting to greet him at the door. The realisation had left him feeling strangely hollow. Hannah was spending more and more time with Ellie, and while he didn't want to push her, he was increasingly concerned about her drinking. But what could he say? If he challenged her, she'd only throw it back at him – *What about you, Dad? Stumbling in at all hours? Keeping secrets about where you've been, and who with?*

He let out a slow breath. It was easier not to think about his daughter at the moment.

Instead, he had called Liz to apologise for missing dinner.

'What happened?' she'd asked, not irritated, just curious.

'Pete's dead. At least we think it's him. What's left of him.'

'Oh my God. What happened?'

He'd told her about the fire, about the body found inside. But he hadn't mentioned the poem. That link seemed too tenuous until they had gathered more evidence.

'Do you think the fire was started deliberately?'

'I don't know yet. We need to confirm the cause of death. But if this was arson and not just an accident, then we're officially dealing with a serial killer.'

Now, as he stood watching the last tendrils of smoke rising into the grey sky, he hoped the forensics team would soon give him the answers he needed.

The CSI van rumbled slowly down the narrow track, its tyres crunching over loose gravel. Holly Chang emerged from it first, clambering ungainly out of the driver's seat, her compact frame weighed down by a heavy-duty utility belt. Her face was impassive, eyes keen as she surveyed the scene. Her youthful and more sprightly juniors, Erin and Jamie, hopped out next, lugging cases of equipment between them.

Holly gave a low whistle as she took in the burnt-out husk of the caravan. 'Looks like someone got a bit enthusiastic with the bacon and eggs,' she remarked dryly. 'Or did bonfire night come early?'

Raven was in no mood for banter. 'Possible arson,' he said levelly, 'although we can't rule out an accident yet.'

The fire officer had explained that the explosion that blasted him to the ground was caused by a cylinder of propane igniting. There was nothing suspicious about the presence of propane, as liquid petroleum gas was commonly used in caravans for cooking. As for the initial cause of the fire, that was still to be determined.

Holly cast her sharp gaze over the scene, unconvinced. 'Accidental, eh? You think someone decided to host their own indoor fireworks display?'

Erin and Jamie began unloading more equipment, their movements brisk and efficient. Holly snapped on a pair of gloves. 'All right, let's get to work. Jamie, check for accelerant residue. Erin, collect soil samples from the perimeter. Let's see if this was a barbecue gone wrong or something more sinister.'

Raven watched them set to work with their usual efficiency. Holly moved around the wreckage with practised ease, her gloved fingers lifting charred fragments, turning them over with a surgeon's precision.

'I'll leave you to it,' said Raven, as a familiar battered Land Rover appeared at the top of the track, bouncing and clattering over the uneven ground before pulling to an abrupt halt. Jess climbed out, followed by Tony.

Raven's eyes flicked past them, searching. 'Is Becca on her way?' he asked, trying his best not to let his disappointment show.

Jess shook her head. 'No idea. I thought she'd be here with you.'

'She's not,' Raven said shortly. His messages to her had gone unanswered. He didn't know if she was deliberately ignoring him, but either way, it was starting to bother him.

He could deal with that later. Right now, they had a crime scene to process.

Tony flipped open his notebook. 'The toxicology report on Robbie came in last night. Cyanide poisoning, just as you suspected.'

'So we're definitely dealing with murder,' said Raven, allowing a moment to let the news sink in. 'Tony, when you get back to base, start digging into potential sources of cyanide. I want to know how the killer might have got hold of it.'

'Will do.' Tony scribbled a note. 'And what about that taxi driver who saw Mickey with someone the night he disappeared? Do you want me to see if he's still around?'

'Good idea. And find out who was SIO on the case at the time.'

'Very good, sir.'

Jess wandered closer to the scorched shell of the caravan, her eyes narrowed in thought. 'Was the door locked when you got here?' she asked, frowning.

'No,' answered Raven.

'Then why couldn't Pete get out in time?'

'Good question.' It was one of the questions that had kept Raven awake the previous night. Had Pete already been dead when the caravan was set alight? Or had he lain there fully conscious as the blaze took hold around him, and if so, why hadn't he been able to escape?

Holly's voice cut through the cold air. 'I think I can help you there.' She emerged from the wreckage of the caravan, holding out a charred, twisted object in a plastic evidence bag. 'I found this in the debris. A hypodermic needle and a syringe. It looks like our victim was injected with something before the flames did their work.'

Raven felt his jaw tighten. 'What about the cause of the fire? Accidental or deliberate?'

Holly puffed out her cheeks. 'You do like your results quickly, don't you? You know what they say around these parts?'

'What?' asked Raven through gritted teeth. He'd already had more than enough of Holly's droll humour for one morning.

'Tha can't rush a good brew,' she declared in her best Yorkshire accent. 'This isn't a guessing game. We haven't even finished processing the scene yet. Then the forensics team will have to pick through all the evidence and maybe send things off to the lab for further analysis before they send you their final report. The wheels turn slowly.' Her eyes gleamed. 'But I can give you an informal heads-up.'

'Yes?'

'It was deliberate. There's a lingering smell of petrol coming from a melted jerry can by the door. Sharp V-patterns on the walls indicate that the fire took hold very quickly. Burn patterns on the floor show petrol was poured in a trail leading to the exit. Classic fire-starter technique.' She glanced back at the blackened remains. 'Whoever did this wanted to make sure the fire spread fast to cut off any chance of escape.'

Raven exhaled, his breath visible in the chilly air.

Someone had dealt ruthlessly with Pete, just as they had murdered Robbie.

He turned to Jess. 'Well done for raising the alarm last night.'

'Not in time, though,' Jess murmured.

'You called me as soon as the poem was posted online.'

She nodded but still looked uneasy. 'I know, but I really wish I'd been wrong about the threat to Pete.'

'True,' said Raven. 'But you've proven there's a link between this online poet and the murder of two band members. *Frost and Fury* is either the perpetrator, or someone very close to them. So establishing their identity is now a top priority.'

Holly's gaze widened as she listened. 'Some anonymous poet posted about the attack online?'

'Yes,' Raven confirmed. 'Jess found the poem last night. It hinted at Pete's death immediately before it happened. And an earlier poem referenced Robbie's murder too. So, whoever *Frost and Fury* are, they knew this was coming.'

Holly turned her gaze to the burnt-out caravan. 'Twisted. Someone's playing a sick game.' There was no trace of her earlier banter.

'Could it really be Mickey?' asked Jess.

Raven stared at the smoking wreckage, his mind already racing through the possibilities.

'That's precisely what we need to find out.'

*

'DCI Raven, what an unexpected honour!'

Raven clenched his jaw. After his early-morning banter with Holly Chang, the last thing he needed was a dose of Dr Felicity Wainwright's habitual snark. If Holly's humour was dry, Felicity's was acidic, designed to corrode. But with Becca nowhere to be seen, and Jess and Tony busy with other tasks, he had little choice but to endure the ordeal.

He knew he should be grateful. Felicity had agreed to conduct Pete's post-mortem at very short notice, but her particular brand of harsh cynicism coupled with their overt and mutual personal dislike of one another was the reason he tried his best never to attend post-mortems himself.

He arranged his features into something resembling civility. 'The pleasure's all mine,' he answered flatly, meeting her sarcasm with a helping of his own.

Felicity's eyes sparkled above her mask, relishing his discomfort. 'Oh, I doubt that very much. Shall we get on with it?'

'By all means.'

Felicity's movements were brisk, efficient and almost graceful. She drew back the blue sheet with a practised flick of her wrist, revealing what remained of Pete the drummer.

Raven's chest tightened. There was hardly anything left – a charred husk where a man had been.

Felicity's gloved hands hovered over the ruined body, her gaze clinical and detached. 'Hmm. Not much to work with,' she remarked with characteristic bluntness. 'Toasted to a crisp, you might say.'

Raven ignored the tactless comment, recalling his failed attempt to enter the caravan as the inferno took hold. Part of him needed to know... had Pete still been alive when Raven arrived at the scene of the blaze? If he'd been quicker, or braver, would there have been a chance to save him?

He swallowed the bile that rose in his throat as the post-mortem began.

Felicity made her first incision with almost tender precision, proceeding to cut and slice with fluid and unhurried efficiency. As she went, she tossed out cold, clinical observations punctuated with caustic remarks intended to rile him.

He ignored her barbs, observing with detachment.

Felicity beckoned for his attention. 'Needle marks on the arm here.' She didn't look up at him. Her eyes were on her work, her tone dispassionate. She indicated a spot on Pete's inner wrist with her gloved hand. 'Toxicology will confirm what was in his system, but I'd wager he was sedated before the fire started.'

'Drugged, more likely,' said Raven. 'Pete was a heroin user, although he swore he'd kicked the habit.'

'Then he was telling the truth,' said Felicity, her tone almost cheerful. She traced faint bruising around Pete's wrists, turning his hands so that Raven could see. 'These marks indicate that he was tied with a rope. So whatever substance was injected into his system, he didn't do it himself.'

Raven took a deep breath. 'So, was Pete already dead before the fire started?'

Felicity paused briefly before giving him the answer he feared most. 'No. The presence of burns in the respiratory tract indicates that the cause of death was asphyxia due to inhalation of carbon monoxide or other toxic gases.' She pointed to the blackened airways within the corpse's throat and lungs. 'Smoke inhalation, in other words. This man was still breathing when the fire took hold.'

The revelation hit Raven hard. Pete had been alive when he reached the caravan, when he'd tried – and failed – to gain entry. If he'd driven faster... if his leg hadn't given way from under him…

His hands trembled with anger and regret. There was a time when he had idolised Echoes of Mercury, had thought of the talented young drummer as a musical genius. Even now, after being confronted with Pete's ongoing battles with mental health and addiction problems, and witnessing the depths to which the musician had fallen, Raven still felt the loss of the murdered man acutely. Perhaps even more so, knowing that, just like him, his idol was only human.

Someone had taken Pete's life in a most cruel fashion just when he was starting to get back onto his own two feet. And Raven intended to make that bastard pay.

Felicity studied him with the detachment of someone inspecting a broken appliance. 'If it's any consolation,' she remarked matter-of-factly, 'the victim was probably unconscious when the fire started. He wouldn't have felt a thing.'

Raven managed a nod, his voice hoarse. 'Thank you.'

Her eyes flicked over him with casual curiosity before she lowered her gaze and began sewing the body back up with brisk efficiency, using surgical tape to close the incisions where organs had been removed.

Raven watched her work, the needle dancing in her long fingers, strangely reluctant to leave the mortuary despite the room's chilly atmosphere and Felicity's own wintry disdain. To his surprise he found himself saying, 'I'm sorry you had to put up with me instead of Becca.'

He wasn't sure why he had said it. He'd meant it as a throwaway remark, an acknowledgement of Felicity's preference for his colleague. But she tilted her head up again, holding his gaze for a fraction too long. 'I wasn't expecting Becca to attend. Not under the circumstances.'

Raven's gaze snapped to meet hers. 'What do you mean? What circumstances?'

She tilted her head to one side, intrigued by his reaction, a flicker of something dark and triumphant in her expression. 'You really don't know?'

'No.'

She hesitated, then proceeded with obvious glee, relishing the opportunity to tell him something he didn't know. Something he ought to have known. 'Becca's grandmother is dying,' she explained bluntly. 'She's in intensive care. Has been since Saturday night. Quite the family drama, by all accounts. So Becca's got other things on her mind at the moment.'

Raven's stomach sank. Not only at the news, but at the realisation that Becca had chosen to confide in the borderline sociopathic pathologist but not in him.

'Becca never said–'

'Apparently, she didn't think you needed to know,' Felicity remarked, milking the moment for all it was worth. 'Interesting, isn't it? Who she trusts. And who she doesn't.'

Raven's mouth went dry. 'I... I didn't know.'

Felicity's eyes gleamed with satisfaction. 'No. You didn't. Maybe you should have asked.'

The words stung, just as they were intended.

He should have.

'Do give my regards to her.' Felicity returned to her work, sewing the corpse back together with methodical ease, humming under her breath.

Raven didn't reply. He turned on his heel and left the mortuary, the door swinging shut behind him. His feet moved on autopilot, carrying him down the hospital's labyrinthine corridors towards the ICU. The cold fluorescent lights buzzed overhead, stark and indifferent.

He hoped he might find Becca there at her grandmother's bedside. He needed to apologise. He needed to tell her that she could take as much time off as necessary.

He just wanted to see her again.

He rounded the corner and came to an abrupt halt.

Becca stood at the far end of the corridor, her shoulders slumped, her face pale and drawn. Her mother, Sue, stood beside her, one arm wrapped protectively around her daughter's shoulders. Her father, David, hovered nearby, his face etched with worry.

A Dying Echo

Raven had met the Shawcross family once at Becca's birthday party back in the summer. A close-knit local family who looked out for one another.

Raven took a step forward, then stopped himself. He couldn't intrude.

Becca was where she needed to be, with the people who meant the most to her. She didn't need her boss complicating things. She didn't need him.

If she saw him now, she would assume he was there to talk about work, or maybe to find out why she hadn't showed up.

He had no place here. He swallowed whatever words he might have said and turned away, his heart heavy, and walked silently back down the corridor.

CHAPTER 22

Liz had missed Raven's company the previous night, but she had been more than adequately compensated for his absence by the valuable snippet of information he'd confided in her. Pete Hollis, the drummer for Echoes of Mercury, had been found dead, his caravan burnt to the ground.

Murder? Liz didn't doubt it for an instant, despite Raven's reluctance to call it.

She couldn't broadcast the news yet – even she wasn't *that* unscrupulous – but knowledge was power. And Liz intended to use hers wisely. When the police were ready to go public with this latest development, she'd already have her facts lined up, ready to hit the airwaves with an exclusive.

But first, she needed more.

She deliberately avoided Chaz McDonald when she spotted him in the hotel lounge ordering a coffee. She had no desire to waste another minute of her life in the company of the lecherous Glaswegian.

Instead, her eyes alighted on Frankie, weaving her way towards the exit. She was dressed for the outdoors, with a hooded jacket zipped up to her chin, and she wore her usual slouchy jeans and combat boots.

Now *that* was a better prospect. Frankie had been embedded with the band for the entire tour, going where they went, seeing what they saw, hearing what they heard. If anyone knew what was going on, it was Frankie.

Liz left the hotel lobby through the revolving doors, feeling like a Cold War spy as she trailed Frankie at a discreet distance onto the Esplanade. The morning was damp with drizzle, the grey sky pressing low over the town. Frankie strode briskly, head down, hood up. Liz kept pace, careful not to get too close.

They walked in step like partners in a strange dance, down the steep slope of Birdcage Walk and across the Spa Bridge. As she reached St Nicholas Café at the far side of the bridge, Frankie glanced quickly back over her shoulder, and Liz froze. But Frankie didn't spot her, and took a left turn, scurrying past the curved façade of the Rotunda museum gleaming pale yellow in the morning mist, before turning right towards the town centre.

Liz allowed the distance between them to grow, then quickened her pace again so as not to lose sight of her quarry once they hit the busy shopping area. She hurried onto the pedestrianised street of Westborough just in time to see Frankie duck into a Starbucks.

Perfect.

Liz lingered outside, waiting for a few more customers to enter before following them in. She joined the queue behind a young couple in matching beanies, watching Frankie from the corner of her eye. The place was crowded. Good. It gave her cover.

Frankie ordered a latte. Liz asked for an Americano – and, at the last second, a chocolate brownie.

She already knew what she was about to do.

Coffee in hand, she made a show of scanning the room for a seat, her eyes widening in mock surprise when she "spotted" Frankie in the corner.

'Oh, hi!' she said brightly, approaching the table. 'It's

Frankie, isn't it? Mind if I join you? It's jam packed in here.'

She didn't wait for a reply before setting her tray down.

Frankie's coat was slung over the back of her chair and she nursed her coffee in her hands, the hot drink making her glasses steam up. She blinked in mild surprise at Liz's arrival, then gave a shrug. 'Sure, yeah. You were with that detective at the concert, weren't you?'

'That's right. My name's Liz.' She held out a hand. 'And you're filming the band, I believe?'

Frankie nodded. 'Yes, I'm making a fly-on-the-wall documentary. But it's going to need a *lot* of editing when I get back to my studio. I've got way too much footage. I hardly know where to start.'

Liz smiled, breaking her brownie neatly into two equal pieces. 'Here, help me out. I can't resist these but I really shouldn't eat the whole thing myself.' She handed Frankie half on a serviette.

Frankie hesitated for only a second before grinning. 'Oh, thanks. That's kind of you.'

Liz gave her a beaming smile in return.

Hook, line and sinker.

Their budding friendship sealed with chocolate, Liz leaned in, lowering her voice to elevate the feeling of intimacy. 'You must have quite the insight into the band,' she murmured, all wide-eyed curiosity. 'I bet you've seen things no one else has.'

Frankie snorted. 'I've seen plenty. And plenty I'd rather *not* have seen.'

Liz widened her eyes encouragingly. 'Ooh, do tell.'

'Well, let's just say that no one needs to see their pop idols first thing in the morning, unwashed, unshaven, and hungover.'

'I bet.' But Liz wasn't here for gossip about greasy hair and bad breath. Time to dig deeper.

She broke off another piece of brownie. 'Shocking about Robbie, wasn't it? What do you think happened?'

Frankie stirred her latte pensively. 'At the time, I

thought he'd had a heart attack, maybe from the stress of touring. None of them are as young as they used to be. But then the police got involved–'

'–and opened a murder inquiry,' finished Liz. She leaned in eagerly. 'Who do you think did it?'

Frankie blinked. 'Wait, are you suggesting it was somebody from the tour?'

'Who else?' Liz countered smoothly. 'It *had* to be someone close to him. Someone with a motive.'

Frankie frowned, considering. 'That would mean one of the other band members. Or someone from the record label.'

Liz nodded. 'You were with them throughout the tour. You must have a gut feeling?'

Frankie took her time to consider, sipping her latte slowly, wiping froth from her lips before replying. 'Well, none of the band members really liked each other that much. I think they'd drifted apart over the years. Skye and Robbie were the closest, but even they had rows from time to time. Stu was a grump. Pete was – well, Pete. Always stoned. None of them liked Chaz, because he'd let them down in the early days – although it was Chaz who brought them back together for the tour. Nobody trusted Rupert, obviously. And then there's Taylor... she pretends to be a bit stupid, but actually she's much sharper than people think.'

'Right,' said Liz, watching her closely. 'What do you make of Pete?'

Frankie shrugged. 'Pete smokes too much weed. It doesn't do him any favours. Just makes his paranoia worse.'

'Paranoia?'

'Depression, maybe. I don't know. I'm not a doctor.'

Liz tilted her head. 'I heard he had a history with hard drugs.'

'Heroin, I heard,' said Frankie. 'Apparently he went off the rails after Mickey's disappearance. Ended up on the streets for a while.'

'Did Pete have enemies?'

'Enemies? Pete? I don't think so. He's just a bit of a loner.' Frankie hesitated, then said, 'Why all the questions about Pete?'

Time to drop the bombshell.

Liz lowered her voice, leaning in conspiratorially. 'Keep this to yourself for now,' she whispered. 'But Pete is dead.'

Frankie froze. 'What?'

Liz nodded. 'Happened last night.'

Frankie looked stunned. 'How?'

'The police are investigating. But his caravan went up in flames.'

'With Pete *inside?*'

'Yes.'

Frankie exhaled sharply. 'Jesus. That's awful. Do they think it was an accident? Maybe he was stoned, knocked over a candle or something?'

'The police are investigating,' said Liz. 'And what I've told you is confidential, so keep it to yourself for now.'

Frankie nodded quickly. 'Of course. I won't say a word.' She shook her head, visibly unsettled. 'Poor Pete. I liked him. You know, he was the only one who truly believed Mickey was still alive.'

Just like Raven said. 'Did he?' said Liz lightly.

'Yeah. Pete swore Mickey never really disappeared. Thought he just went underground. But maybe that was crazy talk. You never knew with Pete.'

'Do *you* think Mickey could still be out there?'

Frankie shrugged. 'Personally? No. But Pete wasn't the only one who thought so. There are loads of conspiracy theorists out there. One guy in particular who goes by the username *EchoOfTruth*. All one word. I think he even lives around here."

Liz sat up straighter. Now this had the makings of a story. She checked her watch. 'Goodness, is that the time? It flies when you're having fun.' She stood up. 'It's been lovely chatting to you, Frankie, but I'm afraid work calls.'

Frankie looked up. 'Wait, what do you do, anyway? Are

you with the police?'

Liz offered her a thin smile. 'Not the police, no.'

Frankie studied her. 'You look familiar. Have I seen you on the telly?'

Liz buttoned her coat. 'Maybe. Anyway, lovely chatting. We should do this again sometime.'

With a final smile, she swept out of the café.

Outside, she whipped out her phone, typed *EchoOfTruth* into the search bar and watched with interest as a profile popped up.

'Found you,' she murmured.

CHAPTER 23

Raven left the hospital chastened by his bruising encounter with Dr Felicity Wainwright. The revelation that Becca had confided in the pathologist rather than him had landed like a punch to the gut. He had assumed they were on more familiar terms, but perhaps he had misread their relationship entirely. After all, he was her boss – nothing more. He shouldn't have fooled himself into thinking otherwise.

He dialled her number again and left a message on her voicemail, telling her to take as much time off as she needed.

When he returned to the station, he found Tony and Jess hunched over their desks, deep in discussion. They looked up as he entered the incident room.

'Any progress?'

'I've been looking into the cyanide question,' said Tony, flipping through his notes. 'There are various ways of obtaining it legally. For example, sodium cyanide and potassium cyanide are used in industrial processes like mining and metal plating, university labs hold small quantities, and it used to be used in pesticides, though its

use is heavily restricted these days. Cya[n]
classified as regulated poisons and require a
for purchase.'

'So our murderer might hold a lice[nse or knows]
someone who does.'

'Right,' said Tony. 'Then again, they might have obtained it illegally.'

'You can buy it on the dark web,' said Jess.

Raven frowned. 'Remind me how that works?'

'It requires a bit of technical know-how,' explained Tony. 'You can't reach it with an ordinary web browser or find it on Google. You need specialist software – something like Tor, for instance.'

'Tor?'

'Stands for The Onion Router. It encrypts communications and bounces them through multiple servers worldwide, making it nearly impossible to trace the original source. Think of it like peeling an onion – each layer adds another level of anonymity. Commercial transactions are often carried out using cryptocurrency like Monero, providing financial anonymity too.'

'Dark web sites often end in dot onion instead of dot com,' chimed in Jess. 'Not everything there is illegal though. There's a mirror version of the BBC, intended for people living in countries with restricted internet access.'

'I doubt the killer bought cyanide from the BBC,' remarked Raven drily.

'No sir,' said Tony.

'So if cyanide was purchased on the dark web, tracing it is near impossible?'

'Not quite, sir. If you could get hold of their laptop, you'd be able to find evidence of activity on the dark web. As long as you had the right cybersecurity expertise, that is.'

Raven exhaled, dragging a hand across his chin. This case was getting more complicated by the day. The killer wasn't just someone with a grudge against a group of ageing rockers. They were meticulous, technically skilled, and capable of high-level planning. That suggested someone outside the band and their entourage. Someone they hadn't even considered yet.

'I also looked up the Senior Investigating Officer from Mickey's disappearance,' continued Tony. 'I'm afraid that the officer in question passed away a few years back. I'm still trying to track down the witness who saw Mickey right before he disappeared.'

Raven folded his arms. 'Do we even know if this witness is still alive?'

'No, sir. But I'm working on it.'

Raven suppressed a sigh. Chasing ghosts. Mickey had vanished so long ago that every lead seemed tenuous at best. But his instincts told him that the deaths of Robbie and Pete were tangled up with whatever had happened to Mickey all those years ago.

'What about this online poet?' he asked Jess. 'Any luck getting an ID?'

'Cyber team's working on it,' said Jess. 'They're tracking IP addresses. But whoever *Frost and Fury* is, they're good at covering their tracks.'

'So they might well be the person who purchased cyanide from the dark web,' said Raven. 'Someone good with computers.'

Jess nodded grimly.

Two murders. A killer who was always two steps ahead. A carefully orchestrated game – and so far, the police were playing catch-up.

Not only had the perpetrator obtained a controlled poison and used it to murder the lead singer of a band in front of a large audience, but they had killed a second band member by arson and had written and published poems forewarning of the murders on an online platform.

Frustration surged through Raven. He slapped a hand against the desk. 'Goddammit!'

The door opened and Becca walked in.

She looked taken aback by his outburst but quickly masked her reaction. 'Sorry I'm late,' she apologised. 'I had some things I needed to take care of.'

Raven immediately regretted his show of anger. Softening his voice, he said, 'It's not a problem at all.'

Becca looked tired, but she was here, and that's what counted. 'I don't want to let the team down,' she said.

He was tempted to ask about her grandmother, but he didn't want her to think he'd been discussing her personal life behind her back. He certainly wasn't going to put her on the spot in front of the others. Instead, he said simply, 'You're not. If you need to take time, just say the word.'

Becca hesitated, as if weighing up whether to say more. Then she shook her head. 'Sorry, I should have called. But I'm here now. Can you bring me up to speed?'

Raven nodded gratefully, seizing the chance to move forwards again. He filled her in on Pete's death and the discovery of the online poet. 'So,' he concluded, 'two people are now dead and we have to assume that the remaining band members, Skye and Stu, could be in danger. Tony, can you get PC Sharon Jarvis to keep a close eye on Skye? I'm going to talk to Stu and warn him.'

'I'll do it right away, sir.'

Raven turned to Becca and lowered his voice. 'Would you like to come with me?'

She met his gaze, steady despite the exhaustion in her eyes. 'Sure.'

Something in his chest loosened and he gave her a grateful smile. She was back, and things were moving forwards again.

*

The drive to Stu's place was heavy with an uneasy silence. Raven didn't push Becca for details about how her grandmother was doing, and she showed no inclination to offer any. He could sense her anxiety, the way she kept her gaze fixed on the road ahead, fingers resting stiffly in her lap. But if she wanted to keep her family affairs private, he wasn't going to press. He just hoped that she knew he was there if she needed him.

According to Tony, Stu rented a place in the Barrowcliff area of Scarborough. The estate had a reputation – high unemployment, pockets of deprivation, and a long-running struggle with antisocial behaviour. At this time of day, the streets were thick with schoolkids heading home. A pair of teenagers shot off the pavement on battered bikes, braking hard as they skidded into the road, narrowly missing Raven's car. One of them raised a middle finger before pedalling away. Others loitered in clusters, vaping, heads bent over their phones.

In Raven's day, it would have been cigarettes. That was progress for you.

They found the address – a drab, two-storey red-brick house identical to the others lining the street and typical of any post-war council estate. The front garden was overgrown, a patchwork of weeds and gravel. Raven rang the doorbell and listened for movement within.

Nothing.

He tried again, pressing harder and longer, making sure the bell actually worked. This time, he heard footsteps descending the stairs and a muffled voice called tetchily from inside. 'All right, all right, I'm coming.'

A chain rattled, and the door creaked open to reveal Stu in the hallway. He looked as though he'd just crawled out of bed – haggard, unshaven, eyes squinting against the afternoon light. He rubbed at his face, yawning.

'You again?' His voice was flat but not entirely unfriendly.

'Can we come in?' asked Raven.

Stu let out a long sigh. 'Aye, go on then.'

The hallway smelt of stale beer, damp laundry and mildew. Raven stepped inside, noting the crumpled pile of clothes by the stairs and the abandoned takeaway cartons on the side table. It wasn't hard to see why Stu preferred to spend his time in the pub.

The front lounge was just as unkempt. A high-tech keyboard dominated the space in front of the window, its

A Dying Echo

sleekness at odds with the rest of the room. A sagging sofa faced a coffee table strewn with empty beer cans, a half-eaten pizza, and the remains of a Chinese takeaway. A dusty bookcase leaned against the far wall, crammed with vinyl records and a tangled mess of unused cables. More records were stacked on top of a pair of floor-standing speakers.

Stu slumped onto a stool by the keyboard, while Becca took the sofa.

Raven pulled up a wooden chair, surveying the room. It was difficult to picture the band's keyboard player as an evil genius capable of two cold-blooded murders with the degree of sophistication demonstrated in this case. But still, Raven couldn't afford to make any assumptions.

'Stu, we need to ask you where you were last night.'

'Last night?' Stu frowned as if he'd been asked to recall an event from a decade earlier.

'It's not that long ago,' Raven prompted.

Stu scratched at his stubble. 'I was out. Visited a few pubs. Caught up with some mates I hadn't seen in a while.'

'We'll need the names of the pubs and who you were with,' Becca said.

'Yeah, yeah, give me a sec.' He rubbed his temple before rattling off a list of bars and people. Becca jotted them down.

'And what time did you get back?' asked Raven.

Stu shrugged. 'Dunno. Late. After closing time for sure. No point leaving early, is there?' He studied Raven, his gaze slowly sharpening. 'Hang on – what's this all about? Has something happened?'

Raven met his gaze. 'Did you speak to Pete yesterday?'

'No, should I have?'

Raven exhaled, bracing himself to break the news. No matter how many times he did this, it never got easier. 'I'm sorry, Stu. Pete's dead.'

Stu stared uncomprehendingly. 'Dead? No... no way. I saw him at the weekend and he was right as rain. I know he had his problems but...' He half rose from the stool, then sank back heavily as if his legs had lost all strength. His face was hollow. 'How? When?'

'It happened last night,' said Raven. 'Pete's caravan burnt down with him inside. We're treating it as arson.'

'Jeez.' Stu pushed a hand through his unkempt hair. 'That's bloody shite.'

'If it's any consolation, we believe he may have been unconscious when the fire took hold.' Raven cast his eyes down, unable to hold Stu's gaze any longer. He could still see the flames, the thick smoke curling into the night sky, Pete's home reduced to blackened wreckage.

Becca rose to her feet. 'Would you like some tea, Stu? I'll put the kettle on.'

'Nah, it's all right, love. I'm all out of teabags anyway. You can fetch me a beer from the fridge though.'

As Becca went to look in the kitchen, Stu took a long, steadying breath, then nodded decisively. 'Go on, then. Ask your questions. I know you've got more.'

Raven leaned in, forearms resting on his knees. 'When I first spoke to you and Skye about Mickey, you both said he was dead. That he'd taken his own life.'

'Aye. The poor bastard was going through a rough patch. The muse had left him high and dry. He couldn't write anything he was happy with. And then Skye left him. It broke him.'

'Right,' said Raven, 'but Pete thought differently. He told me Mickey was still alive. He even pointed me towards an online poet, convinced it was him.'

Stu gave a dry, humourless chuckle. 'That'll have been his guilty conscience talking.'

'Guilty conscience?' Raven pressed. 'What about?'

Stu exhaled, rubbing a hand over his face. 'It was a long time ago, now. But it seems like yesterday. When Skye left Mickey for Robbie, Mickey didn't know what to do. His world had fallen apart. He came to me for help, but it shames me to say this now, I wasn't there when he needed me most. I was too caught up with my own life and I turned him away. And so he went to Pete…'

Becca returned, handing Stu a can of beer. He cracked it open, took a slurp and wiped his chin.

'Pete's idea of helping Mickey was to give him drugs. I suppose he thought it would take the edge off everything. But it nearly killed him.'

Raven sat up straighter, his focus narrowing. 'When was this precisely?'

'About a week before he vanished. I don't know what Pete gave him. I've never done drugs myself.' He raised the can of beer to his lips and took another swig. 'Whatever it was, it put Mickey in hospital. Pete blamed himself after that. I think that's why he clung to the idea that Mickey was still alive. It made it easier to live with what he'd done.'

Raven's mind whirred. Pete had been injected with drugs before his caravan was torched. And here was a near-identical event in the past. Could Mickey really be alive – and out for vengeance on everyone who had let him down or betrayed him?

'Chaz also thinks Mickey is alive.'

Stu gave a bitter laugh, laced with scorn. 'Chaz is an idiot.'

Becca cut in. 'What do you know about a poet called *Frost and Fury?*'

Stu scoffed. 'You heard that from Pete, did you? It's just fanfiction. You're barking up the wrong tree. Forget this idea that Mickey's alive. If you want to catch the killer, stop looking for someone who's dead.'

Raven gave a short nod. 'I hear you, Stu, and believe me, we're considering every possibility. But right now, our concern is that someone may be targeting the members of the band, perhaps taking revenge for some reason we don't yet understand.'

Stu blinked. 'Revenge? You mean some kind of disgruntled fan?'

'Possibly. I don't know. The thing is, Stu, Robbie was murdered, and now Pete. You could be in danger yourself.'

Stu rubbed his temple, clearly disbelieving. 'Why

would anyone come after me?'

'We don't know for certain, Stu, but for now I'd like to offer you police protection.'

Stu took another swig of beer as he considered the idea. It didn't take him long. 'Nah, it's all right. Thanks all the same, but I can take care of myself.'

Raven exchanged a glance with Becca. If Stu didn't want to take up his offer, Raven couldn't force it. But for Stu's sake, he hoped he was right.

CHAPTER 24

As they stepped out of Stu's flat into the damp afternoon air, Raven's phone buzzed in his pocket. He glanced at the screen.

Liz Larkin.

He hesitated. He ought to answer but he was conscious of Becca's presence. What was he embarrassed about? Taking a personal call while on duty? People did that all the time, and no one batted an eye. Or was it Liz herself who was the source of his embarrassment? He knew what Becca would say about his choice of lover. Yet what business was it of hers who he chose to see in his private life?

Becca slowed to a halt, shooting him a sidelong look. 'Aren't you going to answer that?'

Raven hesitated, then sighed. 'Yeah... I guess I better had.' He turned away from her and took the call.

Liz's voice was bright, breathless with excitement. 'I hope this isn't a bad time.'

'Well actually–'

'Don't worry, it won't take long. I've just had a very interesting conversation with Frankie.'

'What about?' Raven asked, glancing towards Becca, who was waiting beside the BMW, observing him in silence.

'Oh, all kinds of things. She's my new BFF.' Liz's voice carried a playful lilt, but Raven didn't bite. 'Anyway, she gave me a name. An online conspiracy theorist who's been pushing the idea that Mickey is still alive. Calls himself *EchoOfTruth*.'

Raven frowned. 'This person isn't connected to *Frost and Fury*, are they?'

'No,' said Liz. 'Unlike *Frost and Fury*, *EchoOfTruth* wasn't hard to trace at all. In fact, he lives locally. I think you should speak to him.'

'Okay,' said Raven, maintaining his business-like tone. 'Send me the details.'

'Done,' said Liz and a message alert popped up on his screen.

'Was there anything else?' he asked.

Liz's voice turned sultry. 'Well, can I look forward to the pleasure of your company later, DCI Raven?'

'Sure,' he muttered. He knew he ought to say more, especially after standing her up the previous evening, but he couldn't bring himself to offer more than a mumbled agreement under Becca's watchful scrutiny. 'I have to go.'

He ended the call, unlocked the car, and slid into the driver's seat. Becca followed, buckling up without a word. He could feel the tension before she even opened her mouth.

'Was that a work call?' she asked.

'Kind of,' he said, starting the engine.

'What do you mean, "kind of"? I heard you mention *Frost and Fury*. Have Tony or Jess found something new?'

Raven signalled and pulled out into the road. 'There's a conspiracy theorist we should track down. Someone pushing the idea that Mickey is still alive.'

'That's an interesting lead. Where did it come from?' Becca's tone was sharp with suspicion.

Raven kept his eyes on the road. 'Just a witness.'

Silence.

'Does this witness have a name?'

Raven's grip tightened on the steering wheel. He didn't answer.

Becca let out a breath. 'Was it Liz Larkin?'

He stopped at a set of red lights, pulled on the handbrake, and risked a glance at her. 'Yes, it was Liz Larkin.'

She turned in her seat, her expression a tight mix of disbelief and frustration. 'How does Liz Larkin even know about *Frost and Fury*? What have you told her?'

'She's a journalist,' Raven said. 'She has a nose for hunting out this sort of thing.'

The lights changed and he moved off.

But Becca wasn't done. Not by a long way.

'I don't think this has anything to do with her being a journalist,' she said coldly. 'It sounds like you've been sharing sensitive information with her, and now she seems to think she's part of the investigation team.'

He didn't respond.

She inhaled sharply, bracing herself. 'Are you two sleeping together?'

Raven kept his gaze firmly on the road ahead. 'That's got nothing to do with anything.'

'Forgive me, but I think it has everything to do with this case if you've been compromising the investigation by sharing details with your... *girlfriend*.'

'She's not my—'

'Isn't she?' Becca cut across him. 'Because it seems to me as if that's exactly what she is.' She folded her arms, turned away and stared out of the passenger window, jaw set.

Raven clenched his teeth and drove in silence.

Becca's words sat heavy in his chest.

Was Liz Larkin his girlfriend?

The label felt wrong. He was too old to have a girlfriend. He wasn't a teenager. He wasn't some lovestruck fool fumbling through a new romance.

Their arrangement was clear and straightforward. They met when they wanted to, spent time together at the dinner table or in her hotel room, then went back to their respective lives.

No expectations. No questions about the future or where their relationship was going. No need for emotional complications.

It was simple, and he liked that. After all the years with Lisa, it felt refreshing.

But Becca had struck a nerve.

He wasn't blind to the fact that Liz loved her job more than she loved him. Not that he expected her to love him at all – they weren't that kind of couple. But deep down, he knew she wasn't the soulmate he was looking for.

Then again, maybe he wasn't looking for one.

Maybe he'd stopped believing that person even existed.

★

PC Sharon Jarvis was relieved to see Skye finally resting. The woman had barely slept, and while an afternoon nap wouldn't fix everything, it was a step in the right direction. It also gave Sharon a moment to herself, and a chance to call her boyfriend, Richard. She stretched out on the living room sofa, phone cradled to her ear, keeping the door ajar in case Skye stirred.

'I don't know how much longer I'll be here,' she murmured, keeping her voice low. 'Skye's getting fed up with me hanging around. Can't say I blame her. There's not much for me to do except hover.'

Richard chuckled on the other end. 'Babysitting duty?'

'Feels like it,' Sharon admitted. 'Raven wants me to stick around for a bit longer, but I reckon I'll be done by the end of the week.'

'That's good,' said Richard. 'I thought we might go and see that new Marvel film at the weekend.'

Sharon smiled. It wasn't really her kind of film, but Richard was a sucker for superheroes. She briefly considered telling him that he was her superhero, but that would be too cringy.

'I'd like that,' she said instead.

A simple plan. Normality. A reminder that there was a life outside this job.

Above her, floorboards creaked, followed by the quiet click of the bathroom door. So much for Skye's nap.

'Sorry, Rich, gotta go. She's getting up.'

'Okay, take care. Love you.'

'Love you too.'

She tucked her phone away just as Skye appeared at the top of the stairs. She looked marginally better than before – less pale, the shadows under her eyes not quite as deep.

'Hi,' said Sharon, pasting on a bright smile. 'Did you sleep well?'

'A bit.'

'That's good. Shall I put the kettle on?'

'I can do it,' snapped Skye. 'You're not my bloody babysitter.' She strode into the kitchen before Sharon could protest.

Sharon sighed and followed, lingering in the doorway as Skye moved about the small space.

The way she busied herself – filling the kettle, setting out mugs, spooning instant coffee with swift, deliberate movements – told Sharon everything she needed to know. Skye was irritated, restless, desperate for normality. It was completely understandable.

But normality wasn't an option. Not today.

Sharon waited until they were both seated at the table before speaking. She softened her tone, but she didn't sugarcoat it. That wasn't her style. 'I'm afraid I have some bad news.'

Skye stilled, fingers tightening around her mug. She looked at Sharon, wary. 'What bad news?'

Sharon took a deep breath. 'It's about Pete. I'm sorry Skye. He's dead.'

The mug slipped from Skye's grip and hit the floor, coffee splattering across the carpet.

'What do you mean, he's dead?' The blood drained from her face, and suddenly she looked worse than ever, her earlier signs of recovery gone in an instant.

Sharon leaned forwards slightly, ready to catch her if she swayed. 'I took a call from DCI Raven. Pete's caravan burnt down last night. He was inside.'

'Oh my God.' Skye pressed the heels of her hands against her eyes. 'Not Pete too. Was it... was it an accident?' Her eyes pleaded with Sharon.

Sharon shook her head. 'We're treating his death as suspicious.'

Skye closed her eyes for a moment, then slumped back in her chair, her whole body folding in on itself as resignation settled over her.

Sharon hesitated. 'I know this is a shock, but if you feel up to it, I'd like to ask you some questions about Pete.'

This was the flipside of Sharon's job. On the one hand, she was here to provide emotional and practical support to the victim. On the other... well, she was a police officer first and foremost. And every victim was also a witness.

For a few seconds, Skye didn't respond. She just sat there, staring at the growing pool of coffee on the floor, watching it seep into the carpet.

'Of course,' she said eventually. 'Anything I can do to help.' Her words sounded flat and robotic.

Sharon studied her carefully, searching for any flicker of emotion. 'Can you think of any reason someone might have wanted to hurt Pete?'

Skye shook her head automatically. 'Not really. Pete wasn't the type to make enemies. He kept to himself, tried to avoid confrontation.' She kept her eyes down, staring at the spilled drink, as if the patterns it made held some deep truth.

Sharon knew there was more. 'But was there someone he argued with?' she probed. 'Some confrontation he couldn't avoid?'

Skye lifted her gaze, something unreadable flashing behind her eyes. 'Pete was always bad news,' she said finally.

A cold, prickling sensation travelled down Sharon's neck. 'Bad news? In what way?'

'Drugs,' Skye said bluntly. 'Pete thought they were the answer to everything. He saw them as an escape, but they were a trap. He dragged others down with him. When Mickey was at his lowest,' – her voice cracked but she carried on – 'Pete thought he was helping by giving him heroin.'

Sharon's stomach clenched. 'Mickey took heroin?'

'Once,' Skye said bitterly. 'He'd never touched the stuff before. But Pete gave it to him anyway. He thought it would help, but the shock to his system nearly killed him.'

Sharon frowned. 'But Mickey recovered?'

Skye let out a bitter, humourless laugh. 'Depends what you mean by recovered. He disappeared just days afterwards, so I suppose you could say no, he didn't. And Pete... well, Pete was to blame, wasn't he?'

Sharon traced the rim of her coffee cup, choosing her next words carefully. 'Skye, I don't know the best way to ask this, but is there any chance Mickey is still alive?'

*

The restaurant of the Crown Spa Hotel was Rupert's kind of place. Moodily lit, secluded and hushed, it was a place where he could escape the troubles of the world and indulge his interest in dining and fine wines. He sat at his usual table in the corner, enjoying a rare steak cooked to perfection, a bottle of full-bodied Malbec within easy reach. He cut into the red meat with practised ease, his movements smooth and composed.

That composure wavered the moment Chaz McDonald stormed in.

Rupert didn't need to look up to know that Chaz was already drunk. The heavy footfalls, the barely controlled sway, the ragged breathing. It was all there, as it so often was. Chaz moved like a man spoiling for a fight. He dropped his stout frame into the seat opposite Rupert without waiting for an invitation.

Rupert ignored his arrival and set about methodically slicing off another morsel of steak.

'I'm getting mighty tired of burying old pals, Rupert.' Chaz's tone was as fiery as his beard, his voice thick with whisky and resentment. The kind of resentment that could only truly be conveyed in a slurred Glaswegian accent.

Rupert lifted the sliver of meat to his mouth, unimpressed by Chaz's opening gambit. He'd once watched the Scot turn another man's face into pulp during a brawl at Granny Black's on Candleriggs, but he didn't think it would come to fists on this occasion. 'Spare me the dramatics, Chaz. I didn't kill Pete.'

Chaz leaned in, knuckles on the table, the chair creaking under his weight. His breath stank of cheap whisky. 'Then who did? And who killed Robbie?'

Rupert finally looked up, his face impassive. 'Seriously, why are you asking me?'

Chaz drew his thick eyebrows closer, a few wiry strands of grey peeking out amid the ginger clumps. 'You dinnae even care that they're dead, you cold-hearted bastard.'

Rupert sighed as if bored by the accusation. 'Of course I care. Go away, Chaz. You're drunk.'

'Maybe I am, but I haven't finished asking questions.' Chaz's eyes were bloodshot, but sharp with suspicion. 'I want to know what's really going on here.'

Rupert set his knife and fork down with a quiet clink, his appetite waning. Trust Chaz to ruin a perfectly good meal. He exhaled slowly, pressing his fingers to his temples before answering. 'What's really going on? Fine. I'll tell you. I recently signed a new deal with Robbie. One that I hoped would be very lucrative. I was going to launch his solo career.'

Chaz went rigid, a storm brewing in his eyes. The words took a second to sink in, but when they did, he was out of his seat so fast that the table lurched. 'You treacherous fucker, Rupert, you had no right to do that.

You know I'm the band's manager!'

Rupert didn't flinch at the outburst. He simply leaned back, lifting his glass and taking a measured sip of wine before responding. 'Robbie was cutting you out, with Skye as his new manager. They were tired of you, Chaz. So if you'd take a moment to think, instead of shooting your mouth off, you'd realise that Robbie's death was bad for business.'

Chaz's face darkened, his knuckles whitening as he gripped the edge of the table. 'You're lying. Robbie and Skye would never do that to me.'

Rupert arched a brow, a flicker of amusement touching his lips. 'Well, why don't you go and ask Skye yourself?' He returned his attention to his plate, picking up his knife and fork as if Chaz's outrage was nothing more than an irritating interruption to his evening.

But Chaz wasn't finished. He planted his hands wide on the table, forcing Rupert to look at him again. 'I'm not budging an inch until you tell me the truth. All of it.'

Rupert sighed, more exasperated than anything else. He set his cutlery down again, fingers brushing lightly against the linen tablecloth. 'You want the truth? Here it is. I don't know who killed Robbie and Pete. And I don't much care. We should leave that to the police. I didn't get where I am today by wallowing in the past.' His gaze hardened. 'If I were you, I'd focus on your career while you still have one.'

Chaz let out a sharp and bitter laugh. 'While you sit high and dry, eh? I'll tell you what I think. Pete was scared. Just before he died, he came to see me. He told me he was being followed.'

Rupert snorted with disdain. 'Pete was always scared of something, even his own shadow. He was paranoid. Decades of drug abuse will do that to a man. If he wasn't ranting about government conspiracies or aliens tampering with his water supply, he was insisting that Mickey was still alive.'

Chaz's expression twisted. 'Well, maybe he was right

about that. Perhaps Mickey is alive.'

Rupert kept his features neutral, but his hand tightened ever so slightly around the stem of his wine glass. 'Mickey's dead, Chaz. We've been over this countless times.'

Chaz leaned in, voice low and dangerous. 'You reckon? Then explain what happened to Pete. Explain what happened to Robbie. Did a ghost kill them?'

Rupert shook his head from side to side. This was like indulging a child with a pointless argument. 'Chaz,' he explained patiently, 'I was there when Mickey disappeared, just like you. The poor guy was in freefall. He couldn't cope. The fame, the pressure… Skye leaving him? That was the final nail in the coffin. He walked out of that studio and was never seen again.'

'True,' he conceded. 'He was struggling. No question about it. But his body was never found.'

'That doesn't mean he's still breathing.'

'Then what about the letter? What about the sightings?'

Rupert's patience finally snapped. 'Let it go, Chaz.'

'That's what you'd like, isn't it?' Chaz studied him closely, his watery eyes struggling to focus. 'What if Mickey's alive and he knows about your scheming? Splitting up the band? He'd come after you. If I were you, I'd be very afraid.' His voice dropped lower. 'And what about the fans? You know how obsessive some of them can be. Did you even consider how the fans would react to your shenanigans, Rupert?'

Rupert's nostrils flared with irritation. 'It was Robbie's decision to go solo, Chaz, not mine. Anyway, it was just business.'

'Business?' Chaz scoffed, shaking his head. 'Greed, you mean. Money is all that matters to you, isn't it?'

Rupert gave a slow, cold smile. 'It's what keeps me alive. It keeps us all alive, which is why Robbie and Skye decided to dump you.'

Chaz's temper finally snapped. He jabbed a stubby finger inches from Rupert's nose. 'You've always been a snake, Rupert. I dinnae trust you one bit.'

Rupert countered smoothly, his voice as sharp as his steak knife. 'Then perhaps you've learned not to be so naïve. It's a pity for Echoes of Mercury that you weren't a little more astute when you signed their contract all those years ago. If you'd trusted me less at the start, you wouldn't have cost them so much money.'

Chaz's jaw worked, his breathing heavy. He looked as if he wanted to lunge across the table and throttle Rupert, but he reined it in. Instead, he hissed, his voice bitter. 'You bastard, Rupert. You're shameless. You're completely amoral. If I find out you know more than you're saying, I swear to God–'

Rupert cut him off, his voice sharp with anger. 'You'll do what, exactly? Kill me?'

Chaz said nothing.

Rupert's lips curled in satisfaction. 'Perhaps the police would like to know your secrets too, Chaz.'

A flicker of something crossed Chaz's face. Fear, maybe. Rupert braced himself for an angry retort, but instead the Scotsman turned and walked out without another word.

Rupert watched him go, then reached for the wine bottle and emptied the last of it into his glass. He sipped it, and allowed his mind to mull over the heated exchange.

Chaz was rapidly becoming a problem.

And fixing problems was what Rupert did best.

CHAPTER 25

EchoOfTruth wasn't a difficult individual to pin down. Tony had managed to find Colin Harris's name and address easily enough from the public records of his website. Perhaps, if Colin truly believed that the government was out to get him, he should have tried a little harder to cover his tracks.

Tollergate was one of the oldest streets in town, and as parking was prohibited on the narrow, steeply sloping street, Raven left the M6 further down the hill in Friargate, not far from his old primary school.

He regretted his decision almost immediately.

The incline was steep, and while Becca strode ahead with ease – probably fitter than ever since moving to her loft apartment on Castle Terrace – Raven lagged behind, his joints protesting with every step. He was no longer the sprightly young lad who had run up the hill from Quay Street every morning, but an old codger nursing a war injury. What did Liz Larkin see in him?

'Are you all right?' asked Becca, as he limped his way along the uneven cobbles.

'Fine,' he muttered, burrowing his hands deeper into

his coat pockets.

He sensed he was still in her bad books after their earlier argument. She had been right, of course – Liz wasn't part of the investigation, and he *shouldn't* have shared sensitive details with her. Yet at the same time, it was thanks to Liz they now had a solid lead – someone actively pushing the idea that Mickey was alive.

He caught up with Becca outside a tall, narrow house near the top of the terrace. Once he'd caught his breath, he leaned on the doorbell.

A minute passed before heavy footsteps plodded down the stairs inside. The door opened to reveal a man in his forties, wearing sagging jogging bottoms and a washed-out T-shirt stretched a little too tightly over his generous stomach. From his flushed face and the way he wheezed after the exertion of descending the stairs, Raven doubted the man had ever jogged a day in his life.

'Colin Harris?'

The man blinked twice, eyes flitting between them. 'Who's asking?' His voice was surprisingly high-pitched for a man of his size.

Raven presented his warrant card. 'DCI Raven and DS Shawcross from North Yorkshire Police. We'd like to talk to you about Echoes of Mercury. We have reason to believe you have posted about them under the username *EchoOfTruth*.'

Raven had expected an outright denial, perhaps a gruff refusal to answer questions, and a demand for a solicitor, but at the mention of the band's name, Colin's whole face lit up. 'Sure, come in,' he said eagerly, stepping back to usher them inside.

The house was narrow but deceptively deep. The front door opened straight into a modest sitting room which led on to a dining area and a long galley kitchen.

Colin seemed delighted to have company. He filled the kettle with water and fished a box of teabags out of a cupboard. 'Would you like some tea?'

'No, thank you,' said Raven. He hadn't come in search

of hospitality.

There was no sign of a laptop in any of the rooms they had seen so far. At the far end of the kitchen, a back door opened onto a tiny courtyard garden and a leaning wooden shed. A cursory glance was enough to tell Raven that the tumbledown shed was no place for electronic equipment.

'Do you have an office or a study, Mr Harris?' Becca enquired.

'My spare room is upstairs,' said Colin. 'That's where I keep my computer and stuff.'

'May we take a look?'

'Of course.' Once again, Colin sounded strangely grateful for the chance to show off his "stuff". 'Mind your head as you go up,' he warned, indicating a low wooden beam over the stairs.

The staircase was steep, winding up through the centre of the house. Colin puffed as he trudged his way up the steps. Raven followed cautiously, ducking under another low beam as they reached the first-floor landing. A second set of stairs twisted upwards again.

The ceilings on the upper floors were even lower than the ground floor. 'Just along here,' said Colin breathlessly, leading the way along the dim landing and pushing open a door.

The moment Raven stepped into the back bedroom, it became clear that they weren't dealing with an ordinary fan of Echoes of Mercury.

This was obsession.

The room had been transformed into a place resembling a shrine. Every square inch of the walls was plastered with posters, old album covers, yellowing news clippings, and printed articles charting Mickey's disappearance. One entire wall was covered in material annotated in Colin's spidery writing, with questions, arrows, pins and strings forming a spiderweb of desperate logic and speculation.

An old CRT computer monitor dominated the battered desk in front of the window. Beside it, a precarious stack of books rose from the floor halfway to the ceiling. Raven scanned the titles on the spines, reading off a handful at random. *Missing But Not Gone: The Truth Behind Celebrity Disappearances. The Disappearance Files: What They Don't Want You to Know. Vanishing Point: Theories That Challenge the Official Record.* The direction of Colin's thinking was abundantly clear.

Raven caught Becca's eye. Her expression confirmed his thoughts: this was deep into tinfoil hat territory.

'What do you do for a living, Mr Harris?' Becca asked.

'I work evenings in the chippy up the road,' explained Colin. 'Leaves me time to pursue my own interests. And it's Colin, please.'

'And what exactly are your interests, Colin?' enquired Raven. He pointed to the posters on the walls. 'I can see that you're quite a fan of the band.'

'They're my favourite,' agreed Colin quickly. 'Ever since I was a teenager. I liked the fact that they were local. Liverpool and Manchester aren't the only places that produce good music.'

'I'm inclined to agree with you,' said Raven pleasantly. 'I saw the Echoes play at the spa with their original lineup, and I was there again for the last night of the comeback tour. Unfortunately, it doesn't look as if they'll be making any more music now.'

Colin's smile faltered. 'Absolute tragedy, what happened to Robbie. I cried when I saw him collapse on stage.'

'You were there?'

'Of course. I saw them in Sheffield, Leeds and Hull too, but I wouldn't have missed their final gig for anything. I took the night off to be there. I told my boss, no way was I showing up for work when history was in the making just around the corner. He wasn't happy, but I said to him there's more to life than chips.'

Raven nodded. A fan like Colin would have done anything to see the band play in his hometown. His attention was drawn to a book on Colin's desk. He picked it up: *The Lost Chord: Deconstructing the Echoes of Mercury Disappearance* by Colin Harris.

'You wrote this yourself, Colin?'

Colin nodded eagerly, his face beaming with pride. 'It's self-published. I've been writing a blog for years, and it's grown to be pretty huge. Some of my followers asked for a condensed version. This is the result.'

'And would you care to summarise it for us?'

'Happy to,' said Colin. 'Basically, I've tried to put together a definitive guide to the facts around Mickey's disappearance. The *true* facts, that is, not the police version of events. So I go into the days and weeks leading up to his disappearance, highlight the lack of a body, the way the police tried to cover up the whole thing… and then lay out the different possible explanations and examine the merits of each one.'

Raven didn't rise to the allegation of a police cover-up. Police *cock-up* seemed like a better way to characterise the flimsy missing persons investigation that had been undertaken. 'And what did you conclude?'

'Well, I try to avoid drawing any specific conclusions in the book,' said Colin. 'As I say, my aim was to give space to every possible theory. So, for instance, there are people who claim to have seen Mickey in Brazil, or on an island in Polynesia. Some say he's still in England but living under a new name. Several writers have proposed variations on amnesia, and there's even the alien abduction hypothesis, but obviously that's not one many people take seriously.'

'Most people think Mickey took his own life,' said Becca.

'I know,' said Colin. 'And I do examine that possibility extensively in the book. But it's not a view I share.'

'So, what is your view, Colin?' asked Raven.

Colin's face grew grave. 'In a nutshell, Mickey has been abducted by person or persons unknown and is being held prisoner.'

It was hard for Raven to keep his face straight, and he

knew that if he caught Becca's eye again he would crumble. He scratched at the stubble on his chin with his thumb and finger. 'Who might be keeping him prisoner?' he asked levelly.

'A deranged fan.'

'Do you have any evidence to support that?'

Colin clasped his hands together and took an eager step forwards. 'It's all there if you know what to look for. Right before Mickey vanished, he gave a TV interview where he kept speaking directly to the camera instead of the interviewer. Sometimes he didn't even answer the question he was asked but said something different instead. He was sending a coded message to somebody. Somebody he knew would be watching.'

Raven was familiar with the infamous TV interview. It was widely regarded as giving an insight into Mickey's precarious mental state during his final days. But Colin clearly had his own interpretation. 'And what was that message?'

'Not everyone wanted the band to go to America. Some fans were vocal in accusing the Echoes of selling out. Mickey was talking to them, not to the interviewer. And then, suddenly, he disappears. On the very eve of the trip. Someone stopped him from going.'

'A fan abducted him?' said Raven.

'That's right.'

'And – let me get this straight – you believe that this fan has been holding Mickey against his will all this time?'

'Precisely.' Colin looked relieved that he had finally been listened to by the authorities. 'So, what are you going to do about it?'

'Us?' said Raven. 'Well, we're investigating the murder of Robbie Kershaw, not a historic missing persons case.'

Colin's face fell. 'I knew it!' he declared. 'You're part of the cover-up!'

'No,' said Raven firmly. 'We're not here to cover anything up. We're here to find the truth. So tell me, what do you know about a poet called *Frost and Fury*?'

Colin's face lit up again, his enthusiasm redoubled. 'You've heard of *Frost and Fury*? That's awesome. Well, the author of the poems is obviously Mickey. He's writing them, but his kidnapper is posting them online for him.'

'And what makes you think that, Colin?' asked Becca.

'You just have to read the words,' said Colin. He clicked his mouse and the screen of the CRT monitor sprang into life. 'Look, I'll show you.' Colin sat in his chair and tapped away at his keyboard. 'Look at this one. It's called *Never is a Place*.'

Raven peered over Colin's shoulder as the screen filled with lines of verse. Colin read them aloud, giving the impression of reciting from memory:

Never is a place I heard you mention.
Never is a place I yearn to know.
Never is a place without beginning.
Never is a place I have to go.

In these four walls, this darkened space,
Where shadows writhe and time leaves no trace.
The air is heavy, thick with despair,
The ceiling whispers secrets to the empty chair.

Never is a place where doors don't exist,
Where silence howls, and memories twist.
Each step I take is a loop to the start,
Each beat of the clock another crack in my heart.

I claw at the walls, but they never give way,
The echoes of screams are here to stay.
Never is a prison, a sentence, a vow,
A place where tomorrow is never now.

'See?' said Colin, fixing Raven with an expectant look. 'That's proof. This is Mickey's cry for help from wherever he's being held.'

'Hmm.'

Raven was unconvinced, to say the least. It seemed to him that you could read any interpretation into those words. He was reminded of English classes at school where the teacher had asked about the hidden meaning of a famous poem. It had seemed to Raven that there was no wrong answer.

'It's just a poem, Colin. We can't base a police investigation on that. But if you had reason to believe that Mickey was being held captive, why didn't you go to the police?'

'I did,' Colin protested. 'They arrested me for wasting police time, but I was released without charge. They knew they couldn't risk me giving evidence in court. I even went to Mickey's parents, but they hired a solicitor who got a court order against me, preventing me from contacting them again. They should have listened to me. I was right. And now the kidnapper has killed Robbie. And Pete too.'

That last bit got Raven's attention. So far, the police hadn't gone public about Pete's death. 'What do you know about Pete?' he snapped.

Colin shrugged. 'Just what's online. Everybody's talking about it. Look!' His fingers worked again at his keyboard, tapping out the web address of a forum. Sure enough, word of Pete's death had leaked out, and speculation in the online community was rife. There were already hundreds of replies to the original post reporting the fire at Pete's caravan.

Becca shot Raven a sharp look, and he took her meaning quickly enough. *Liz Larkin.* But there were lots of ways the information might have leaked, and no reason to point the finger at Liz. Raven would have to put out an official press release as soon as he got back, to quell the wild speculation.

'Who originally posted the news of the fire?' asked Becca.

Colin clicked on the post. It came as little surprise to Raven to see that the username of the source was *Frost and Fury.*

'And what is your username on this website?' she asked.

Colin pointed to his profile details at the top of the page. '*EchoOfTruth.*'

'Okay,' said Raven. 'Just one more thing before we go. Do you have a name for this alleged kidnapper, or any information that might help us to identify them?'

Colin's face fell. 'Sorry, I wish I did. I think Mickey might be inserting clues into his poems but obviously *Frost and Fury* is censoring them before making them public.'

'Obviously,' echoed Becca, her voice deadpan.

It seemed like they had reached a blank. They had found no link between Colin Harris and the online poet other than a shared interest in Echoes of Mercury, and nothing to suggest that he was any more than a harmless, though obsessive fan.

'Okay,' said Raven, 'Thanks for your time. We'll see ourselves out.'

He carefully retraced his steps down the creaking staircase and out onto Tollergate. It was a relief to be back in the fresh air and to discover that the world was still turning on its axis.

'What did you make of that?' he asked Becca as they walked back to the car.

Becca grinned at him – the first time he'd seen her smile in days. 'I think we briefly entered some weird parallel universe.'

'You're right,' said Raven. 'We need to stop chasing ghosts and lunatics and get this investigation back onto solid ground.'

CHAPTER 26

'Well,' said Tony, scratching his chin in thought. 'These things do happen. Back in the sixties, Frank Sinatra's son was kidnapped. The kidnappers demanded a ransom and once it was paid they let the kid go.'

Jess nodded. 'And Madonna had that stalker. Some unhinged fan broke into her home and threatened to kill her unless she agreed to marry him.'

Raven glanced around the incident room. 'All right, so we're agreed that celebrities attract criminals and crackpots. But is it really plausible that an obsessed fan has been keeping Mickey under lock and key for over thirty years?'

Jess snorted with derision. 'That's next-level crazy.'

Raven nodded. 'So let's forget about Conspiracy Colin and focus our attention on known facts. Jess, what have the cybercrime team managed to find out about *Frost and Fury*?'

Jess's expression soured, her shoulders sagging with frustration. 'Basically nothing. Whoever's behind it knows what they're doing. They've erased every trail the cyber team has tried to follow. The forums are all hosted abroad, so we've got no power to demand access to user data.'

'A dead end, then,' said Raven grimly.

'For now,' said Jess. 'But I've set up an alert on my phone in case *Frost and Fury* post again.'

'Good thinking,' said Raven. 'Tony, any luck with your enquiries?'

Tony tapped his pen against his notebook. 'I've been digging into Mickey's disappearance, seeing if there's anything we might have missed. I tried tracking down any relatives of Mickey who are still alive. His parents are dead, but he has a younger sister called Emily. She was just a girl at the time Mickey went missing, so I doubt she'd be able to help us. There's no record of any police interview with her at the time. In any case, she got married and moved away from the area after her parents died.'

'So that's another blank,' muttered Raven.

'There is one lead, though, sir. I found the address of the taxi driver who claimed he saw Mickey with someone the night he disappeared. His name's Gordon Williams. Still lives in Scarborough. Still driving taxis.'

Raven brightened at the prospect. 'So we can speak to him?'

'Not yet, sir. Not in person anyway. I spoke to the taxi firm he works for and they said he's out of the country on holiday, but he's due home in a day or two.'

It seemed like every avenue they turned down was blocked for some reason. 'Fine, well as soon as he's back, let's talk to him.' Raven thought for a moment. 'We also need to check Stu's alibi for the night Pete died. Where's that list of pubs he gave us?'

'Here,' said Becca, holding out a slip of paper.

Raven took it. 'Tony, Jess, did you have any plans for this evening? If not, I'd like you to do the rounds and see if you can find anyone who remembers seeing Stu.'

Jess took the list, grinning. 'Pub crawl in the name of justice? Sounds good to me.'

'All expenses paid?' Tony asked hopefully.

'I think the budget can stretch to fizzy water,' said Raven. 'Maybe even a packet of crisps too. To share, mind you.'

Jess rolled her eyes but still looked excited at the prospect of a night out at the expense of North Yorkshire Police.

As the pair started gathering their things, Raven drew Becca aside.

'How is your grandmother?' he asked gently.

Becca turned, a flicker of surprise crossing her face. 'Who told you?'

'Felicity mentioned it during the post-mortem,' Raven admitted. He hesitated, then added quietly, 'I'm sorry, I don't mean to intrude. I should have asked you how you were earlier.'

'No,' said Becca. 'You didn't do anything wrong. I should have explained why I needed time off.'

Raven reached out to touch her shoulder, then thought better of it and let his hand fall back to his side. 'Well, it's not a problem. If you need time off, that's absolutely fine.'

She held his gaze for a moment longer before dipping her head. 'I haven't been much of a team player recently.'

Raven cracked a smile. 'That's usually what people say about me.'

To his surprise, a tear welled up in the corner of one eye. She blinked quickly and wiped it away. 'I'm sorry,' she whispered. 'I guess I'm just a bit fragile at the moment.'

'Are you sure you're okay to be here?' he asked softly.

Her reply was firm and unwavering. 'Yes. If something changes, I might have to go back to the hospital, but for now, this is where I belong.'

Raven got that.

For him too, work had always been a way of coping, of keeping the chaos of life at bay. Lisa used to accuse him of hiding behind it, of running from his problems and ducking his responsibilities. Maybe she'd had a point, but she had never grasped that work wasn't an escape – it *was* his responsibility. Becca understood that instinctively. She was more like him than Lisa had ever been.

They stood in silence for a few seconds, the office humming faintly in the background – a phone ringing, chairs scraping, Jess and Tony laughing over something.

Raven straightened. 'Right then, enough talk about work, let's get back to it.'

★

After Becca had finished entering her notes from the interviews with Stu and Colin into the HOLMES police database, she returned to the hospital, where she had arranged to meet her mum and dad. It was more peaceful at this time of day, the car park almost deserted. In the intensive care unit, the main background noise was the low hum of machinery. The hustle and bustle of earlier in the day was over, although a hospital was never a quiet place. Nurses were always patrolling the corridors, and the usual restrictions on visitors didn't apply in the ICU.

Sue and David sat beside her grandmother's bed, their expressions strained with exhaustion.

'How is she?' Becca asked softly.

Sue looked up, a weary smile on her face. 'Just the same.'

Her father nodded in quiet agreement.

'I'll sit with her for a bit if you two want to go and grab a bite to eat,' Becca offered.

Sue hesitated. 'Are you sure, love? You've been working. You must be hungry too.'

Becca didn't really feel hungry. Or tired. She was too numb, and didn't know what she felt. She certainly didn't want food right now, she just needed a chance to process her emotions. 'It's all right, you take your time. I'd like to sit quietly for a while.'

Sue studied her for a moment as if sensing there was more beneath the surface, but for once she didn't press. 'Thanks, love. We won't be long.'

Becca took the vacated seat, still comfortably warm

A Dying Echo

from her mother's presence, and watched her parents as they made their way down the corridor. She noted the stiffness in Sue's hips, the way her father favoured his left leg over his right. It wasn't just from sitting – her parents were growing old too, and one day it would be them lying in the hospital bed, while Becca waited anxiously at their side. She wondered whether she'd be alone when that happened. The prospect of having her own children seemed remote.

She shook her head to dismiss the maudlin sentiments. She had come to see her grandmother, not indulge in worries about her own affairs.

'So, Nana,' she murmured, her voice barely above a whisper. 'Here I am again. Another crazy day at work. We talked to a right one this afternoon. Conspiracy Colin. You always said, it takes all sorts.'

Her grandmother looked so small and vulnerable in her flimsy hospital gown. Becca reached out, taking her cool, fragile hand in hers. The old woman didn't stir.

Becca smiled faintly, running her thumb over the wrinkled and age-spotted fingers. 'Nothing to say, eh, Nana? That's not like you.'

Her grandmother's eyes didn't even flicker, and Becca felt her absence pierce her like a dart. The thought of losing her was horrible. She'd almost lost Sam once, but Sam was young and strong and had made a full recovery. The old woman in the bed was weak and seemed to be slowly fading from view. One day – sooner or later – she would be gone forever.

A nurse walked in, acknowledging Becca with a curt nod. She adjusted one of the machines and made some notes on the chart at the foot of the bed. Becca fell silent, waiting until they were alone again before continuing. There were things she could only tell her grandmother. Things she didn't want to acknowledge, even to herself – but she couldn't lie, not here. Not now.

'If I'm honest, Nana, I'm feeling pretty down at the moment.' Becca's own troubles seemed trivial compared with those of her grandmother's, yet she knew that if the old woman in the bed could speak, she would encourage Becca to pour out her heart and give full vent to her feelings.

Her grip on the frail hand tightened. 'It's to do with Raven. He's started having an affair with Liz Larkin and' – she took a breath, the words sticking in her throat before she forced them out – 'I'm not proud of this, but the fact is… I'm jealous of her.'

The admission hung in the air, weighty and undeniable.

But now that she'd said it out loud, something inside her settled. The road ahead seemed a little clearer.

'You mustn't tell anyone, Nana. This is our little secret, all right? I won't say a word to anyone else. I'll just bury my feelings deep in the sand and soldier on. That's the right thing to do, isn't it?'

She scanned the old woman's face for a sign she could hear. But there was nothing. Her features remained as serene as a mask, and Becca took comfort from that. Whatever her grandmother could feel, she was in no pain.

'I've been doing a lot of thinking, Nana, and I know that my feelings for Raven aren't appropriate. He's far too old for me, and he's my boss. It could never work. So I'll keep our relationship professional, and I'll do my best to be happy for him. If he wants to be with Liz, that's up to him.'

There was still no response. Just the steady beep of the heart monitor. But Becca liked to imagine that if her grandmother could speak, she'd tell her to stop being a fool and go after what she wanted – or to let it go, truly let it go, and move forward.

But what did she want, really?

'I'm supposed to be studying for my inspector exams, but I'm questioning whether I want to become a DI. I think I should have gone to Australia with Sam when I had the chance. Who knows what I'd be doing now if I'd gone with him? A surfing instructor or a tour guide, perhaps.'

The idea made her laugh softly. She didn't know one

end of a surfboard from the other.

'What are you smiling about?'

Becca looked up, startled to see her mother standing in the doorway.

Back so soon.

She swallowed her disappointment at the intrusion. 'Oh, nothing,' she said, giving a shake of her head. 'I was just having a little chat with Nana. She always gives good advice.'

She squeezed her grandmother's hand one last time before gently placing it back on the sheet. She already knew the advice her grandmother would have given. Maybe she just needed the courage to act on it.

CHAPTER 27

It was Hannah's evening off, and that could only mean one thing. More time for drinking with Ellie. 'Why don't we go out for a change?' Ellie suggested when she came knocking at Hannah's door. 'We'll head into town and see how many pubs we can manage before closing time.'

Hannah wasn't sure that a pub crawl was the wisest choice for her evening off. Wouldn't one dry day a week be a sensible move?

Quincey rubbed his nose against her legs, as if offering moral support, but Ellie clearly wasn't going to take no for an answer.

'Come on,' she insisted, sensing Hannah's reticence. 'It'll be fun. We need to work on your beer education. Do you even know your stout from your IPA?'

Hannah wasn't one to back away from a challenge. She placed her hands firmly on her hips.

'Of course I do. I've just finished a three-year Law degree, remember? Every student has to complete a test of basic beer literacy before graduating. It's written into the university constitution somewhere.'

'Is it, indeed?' Ellie grinned. 'Well, Hannah Raven, let's find out if you can pass *my* test. I'm the resident beer expert, not some bunch of students.'

They set out together, Quincey on his lead, tugging gently towards the beach. He clearly wanted to play ball on the sand again, but Hannah steered him in the direction of a dog-friendly pub that served food. It wasn't up to the standard of the bistro – more a pie-and-mash sort of place – but she wanted to get some food inside her before embarking on a night of beer swilling.

She chose a steak and ale pie and, under Ellie's guidance, paired it with a pint of best bitter. Quincey lay contentedly beneath her chair, his nose twitching as the two girls laughed and joked. Hannah surreptitiously fed him an occasional chip, although she knew it wasn't the most doggy-friendly diet.

'A little bit of what you fancy does no harm,' Ellie assured her. 'Speaking of which, let's finish here and move on.' She downed the last of her beer and rose to her feet.

At the second pub, Hannah decided to steer the conversation onto more serious territory. 'I still need to think about my future,' she reminded Ellie. They had broached the subject once before but had quickly run aground. 'There are just so many options. I barely know where to begin.'

'True,' agreed Ellie. 'It's a conundrum. I think this calls for a pint of stout.'

She returned from the bar with two pints so dark they were almost black. A finger of creamy froth floated on top. She placed the glasses carefully on the table without spilling a drop and perched herself on a stool. 'Have a mouthful and then tell me your thoughts.'

'About the beer?' asked Hannah.

'No, silly! About your life!'

They laughed, and drank, then settled down to some serious discussion, Hannah pouring out her uncertainties and self-doubts. It took her quite a while before she finished. She hadn't realised until she tried to articulate her uncertainties just how muddled she was about her own future. The one thing she felt she ought to know best appeared to be utterly elusive.

'So the thing is,' said Ellie after listening to Hannah's outpouring, 'is that you basically want to save the world.'

'Well, yes,' conceded Hannah. 'I suppose I do.'

Ellie studied her over the rim of her near-empty glass. 'And that's not such an easy thing to do.'

'Well, no.'

'Me?' said Ellie. 'I'm happy to make beer. And while there's a case to make for beer saving the world, you're looking for something more direct.'

'Exactly,' said Hannah, with bated breath. Ellie seemed to have put her finger on her needs, and she waited to find out what she was going to suggest.

'But,' said Ellie, 'you've worked hard for your Law degree and it would be a pity to waste that–'

'I've already tried being a defence lawyer,' Hannah interrupted, 'and I don't just want to defend criminals.' She recalled her stint with a local firm of solicitors. Not only had the clients seemed shady, but her boss hadn't been much better, and she had quit after less than two weeks.

'So how about working for the good guys instead?' said Ellie.

'Who do you mean? The CPS? I don't really want to be a prosecutor.'

'Okay. Then what about being a human rights lawyer, or a legal aid solicitor?'

Hannah gave the suggestions some thought. 'A human rights lawyer would probably have to be based in London. I don't really want to move away from Scarborough.'

Ellie cocked her head to one side. 'Most folk would jump at the chance of a glamorous career in the city.'

'Well, I'm not most people.'

'We've already established that,' Ellie said with a grin. 'So what about legal aid work?'

'I'd still be defending criminals, though.'

'Sometimes,' said Ellie. 'But everyone deserves a fair hearing. Some people are just in the wrong place at the wrong time.'

'I suppose so,' said Hannah. It was an argument she had made to her dad when he had moaned about lawyers making his job difficult.

'Speaking of which,' said Ellie, regarding her empty pint glass with a look of consternation. 'It's time we moved on to our next pub, with some fresh glasses in front of us. Come on, grab your coat!'

★

Raven pulled the M6 into the last remaining space on the Esplanade, silenced the remorseless growl of the V10 engine and sat in still contemplation for a few brief moments. Then, leaving the warmth of the car behind, he walked to the seafront railings, leaning into the light evening breeze and training his gaze towards the black horizon where silent sea merged seamlessly with cloud-heavy sky. No matter how hard he searched for that distant line, he found himself unable to distinguish one watery element from the other.

Neither, he reflected, had he been able to fathom Becca's changeable moods – until Felicity Wainwright had bluntly brought the facts of the matter to his attention.

A dying relative.

No wonder Becca had seemed distracted, taking unannounced time off work to deal with a family crisis. And yet she had felt unable to confide in him.

He sighed, rubbing his tired eyes with his fingers. The wind tugged at his hair and flapped his coattails. He drew a deep breath, filling his lungs with damp salt and sharp ozone and felt his senses come alive.

Enough with introspection. He had come here to enjoy an evening with Liz. She had messaged earlier to say she had rebooked the hotel restaurant where they were supposed to have dined the previous night. Apparently she was willing to give him a second chance.

If Raven had learned anything in life, he should seize it with both hands.

With one last glance at the darkened sea, he crossed the road and entered the hotel, letting his nose lead him in the direction of the restaurant. He hoped they did steak and chips. He was ravenous.

Liz was already seated at a table, a glass of white wine in front of her, her quick fingers busily tapping away on her phone.

He paused for a moment to admire her.

She looked relaxed and carefree, untainted by the dark thoughts that lingered in his own head. Her blonde hair tumbled casually over her shoulders, and once again he was struck by their age difference. Fifteen years between them? More? However many it was, he wasn't about to complain. Liz was exactly the tonic he needed in his life right now. An attractive and uncomplicated woman to stop him brooding about his own failings.

As he approached the table, she set her phone aside and greeted him with a warm smile. 'Glad you could make it, DCI Raven,' she teased. 'Nothing to keep you away from me tonight?'

'Nothing,' he answered, greeting her with a kiss and sliding into the chair opposite her. 'Have you been waiting long?'

'Only a minute.' She raised her glass. 'I ordered a drink to keep me company, just in case you were called upon to be a hero again and couldn't make it.'

A brief flicker of fire and the stench of burning plastic intruded on Raven's memory, reminding him just how badly he had failed to be a hero in Pete's hour of need, but he pushed it away, angry with himself for allowing guilt to haunt his night out.

'Nothing like that tonight, thankfully.'

'Good.'

He studied the menu, relieved to find sirloin steak and chunky chips, then folded it away again.

Liz watched him with amusement. 'I do like a decisive man.'

Raven knew when he was being gently mocked, but there was no malice in it. Unlike Lisa, who had delighted in pointing out his unimaginative food choices. He sighed inwardly. Did he constantly have to compare every woman he encountered to his ex-wife?

'I expect you've chosen already,' he remarked, keeping his tone light to match hers.

'Of course. It's important to stay ahead of the game.'

When they had placed their orders – Liz chose salmon to accompany her wine, although Raven tended to the view that a drink should match the food rather than the other way around – she reached across the table and lightly traced the backs of his hands with her fingers. 'So how was your day?'

'Busy.'

She feigned disappointment, exaggerated for effect. 'That's all I get from you? Busy? It's just as well we're not on television. This would make a car crash of an interview.'

He smiled yet hesitated before elaborating. Becca's rebuke was still fresh in his mind. *You've been compromising the investigation by sharing details with your...* girlfriend.

He'd been stung initially by the suggestion that he had a girlfriend. But that was silly. The substance of Becca's accusation was far more serious – that he'd compromised the investigation.

Had he?

It was true he'd told Liz about the fire which had claimed Pete's life. And it was equally true that the information had subsequently leaked into the public domain. But Liz could hardly be held responsible for that. Several people must have known about the blaze at the caravan, not least the site manager and the owners of other caravans. Liz hadn't gone on TV with the news, so there was no reason to suspect her, and no harm done. And hadn't she provided him with a useful lead in return? Perhaps that was how it worked in her world. Nothing for free. A two-way trade in information.

All the same, he should be careful about what he told her.

'So,' she said, breaking the silence, 'did you manage to track down *EchoOfTruth*?'

'Conspiracy Colin,' said Raven with a wry smile. 'My assessment? Deranged, but probably not dangerous.'

Liz's gaze sharpened. 'I'll need more than that.'

Raven didn't see the harm in elaborating. She could dig up the same information as Tony, and just as easily. Maybe she already had and was simply testing him. 'His real name is Colin Harris. Lives on Tollergate.'

Liz sipped her wine. 'In what way deranged?'

'More obsessive than deranged. He seemed like a regular bloke at first. Very friendly. Works in the local chippy. But he's totally obsessed with Echoes of Mercury, and Mickey's disappearance in particular. He runs a blog about it and has written a book summarising all the possible explanations.'

'He sounds quite rational to me.'

'Yes,' said Raven, 'except that he believes Mickey is being held captive by a fan.'

'A deranged fan?'

'Clearly.'

'And a dangerous one.'

Raven regarded her through narrowed eyes. 'Seriously, don't tell me you're buying his idea?'

'All ideas are worthy of consideration until proved to be false.'

Raven smiled, unsure if she was playing him. 'Some are more worthy than others.'

'There's a Stephen King book,' Liz mused, 'where a deranged fan keeps an author prisoner because she wants him to keep writing about her favourite character.'

'But's that's fiction,' said Raven. 'This is real life.'

'True,' she acknowledged. 'So what about *Frost and Fury*? Any progress with them?'

'It could be anyone. But whoever they are, they know

how to outwit our cybercrime division.'

'Hmm,' said Liz pensively. Her tone suggested scant regard for North Yorkshire's cyber elite.

Raven shared her frustration, but facts were facts. 'Essentially, we're dealing with a serial killer who's highly capable of evading detection. Not only are they one step ahead of us, but they seem to delight in posting their intentions in advance in the form of cryptic verses of poetry. It hardly seems like the work of a deranged fan.'

'Possibly. I assume you're monitoring *Frost and Fury's* account in case they post again?'

'Of course.'

'Do you think they'll strike again?'

Raven shrugged. 'Without knowing their motive, it's impossible to say, but I've offered protection to the surviving band members.'

'Did they accept?'

'Skye had no choice. There's already a family liaison officer assigned to her. But Stu refused. I can't force him.'

'He's a bloody fool to say no,' said Liz. 'If I was him, I'd be scared.'

Their conversation became more animated as dinner progressed, theories and counter-theories tossed back and forth. Raven was so engrossed, he hardly noticed the taste of the steak as it disappeared from his plate.

'It always comes back to Mickey,' he concluded after the waiter had cleared their plates. 'Do you still think he was murdered?'

Liz poured the last of her wine into her glass and gave it a thoughtful swirl. 'I was convinced that Robbie had killed him, but with Robbie dead...'

'The journal you showed me proved that Mickey was afraid of Robbie. But that doesn't mean Robbie murdered him. We now know that Pete gave heroin to Mickey shortly before he died. His paranoia may have been caused by the drug overdose.'

'Really?' Liz raised a delicate eyebrow as she absorbed the information. 'So it could be that someone killed

Robbie and Pete in order to avenge Mickey. That puts Skye in danger too.'

'That's why I insisted on round-the-clock protection for her.'

'Pete believed that *Frost and Fury* is Mickey's online persona – that Mickey is alive and writing from the shadows.' Liz held him in her gaze. 'If Pete was right, then Mickey isn't just writing anymore. He's killing.'

'Or perhaps Mickey was the killer's first victim, in which case we're dealing with three murders in total.'

'Three members of the same band.'

Raven was reluctant to give voice to his thoughts, but the more he considered the possibilities, the more he was able to persuade himself that Mickey really was alive and had come out of hiding to take revenge on his former band mates. The poems, the clear motive, the fact that no body was ever discovered, the reported sightings of Mickey after his disappearance – all the facts pointed in the same direction – if you could get over the colossal hurdle of believing that the lead singer of a cult band could fake his death and go undetected for three decades.

What would Becca make of his analysis? Would she be thinking along the same lines? Or would she dismiss the apparent connections as mere coincidences? She had been quick to reject Colin's ideas as a ridiculous fantasy.

Liz tapped her fingernail against the stem of her wine glass, making it sing. 'What are you thinking?'

'Just something Becca said.'

'Ah, yes, DS Shawcross, the local girl.'

'I'm worried about her,' Raven admitted.

Liz frowned. 'She always seems very capable to me.'

'She's one of the best,' said Raven. 'She'll make DI soon, no question.'

'So what are you worried about?'

Raven exhaled. 'Her grandmother is critically ill in hospital. Reading between the lines, she probably won't make it.'

Liz made a sympathetic noise but said nothing.

'But there's something else bothering her,' Raven continued. 'I think it might be me.'

Liz laughed. 'She probably has a crush on you or something.'

'I doubt it.'

'Come on,' she said, rising from her chair. 'Let's go upstairs.'

They left the restaurant together, Liz's hand slipping easily and automatically into his. It felt natural now.

And yet, as they waited for the lift doors to open, Raven found his mind drifting again.

To Becca.

CHAPTER 28

Jess followed Tony into their fourth pub of the evening, her enthusiasm for their assignment wearing thin. The night was damp and chilly, and Stu's regular haunts were turning out to be a grim collection of the town's least appealing venues, each one dingier than the last. But at least she was getting her steps in – not that trudging up and down the streets of Scarborough would prepare her for the Coast to Coast Walk. For that, some proper training would be needed. But it was better than spending the evening at the station, staring at her screen while the cybercrime team continued to hit dead ends.

So far, Stu's alibi remained unconfirmed and Jess didn't hold out much hope that this place would be any different. The pub was nearly deserted: a few regulars hunched at the bar, a man and woman at a corner table, and that was about it.

Tony, methodical as ever, pulled out his list and ticked off the pub's name before heading up to the bar. He held up a mugshot of Stu taken from one of the band's recent press photos. Jess thought it was a rather flattering likeness. The real Stu looked rougher around the edges these days.

A Dying Echo

'Was this bloke in here last night?'

The barman, a lad in his twenties with a buzz cut and a bored expression, took the photo and studied it. 'Yeah, he was,' he drawled eventually.

'Do you remember what time?'

'Turned up around ten. Left at closing time. Worked his way through a couple of pints.'

'You're sure it was him?'

'Yeah, it was pretty dead here last night.' The lad glanced idly around the room as if expecting it to be any busier this evening. Then again, it was Tuesday night in late October. Not exactly the height of tourist season. He handed the photo back to Tony. 'Bloke was stood right where you're stood now. Said he plays in some band doing a comeback tour. Bit past it for all that, if you ask me.'

Tony exchanged a look with Jess. Clearly in the barman's world, anyone over the age of forty was ancient, and anyone over fifty should be collecting their pension, not playing music gigs.

'Thanks, mate,' said Tony, making a note of the time Stu had arrived and left the pub.

His alibi was finally beginning to stack up.

Tony passed the photo around the others at the bar, who all perked up and showed interest. No doubt this was the most exciting event of their evening.

'You police?' asked one of them, an older bloke in a leather jacket with grey whiskers and the weathered look of someone who'd spent more evenings in bars than out of them.

'That's right,' said Tony.

'That's Stu Lomas, yeah? He's often in here. You don't reckon he had owt to do with Robbie's death, do you?'

'We're just making routine inquiries, sir,' said Tony smoothly. 'Do you recall seeing him here last night?'

'Yeah. Same as Leon said.' The man indicated the barman with a nod. 'He left at eleven.'

'Did he mention where he was going afterwards?' asked Jess.

'Yeah. Summat about that club on Ramshill Road.'

'I know it,' said Jess. She'd been dragged there a few times by friends. It was the sort of place that didn't even start to get lively until after the pubs closed. A dingy, overcrowded pit of pricey drinks and bass so loud you could feel it in your bones. Not exactly her scene. She enjoyed music, but she preferred fresh air, hills and hiking boots over sticky dance floors.

Her phone buzzed in her pocket and she pulled it out, reading the name on the screen.

Gavin.

The dark-haired guy from the Coast to Coast meeting who'd bought her a drink.

She hesitated, watching the call go to voicemail. Everyone in the group had swapped numbers, but there was no reason for him to be ringing now. The next meetup wasn't until next week.

Unless this wasn't about the walk.

She'd sensed he was interested in her, and she had taken an instant liking to him too. He seemed kind. Steady. Nice.

But lately, "nice" wasn't enough. Not anymore. She'd had her heart broken, and she wasn't eager to risk a repeat. Keeping her distance felt safer. And she'd grown good at being on her own – too good, maybe. Still, some small part of her ached for something more.

She sighed as she slid the phone back into her pocket. Gavin hadn't left a voicemail. But if he really wanted to speak to her, he could call again.

'All okay?' Tony asked, catching her expression.

'Yeah, fine.' She shook off her thoughts. 'Shall we check out this nightclub?'

'Sure. Might be someone there who saw Stu earlier in the evening. We still have a blank to fill between six and ten.'

'And then we can finally call it a night.'

Tony grinned. 'Best news I've heard all evening.'

From the town centre, it took them just under ten

minutes to walk across Valley Bridge Road and up the Ramshill Road to a row of small, shuttered shops that lined the street. The entrance to the club was wedged between a closed tanning salon and a kebab shop. By day, it could have passed for a discount electronics store. At night, however, it was the only unit still lit, a flickering neon sign above the doorway casting a bluish glow onto the pavement.

The bass thump of music leaked out through the door with a dull pounding that vibrated in Jess's chest even before they stepped inside.

A pair of bouncers loomed in the doorway, shoulders squared beneath thick jackets. One of them had a neck tattoo that curled up behind his ear like a snake. He looked them up and down with the bored suspicion of someone who'd seen it all.

'What have we here?' he said, lips curling into a smirk. 'A couple of love birds?'

'Just slipped out of the office, have you?' added the second, his gaze lingering a moment too long on Jess, eyes filled with sly amusement.

Jess didn't reply, but the look she gave him was sharp enough. In their work clothes – Tony in his plain suit and she in her practical coat and boots – they hardly looked like club regulars. Tony in particular gave the impression that he'd never willingly set foot inside a place like this before.

She flipped open her warrant card and Tony followed suit.

The shift in tone was immediate.

'Oh, police, is it?' said Tattoo-neck, taking a hurried step back. 'Right, sorry. We don't want any bother.'

'I'm sure there won't be any if you'll let us straight through,' said Tony crisply.

Inside, the sound hit them like a wave. Spilt beer, cheap aftershave and body odour hung thick in the stuffy atmosphere. Strobe lights flared and lasers flickered, casting dancers in fractured bursts of movement – arms lifted, hips grinding, heads nodding in time with the beat.

The music was deafening, each drumbeat rattling in Jess's chest like a punch.

And yet for all the noise, the club didn't seem overcrowded. The writhing bodies on the dance floor were few and far between, although away from the dance floor, the seating was so dark it was impossible to make out much.

It was far too loud to talk. Jess led the way to the bar, weaving between clusters of clubgoers, Tony visibly unimpressed by the venue and its clientele, his mouth set in a grim line as he followed in her wake.

Behind the bar, a pair of bartenders were operating with efficient but mechanical monotony, slamming glasses down, pouring shots, shouting to the punters above the noise.

Tony held up Stu's photo and leaned in, raising his voice to be heard. 'Do you recognise this man? Was he here last night?'

One of the barmaids glanced at the photo without much interest. 'Dunno,' she shouted back, already turning away to deal with the next customer.

Jess motioned for them to circle the room. Tony nodded, grim-faced.

They made a slow sweep of the booths lining the club's walls, pausing to flash the photo and ask questions. Less than half of the booths were taken, their occupants either talking and laughing at the tops of their voices, or staring vacantly at their drinks, too drunk to dance.

Most of the responses were shrugs, half-heard comments or blank looks. A few people leaned in with vague interest, but nobody recognised the man in the picture. Most of them looked too young to remember the band, let alone care.

None of them had any recollection of Stu.

Jess couldn't say she was surprised. Stu wouldn't have fitted in easily here. Most of the clientele were around thirty years younger than the band's keyboard player. Then again, maybe Stu hadn't come for the atmosphere – maybe he just wanted somewhere that served drinks late into the night. Or perhaps he was trying to relive his youth.

She was about to suggest calling it a night when she noticed something.

In the far corner of the club, half-hidden behind a support pillar, one booth lay in deeper shadow. A man's form was slumped in the seat, head resting against the padded backrest. She couldn't make out his features in the stygian gloom, but he was alone and something about his pose didn't feel right. His body language was wrong – too still, too heavy.

She stepped away from the main floor and moved towards the booth, threading past dancers without taking her eyes off the figure. Still no movement. As she drew closer, flickering strobes momentarily lit up the man's face.

Her heart skipped a beat.

'Tony,' she said, turning back sharply. She pointed to the booth and mouthed the word: 'Stu.'

Tony's expression hardened in an instant. They sidled around the pillar, slipping into the booth on either side.

Up close, the scene was worse than she'd feared. Stu was slouched awkwardly, head lolling at an unnatural angle, jaw slack. His skin looked pallid in the strobe light, and his chest wasn't rising.

The table in front of him was scattered with pint glasses, most empty, one knocked over, leaving a thin puddle of beer that had spread across the sticky surface. The stench of alcohol was strong.

Jess reached out and tapped his arm. Nothing. She shook his shoulder. Still no response. His lips were blue.

A cold weight settled in her stomach.

Tony leaned in, pressing two fingers to Stu's neck.

Jess waited breathlessly until finally he gave a slow shake of his head.

Stu was dead.

CHAPTER 29

Raven stood in the middle of the emptied nightclub, surveying the scene with heavy-lidded eyes. The call had come through shortly before midnight, just as he and Liz were drifting off to sleep in her hotel bed.

A third death, exactly as he had feared. Someone, it seemed, was intent on picking off every member of Echoes of Mercury, and Raven's first action on hearing the news had been to call PC Sharon Jarvis and brief her on the latest development. 'I'll get someone in to provide full protection for Skye, don't worry,' he had assured her. He just hoped Gillian would agree to his request for more manpower in the morning.

He rubbed the back of his neck and surveyed the scene. Without the throb of music and the cover of darkness, the nightclub had lost what little glamour it pretended to possess. Harsh overhead lights cast a pallid glare over the sticky floors and scuffed furniture. The tables were littered with empty glasses and marked by syrupy rings. Crumpled tissues, cigarette ends and other debris clung to the floor like damp confetti, ground in by careless feet.

The booths, now deserted, looked tired and worn, the

faux leather upholstery cracked and peeling at the edges. A sour mix of stale beer and sweat clung to the air, making Raven's nose wrinkle in disgust. Even the dance floor seemed small, the space so recently pulsing with bodies now glittering with shards of broken plastic cups.

Stu's body had been removed to the mortuary. In the foyer, the last few clubgoers were being questioned by uniformed officers, their statements taken and meticulously recorded, although the likelihood that any of them had anything useful to offer felt remote.

The killer was too adept at covering their tracks.

Two bouncers stood awkwardly beside the bar, arms folded, watching with wary eyes as the CSI team in their white suits began their work. Behind the bar itself, the bartenders busied themselves wiping down surfaces, though it was clear from their glazed expressions that they'd rather be anywhere else. At home in bed, probably.

Raven, too, wished he was still curled up in the warmth of Liz's embrace. It gave him no satisfaction to see his suspicions consolidated into an even clearer pattern. Three band members dead, one missing. Only Skye remained.

He studied the booth where Stu had met his death. It was squalid, there was no other way to describe it. Beneath the sticky surfaces and reek of lager, something uglier lingered. It was the residue of loneliness, of desperation, and of the quiet chaos that crept in when the music stopped.

Jess stepped up beside him, her face pale and drawn. 'It looks different in the light,' she murmured.

'It always does.' Raven had seen more than his fair share of crime scenes over the years. Each one was different, yet after a while they blurred into one. A corpse, a murder weapon, a telltale trail of violence. Details changed, yet the overall impression endured. The trick was to look with fresh eyes every time. No two victims were the same, nor any crime. The perpetrator always left a unique fingerprint, even if – as Raven strongly suspected in this case – they successfully avoided leaving any actual prints for CSI to find.

'With the lights off,' said Jess, 'anyone who looked in this direction probably just thought he'd closed his eyes for a moment or nodded off.'

It was a depressing thought. Stu had been murdered just yards from dozens of potential witnesses. Men and women had danced before him as he drew his final breath, and his heart had beat for the very last time to the sound of a relentless bass line.

Yet in a way, perhaps Stu would have appreciated the irony. He had spent his life making music. He had died while the music played.

'You did well, Jess,' Raven told her. 'He can't have been dead for long when you found him.'

'That's what's so frustrating,' she said. 'If we'd arrived a bit sooner, we might have been able to save him. We might even have caught the killer red-handed.'

Raven shook his head to reassure her. 'The world of "ifs" leads nowhere, Jess. It's no use thinking that way.'

And yet who was he to talk? Flickers of flame and billowing smoke haunted his every dream. He should take his own advice and move on.

When the killer is behind bars.

A familiar figure waddled towards him, shrouded in white. She removed her face mask and treated him to a scowl. 'DCI Raven, glad to see you up and about like the rest of us. Nothing like your early morning cheer to bring sunshine to my day. Or night, in this case.'

Holly Chang.

Her blunt Yorkshire demeanour was unwelcome at the best of times. Right now, Raven didn't think he could handle much of it.

'I don't suppose you thought to bring us a cup of coffee?' she enquired. 'Or a bacon butty, for that matter. It's funny, but I'm quite partial to a dollop of fried pig grease at three in the morning.'

'Sorry,' said Raven. 'Next time.'

'Lucky I brought a Mars bar with me, then.' Holly

stripped off her gloves and pulled a bar of chocolate from her pocket. 'Breakfast of champions,' she informed him, peeling off the wrapper and taking a hearty bite.

'So,' said Raven with ill-concealed irritation. 'Anything?'

Holly gave Jess a wink as she chewed. 'Doesn't hang about, does he, your boss? Always wants to know. Reckon he'll make a decent detective with that attitude.' She turned to face Raven. 'Unless somebody gives him a good clobbering first. I was just saying to Jamie–'

'Holly–' warned Raven. His patience for her banter had finally run out.

'All right, all right.' She returned to the booth where Stu's lifeless body had been slumped just hours earlier, pulled her gloves back on and lifted a half-finished pint of beer off the table. 'Erin's already dusted this for prints, and we'll be sending it to the lab for analysis. I'm no expert on poisons, but my gut's telling me your man may not have found it to his liking.' She held out the glass. 'Want to give your nose a whirl?'

Raven bent closer, gingerly taking a sniff of the drink and searching its aroma for any trace of bitter almonds. Nothing. Just flat, warm beer, its sour smell cloying in the back of his throat.

'Can't tell,' he admitted, but Holly was right to suspect it had been spiked. According to Jess and Tony, there were no obvious indications of violence on Stu's body. No blood, no bruising, no needle marks on his arms. His lips were blue, however, and his tongue swollen, suggesting he had died from asphyxiation caused by some ingested substance. Poison or a drug overdose certainly fitted the perpetrator's style.

Jess was busy with her phone. She gave a short cry of surprise and passed it to Raven. 'Boss, take a look at this. It's another poem from *Frost and Fury*.'

Raven's heart sank, but he ought to have been expecting the news. If there was one thing they had learned about the killer, it was that he or she was a creature of habit. Taking Jess's phone, he scanned the lines of verse, his stomach tightening as he read the words posted in the dead of night.

You sought that sweetness,
In a house of sin.
Found a taste of ruin,
A black toxin.

With hollow truths,
And weighty lies,
You bartered your soul,
And paid with your sighs.

Disgust turned to fear,
Then blindly to shame,
You withered away,
And feasted on blame.

'Does "house of sin" refer to this nightclub?' asked Jess, peering over his shoulder. 'And "black toxin", surely that means some kind of poison.'

'Potentially.'

Raven was wary of reading too much into the words. Like the other poems, it was cryptic and vague, capable of being twisted to fit any number of narratives. Conspiracy Colin would be all over this, putting two and two together and making fifty-five.

Yet despite his misgivings, Raven couldn't ignore the fact that a poem appeared immediately before or soon after each death of a band member. And the words did point to inside knowledge.

But what did the rest of it mean? *Fear, disgust, blame, shame.* There was so much he didn't yet understand.

*

A pale sun bled above the rooftops of the Barrowcliff estate as Raven nudged the M6 into the same parking spot he'd used the day before. Schoolkids dawdled along the pavement, kicking at stray cans, munching breakfast bars or bags of crisps, dragging heavy feet towards another dull school day – while his had never really ended.

He hadn't slept. Not a wink. Just hours of pacing the nightclub, watching CSI sweep the scene, pretending the ache in his bones was fatigue and not a growing sense of failure. Holly Chang might grumble about being wrenched from her bed in the dead of night, but at least she could return to it when her job was done. For Raven, the real work was only just beginning. He'd be relying on caffeine to get him through the day.

Jess hadn't been home to bed either. She'd curled up in one of the booths in the nightclub for a while, but she looked dog-tired. Her eyes were shadowed, her skin drawn. She gave him a dubious glance as he killed the engine. 'Boss, don't we need a search warrant to gain entry to a victim's home?'

For some reason, she had never been able to call him Raven – perhaps because he had never invited her to. On balance, he was quite happy with "boss".

'Not if we have reason to believe it may form part of the crime scene or is likely to contain evidence.'

'And do we?'

'Ask me again when I'm not feeling so sleepy,' said Raven.

He stepped out of the car, cold air biting his face, providing some welcome stimulation. In his pocket, he fingered the key he'd taken from Stu's body. He drew it out as he walked up the path to the house.

The lock resisted at first, then clicked open with a reluctant groan. The door creaked inward.

Music greeted them – soft, eerie, incongruous. A record playing from somewhere inside the house. Raven recognised it instantly and his chest tightened in response. *Twin Track*.

Steel wheels scream against the rail,
A banshee's wail of a love that failed.
Parallel lines that never bend,
No crossing, no meeting,
Just an endless end.

This was the original version, with Mickey's deeper vocals in place of Robbie's. The song was from the band's debut album. A tale of doomed love, as if Mickey had glimpsed his future as he penned the verses all those years ago. As if this had all been predetermined from the outset.

Jess shot Raven a questioning look, but he raised a finger to his lips and stepped over the threshold. Creeping stealthily into the hallway, he pushed open the door to the front room with his foot.

The place was as cluttered and chaotic as Raven remembered from his first visit – a battlefield of empty pizza boxes and crushed beer cans. Ashtrays overflowed onto a carpet peppered with cigarette burns. Dust motes floated in a shaft of pale light leaking through a grimy curtain.

The music was coming from a battered old record player in the corner, a faint hiss and crackle as the needle tracked around the vinyl groove. Raven slipped on nitrile gloves, crossed to the machine, and lifted the needle with a faint *click*.

'It was playing on repeat,' he murmured.

'Bloody hell, boss,' said Jess as she took in the state of the room. 'Has it been ransacked?'

'No,' said Raven. 'This is just how Stu lived.'

Apart from the general untidiness, nothing appeared disturbed. There were no signs that anyone else had got there first.

A laptop stood open on the coffee table, sandwiched between a stack of well-thumbed vinyl singles and an empty can of lager. A green LED indicated that it was powered on. Raven tapped the mouse pad with his gloved finger. The screen blinked into life, revealing an open inbox. No password. No lock screen.

'No security,' muttered Jess, incredulous. 'Anyone could get in.'

'We just did,' said Raven, delighted it had been so simple. He doubted they would be able to gain such easy entry to *Frost and Fury's* computer, should they ever find themselves in a position to try. No doubt it would have every type of encryption and protection going.

At the top of the inbox was a single received message.

'Look,' said Raven. 'This must have been the last thing Stu looked at before he went out to the nightclub.'

Raven clicked on it, and his blood turned to ice.

Sender: Mickey Flint
You let me down, Stu. When I needed a friend, you turned me away

Jess gasped. 'That's it? That's all it says?'

Raven exhaled slowly. 'It's enough.'

'Could it really be from Mickey?'

Raven shrugged. 'The question is whether Stu believed it was from Mickey.'

'There's a reply.' Jess pointed. 'Go to Sent Mail.'

Raven navigated to the Sent folder, and there it was: Stu's final email.

Mickey,
Man, I'm sorry. I should have been a better friend. I never meant to let you down.
If you're out there, if this is really you, let's meet at the club. I want to put this right. I owe you that much.

'That's why he went to the nightclub last night,' breathed Jess. 'He suggested it because he knew it was a place Mickey would remember from the old days. He thought he was going to a reunion with his old friend. A chance to apologise and make up.'

'But he was going to his own execution.' Raven clicked

on the email address of the sender. 'Can we trace this?'

They looked at it together. The address was a random sequence of numbers and characters, the domain name equally meaningless.

Jess grimaced. 'What I've learnt from working with the cybercrime team is that hackers use addresses like these as burner addresses. The domain name is disposable and the address self-deletes after a few hours, erasing all records. It's designed to be completely untraceable. Sometimes there's a way to find the originating IP address, but if the sender used a VPN, then forget it. We'll be running in circles.'

Raven groaned in despair. The killer had anticipated everything – again. 'They're running rings around us.'

'It seems that way.'

Raven slammed the laptop shut. 'Let's get this over to cybercrime immediately. If they can find even a single crumb of data, I want to know about it. Find out if Stu had any previous contact with the killer. Find out if he messaged anyone else about Mickey.'

Weariness crashed over him like a wave. His limbs were heavy. But he needed to be at the top of his game. The killer was always a step ahead of them, even finding the time to write poetry about his or her crimes.

Raven pushed the exhaustion away, refusing to give in.

'We still don't know if it's Mickey,' he told Jess, as he surveyed the wreckage of Stu's life. 'But if it is, we're no longer searching for a missing person. We're chasing a man back from the dead – and hell-bent on vengeance.'

CHAPTER 30

'This is turning into a bloodbath, Tom. Three deaths now. What's going on?' Detective Superintendent Gillian Ellis planted her elbows on the desk and leaned forwards, her chair creaking beneath her heavy frame. Her eyes narrowed beneath a furrowed brow, her face twisted into an expression halfway between horror and disbelief.

Raven rubbed at his temple, trying to push back the tension crawling across his scalp. Encounters with his boss always set him on edge, and this was no exception. Gillian Ellis didn't tolerate failure. And this case was nothing short of a disaster.

'I believe the motive is revenge, ma'am,' he said carefully. 'The three victims were all members of Echoes of Mercury. I think they were targeted because they let Mickey down when he needed them most.'

Gillian gave a sharp grunt, shifting her bulk in the chair as she folded her arms across her chest like a judge about to pass sentence. Her lips pursed. 'You mean Mickey Flint, the singer presumed dead. So who might want to avenge him?'

Raven shifted uncomfortably, knowing that the answer he gave wouldn't be what Gillian wanted to hear. He had no choice but to spit it out. 'We have two working theories, ma'am. The first is that an obsessive fan is carrying out the murders. We've linked the killings to an online user called *Frost and Fury*, but the cyber team has been unable to trace them. Whoever *Frost and Fury* is, they're expert at covering their tracks online.'

'Do you have suspects?'

Raven dipped his head. 'Not really.'

Gillian drummed her thick fingers against the desk, loud and impatient. 'And your second theory?'

Raven took a deep breath. He could already feel her reaction coming. 'That Mickey Flint is still alive and he's picking off his former band members one by one.'

Gillian's thick brows rose together. 'You have evidence to support that?'

'The latest victim received emails from someone claiming to be Mickey. The poems posted by *Frost and Fury* resemble the band's lyrics, no body was ever found–'

'All right,' she snapped, slicing the air with a dismissive wave of her hand. 'Get a computer-generated image of Mickey as he would appear now and circulate it to officers on the ground.'

'Yes, ma'am.'

She shifted again in her seat, the leather creaking. 'And make sure anyone else at risk has proper protection in place.'

'That's what I wanted to ask you about, ma'am,' said Raven. 'The last surviving band member is Skye Kershaw, Mickey's former girlfriend. She broke off their relationship shortly before his disappearance. So if the revenge theory is correct–'

'She'll need round-the-clock protection until the killer is caught,' Gillian barked, already reaching for her phone. 'All right, I'll make the necessary arrangements immediately.'

Raven exhaled, the knot in his chest easing just slightly.

'Thank you, ma'am. Much appreciated.'

He rose to his feet, but Gillian's voice halted him halfway to the door.

'And Tom,' she said, fixing him with a stare sharp enough to pin him in place, 'the next time I see you, I want this case solved.'

Raven gave a tight nod and left before she could say another word.

As he made his way back along the corridor, he rolled his shoulders to shake off the encounter. He'd got what he needed, but it didn't feel like much of a victory. He was just about to enter the incident room when his phone rang.

'Raven.'

'Sir, it's PC Sharon Jarvis here.' The family liaison officer sounded flustered, not like her usual calm self.

'What is it?'

'It's Skye, sir. She's gone.'

Raven froze, mid-step. 'Gone where? How?'

'I don't know. She slipped out while I was using the bathroom. She's taken her phone. I'm so sorry.'

'It's not your fault,' he said briskly. 'But we need to find her. Fast. She could be in serious danger. Did she say anything? Mention anyone she wanted to meet?'

'Nothing. She just vanished.'

'All right,' said Raven. 'Stay calm. Stay put in case she returns. I'll send backup.'

*

Becca had left the hospital the previous night feeling calmer than she had in ages. There was no change in her grandmother's condition, and perhaps that was good news, or at least the best that could be hoped for under the circumstances. After her chat at her nana's bedside, she had finally reached clarity about her feelings for Raven – or so she hoped.

She slept well, and when Raven called her first thing and asked her to attend Stu's post-mortem, she went immediately.

Felicity was already laying out her tools on a tray as Becca arrived in the mortuary.

Becca had never known a post-mortem to proceed at such short notice. Then again, this was the third murder in less than a week. Urgency was required before the killer struck again.

The latest body lay under a blue sheet on a gurney.

'How nice to see you again, Becca,' said Felicity from behind her mask. 'We seem to be making a habit of this. Other people meet for tea or coffee, but I've never understood the appeal. A glass of water serves the same purpose and is much less fuss.'

Becca nodded, not wanting to give Felicity any encouragement. She hoped the pathologist wasn't going to indulge in her usual brand of barely concealed sarcasm and spite as she conducted her forensic examination.

Felicity adjusted one of her instruments and placed it carefully on the metal tray with a *clink*. 'So, Raven's keeping his distance again, I see,' she continued breezily. 'I much prefer it that way. He attended the previous PM, but I'd rather have you here. How is your grandmother, by the way? I do hope she makes a recovery. Although, a stroke at her age… it would be wise to brace yourself for the worst.'

Becca regarded her icily. 'I understand that you told Raven about her illness.'

'Yes,' said Felicity. 'To my astonishment, he knew nothing about it. He's your boss, after all. He should have realised something was wrong. I told him he ought to show more consideration to the members of his team. But that's so typical of men like him, isn't it?'

'I'm sorry, Felicity, but Raven's not a mind reader!' Becca snapped, not in the mood for more of Felicity's Raven-hating rhetoric. 'In fact he's been very kind and considerate. He may not be perfect, but he' – she paused, groping for the right word – 'tries.'

'I find that hard to believe,' scoffed Felicity. She

sounded unapologetic – almost sharp in her response. 'I think you're being far too soft on him. That's so like a woman to do that – to apologise for something that isn't her fault.'

'Well, I'm not being soft, and none of this is Raven's fault. You should have let me tell him myself about my grandmother's illness, instead of discussing personal matters behind my back. You breached confidentiality, not to mention putting Raven in an awkward position.'

The rebuke came out sharper than Becca had intended. Felicity had obviously touched a raw nerve, or perhaps the outburst had been building for a long time. In hindsight, Becca realised she hadn't yet said all that needed saying.

'You've hated Raven ever since he arrived in Scarborough,' she accused. 'What have you got against him?'

Felicity's fingers froze around the handle of the scalpel she was about to pick up. Her eyes widened, a look of surprise spreading across her face as if she'd been struck. 'Really, Becca, you mustn't make excuses for a man like that. He doesn't deserve it.'

'A man like what?'

'Like any man!' wailed Felicity, her voice cracking. She stopped cold, as if she had given away far more than she intended. As if, for the first time in her life, she had lost control. Her fingers trembled and slid along the blade. A drop of blood welled up and she yanked her hand away from the scalpel as if burned.

'Look what you made me do,' she complained, her voice quieter, the control beginning to return. But she couldn't disguise what had happened, nor could she hide the single tear that appeared in the corner of her eye.

Becca had scarcely seen the pathologist express emotion before, let alone reveal an ounce of vulnerability. She hesitated, then took a step closer. 'Felicity?' she said, her voice gentle. 'Are you okay?'

'Perfectly.' Felicity peeled off her gloves and moved to the stainless-steel sink to attend to her finger. 'I'm quite all right, thank you.'

She washed the cut, dried her hand briskly and applied antiseptic and surgical gauze, her movements brisk and efficient. When she turned back to face Becca, her eyes were dry, her features composed once more.

'I'm sorry for my outburst,' she said, her gaze not quite meeting Becca's but gliding to the sheeted corpse between them. 'I have... issues with male authority figures.'

Becca watched her closely. 'But why?'

A silence stretched between them before Felicity answered, speaking in a tone devoid of its usual sharp edges.

'My mother died when I was eight.'

'I'm so sorry. I didn't know.'

'I don't talk about it.' Felicity's voice was brittle, and Becca got the impression that she had never spoken about this to anyone. 'Losing my mother would have been bad enough. But my real problems had only just begun. You see, my father was weak, a failure. He couldn't cope on his own, and just when I needed him most, he left. Inexcusable behaviour, don't you think, for a father to abandon a small child in that way? Unforgiveable.' She picked up the scalpel again, turning it over absentmindedly. 'I was placed with a string of foster parents and ended up in care. Apparently, I was a difficult child to place.' She lifted her gaze to meet Becca's at last. 'So now you know my secrets. I don't form attachments, and I don't trust men. I have a pathological ability to control, and an obsession with understanding death. I'm like a case straight out of a psychology textbook, aren't I?'

She laughed lightly, a hollow sound, her voice barely a tinkle above the hiss of the air conditioning. Then she turned her attention back to the cadaver and snapped on a fresh pair of gloves.

'Anyway,' she said briskly, business-like again, 'we'd best crack on. We've got a body to slice open. Ready?'

CHAPTER 31

It was liberating to be outside again, free from Sharon's unrelenting scrutiny. Skye strode along the pavement, feeling the wind in her hair, the weak winter sun on her face. The police might pretend that the family liaison officer was posted to give emotional support and provide protection, but Sharon knew what her true purpose was. To keep a watch on her and find out everything she knew.

Anyway, Skye didn't need emotional support. Or protection.

It had been easy enough to give her minder the slip. With any luck, Sharon wouldn't even notice she'd gone. It was a fair walk from Ramsey Street to the Crown Spa hotel, and by the time she arrived, her initial rush had faded and trepidation was beginning to set in. This would have been easier when Robbie was still alive. He had always had a knack for getting what he wanted. He'd wanted her, and she had become his wife. He'd wanted to be the band's frontman, and nobody had stood in his way. He'd wanted a solo career and even that bastard Rupert had been persuaded to sign a deal.

Now it was her turn to fight for what she wanted. She

could do it. She had to. With a toss of her head she pushed open the hotel doors and strode in, ready to do battle.

She didn't have to look hard for Rupert. He was lounging in an armchair by the window, newspaper in hand, radiating smugness as he always did. He must have been born like that, with a silver spoon stuck up his arse.

She psyched herself up, just like she did before a show, and strode towards him.

'Rupert!'

Rupert glanced up, his haughty features registering a glimmer of surprise. 'Skye, what a pleasure to see you again. I wasn't expecting you out and about after…'

'After Robbie died?' She stood before him, her hands trembling. 'You didn't want to see me, is that what you meant?'

He wrinkled his Roman nose. 'Of course not. I would have dropped by to say hello, but I didn't think the police would want me poking my nose in.'

'Is that right?' Rupert was the only one who hadn't called to offer sympathy and support after Robbie's death. Pete, Stu, Chaz, Taylor, Frankie – they had all been there for her, offering condolences, promising to help. Not that she needed their help. But Rupert? There had been no profit in it for him, and so he hadn't bothered. It maybe hadn't even occurred to him.

He gestured at an empty chair. 'Why don't you take a seat, Skye? I'll order coffee and tea.'

But Skye didn't want to sit. 'We need to talk.'

Rupert folded his newspaper away with measured ease. 'Yes? What about?'

'The rights to our songs. I want them back. Our songs are charting again after all the publicity. Those royalties belong to me!'

A faint smile tugged at the edges of Rupert's thin mouth. Then he threw his head back and roared with laughter. 'Oh, Skye, you must understand you signed those away years ago. You were paid for them at the time. Fair and square.'

'There was nothing fair and square about it.' Skye glared, her anger making her nostrils flare. 'You know full well you screwed us over. You wouldn't get away with a deal like that now.'

Rupert smirked. 'Maybe not. But this is now and that was then. You were a bunch of nobodies when I signed you. Without me you'd have remained just another pub band playing for free drinks.'

'You took advantage of us,' said Skye, tears smarting her eyes at the injustice, but determined not to back down. 'And of Chaz's inexperience. He tried his best for us, but you took him for a ride too.'

'Perhaps you ought to take your temper out on Chaz, then. That Scottish oaf's as good as useless.'

A shout came from across the hotel lobby. 'Hey! Who're you calling a useless oaf?'

Rupert's smirk slid from his face. His face paled as Chaz appeared, striding belligerently across the lounge, his face flushed with fury, his broad shoulders squared like a boxer stepping into the ring.

Had he been eavesdropping, or had fate simply orchestrated his entrance at precisely the right moment?

'You stuck-up English bastard!' cried Chaz. 'You're like a spider in its web, pulling the strings, collecting the cash. You sit there watching with your beady eyes as the rest of us go blundering about. You dinnae care if every last one of us gets murdered.'

'Steady on now, Chaz,' said Rupert, but the Glaswegian was beyond reasoning.

He seized Rupert by the collar, hauled him out of his chair, and drove the crown of his head into the bridge of Rupert's nose with the casual brutality of a bare-knuckle brawler.

The sickening crack of skull against bone echoed across the lounge. Rupert crumpled back into his chair, his hands flying to his face as blood gushed from his nose, staining his pristine white shirt a deep scarlet.

For the first time in Skye's memory, Rupert Devizes

was too stunned to utter a word.

Chaz stood back, dusting himself down. He grinned with the satisfaction of a job well done. 'That'll teach ye tae call me a Scottish oaf,' he declared.

He turned to Skye. 'You all right, hen?'

'I think so,' said Skye.

'I should have done that years ago,' said Chaz.

And with that, he turned on his heel and left, leaving Skye standing between a bleeding record executive and a room of stunned onlookers.

Rupert groaned, his fingers groping for something to stifle the flow of blood.

'So,' said Skye, handing him a napkin. 'Now that we've got that out of the way, let's talk again about my songs.'

★

Raven sat in the interview room, fists clenching and unclenching, his barely restrained anger simmering just beneath the surface. He had three murders on his hands, not to mention the cold case of Mickey's disappearance, and now he had to waste time chasing a missing witness under his protection and dealing with a charge of common assault.

Across the table, Chaz McDonald sat sulking in his chair, arms folded tightly across his chest, features twisted into a ruddy scowl. The duty sergeant had brought him a cup of black coffee from the vending machine. For once, the usual stench of whisky was absent from the Glaswegian's breath. Apparently he had decided to batter his victim while stone-cold sober.

After reading him his rights, Raven leaned forwards. 'Explain yourself, Chaz.' He had no patience for a fruitless interview, not while a serial killer was at large, striking with ruthless precision.

He had already spoken to Skye after retrieving her from the hotel and ensuring that she was safely back home, now under the watchful eyes of not only Sharon Jarvis but also a uniformed officer who had been sent to guard her. Raven couldn't keep her under lock and key, but he had done his best to convince her of the reality of the danger she faced and the need to stay out of harm's way.

It was a lesson that Rupert Devizes had learned the hard way. A visit to the emergency department of the hospital to patch things up would most likely have to be followed by more invasive surgical procedures to repair the bone structure once the initial swelling had subsided. His noble Roman nose might never look the same again. Poetic justice, perhaps. Things would have gone better for Rupert if he'd returned to London immediately after Robbie's death, instead of hanging around Scarborough, apparently with the intention of gloating and wallowing in other people's misery.

Chaz gave an unapologetic shrug. 'The smug bastard deserved it. He's had it coming for a long time.'

Raven sighed, finding it hard to disagree. He'd been tempted to hit Rupert himself during their meeting at the hotel's health club. Yet it was his job to uphold the law and to hold to account those who broke it. 'You admit to causing grievous bodily harm?'

'Aye. And I'd do it again.'

Raven leaned his elbows on the table, his head in his hands. Exhaustion was creeping into his bones, clouding his thinking, sapping his very will to move forwards. He glanced at Becca, who had returned from the post-mortem with nothing more to report than what they had already surmised – that Stu Lomas had died from acute poisoning from a toxin as yet unidentified, but which the laboratory analysis of the beer would no doubt reveal. The ingested toxin had caused Stu's throat and tongue to swell up, leading to rapid asphyxiation and loss of consciousness. Just like the cyanide and heroin that had been used to murder Robbie and Pete, it had most likely been obtained from the dark web by the elusive *Frost and Fury*.

'Give us something, Chaz,' said Raven. 'Help us catch the killer.'

Chaz's eyes peered out belligerently from beneath his bushy red brows. 'You think I know who it is? You think it's me?' His voice rose in indignation. 'Because if you're looking for someone to pin this on, then look no further than that bastard Rupert.'

'Enough!' Raven brought his fist down hard, making the plastic cup jump on the table and the coffee spill. 'Do you think I've got time for your playground spats? Three people are dead, and you're out there throwing headbutts like it's chucking-out time in Easterhouse!'

Chaz held up his hands. 'I'm no' sorry for that, and I won't apologise, but I'll help you if I can. It's my pals who are dead. You might think I wasn't much of a manager, with the money and the contracts and all, but I always did my best for the band. It was me that got them back on their feet, out on the road again. It was me that stuck by them through the darkest days. And I'm not letting Skye down now. No way.'

For all his temper, the Scotsman had heart, and it was hard to stay angry with him for long.

'Then tell me something, Chaz,' Raven pleaded.

'Aye, all right. Anything to help the *polis*. What exactly do you want to know?'

It was time to level with Chaz. If Raven wanted useful information, he would have to steer him in the right direction. 'The theory we're working on is that the motive for the murders is revenge. So, who was close enough to Mickey to know how the others betrayed him?'

Chaz frowned in consternation. 'What are you saying? Those guys were his pals. They wouldnae–'

'Stop!' Raven cut him off. 'We know Robbie took Mickey's girlfriend from him. Pete gave him heroin. Stu turned his back on him when he was at his lowest ebb. What I want to hear from you is who knew.'

Chaz looked genuinely shaken by the weight of the accusations. 'Well, now you mention it, I guess that's all true. Those lads should have done more to help Mickey. We all should have done more – me, Skye, and that bastard

Rupert too. And so I guess those are the ones who know what happened.'

'Just the three of you?' Raven pressed.

'I cannae think of anyone else. But you cannae be serious. Skye would never hurt anyone! As for Rupert, he's a cold-hearted bastard and I wouldnae put it past him to kill, but not to avenge Mickey. No! Rupert cares for no one but himself.'

'Then what about Mickey? What if it's him?' Raven watched closely to see how his suggestion would land.

Chaz looked stunned. 'Mickey, the killer?' He leaned back in his chair, eyebrows raised high. 'Now I know you're joking.'

Becca took the lead. 'Why do you say that, Chaz? Previously you insisted that Mickey was still alive.'

Chaz tugged at his unruly beard. 'I did, aye, but I didn't think...'

'What aren't you telling us?' Raven's patience was threadbare.

Chaz's gaze darted around the room, as if searching for a way out. But there was nowhere for him to go. Finally, he exhaled. 'I suppose it had to come to light someday. Sad news, but the fact is...'

'What?'

'Poor Mickey's dead. May his soul rest in peace.'

'How can you be so certain?' asked Becca.

'Well, I cannae know for sure, but he's not been seen for a long while now, so I doubt he's still kicking.'

'But you were the one who received a letter from him,' pointed out Becca. 'You drew our attention to the sightings.'

Chaz stared down at his boots. 'Well, about that...,' he mumbled. 'Maybe I penned that letter myself.'

Raven shook his head, incredulous. 'You forged it? And what about the sightings?'

Chaz winced. 'That was me too. I paid a bloke to say he'd spoken to Mickey in Whitby. And I hired an actor to pretend to be him.'

'You deliberately created a false trail,' said Raven. 'Why would you do that?'

'To sell records,' admitted Chaz miserably. 'Echoes of Mercury were my life. They were all I had back then. And it turned out that a half-dead rockstar's worth a lot more than a dead one or even a living one. Mystery created the myth. And the myth became legend.'

'All you've done is fuel the conspiracy theories,' said Raven. 'There are fans out there holding onto the idea that Mickey is still alive.'

Chaz hung his head. 'I'm not proud of what I did.'

Raven pushed back his chair and stood up. 'Stay here.'

He signalled to Becca and the two of them stepped into the corridor, out of Chaz's earshot.

Raven leaned against the wall, his palms pressed to the hard surface, his arms heavy with fatigue. 'If all that evidence was faked, then Mickey's dead after all.'

'That leaves us with three people who were close enough to Mickey to know the truth: Chaz, Skye, and Rupert. And none of them has a good reason to avenge his death.'

Raven looked at her sideways, catching something in her tone of voice. 'What?'

'This is a pretty wild idea,' she admitted. 'But right now I'm starting to think anything's possible.'

'So what are you thinking?'

'Just what Colin Harris said – that Mickey is still alive and a deranged fan is holding him prisoner.'

Raven tilted his head, wondering if he'd misheard. 'A deranged fan? But the only obsessive fan we know about is Conspiracy Colin himself.'

Becca smiled faintly. 'Exactly.'

CHAPTER 32

Raven wasted no time before applying for a warrant to search Colin Harris's house on Tollergate. He half expected his request to be denied. If that happened, he would have to get creative.

He didn't mention his hunch that a missing rockstar, long since presumed dead, was being held captive in a garden shed at Colin's house. That would have been laughed out of court. He simply stated his suspicion that the suspect was in possession of computer equipment of relevance to an ongoing murder investigation.

Then came the waiting. Long, grinding, and tedious. He fought the temptation to give in to fatigue and lay his head on his desk.

Becca brought them both a hot drink. 'Get some more caffeine inside you,' she urged. 'Try to stay upright.'

Just when he was beginning to give up hope, the authorisation came through.

'We're on,' he told her. 'Grab your coat.'

By the time they reached Tollergate, marked cars with flashing blue lights had already taken up position at the top and bottom of the road, sealing off the street to traffic.

Raven parked his BMW behind the lead vehicle and joined the four uniformed officers standing ready to proceed with the search.

'We don't believe the suspect is armed,' Raven told them, 'but he may be dangerous. Don't take any risks.'

'Understood, sir,' the sergeant in charge informed him. 'We'll take it from here.' He turned to his team. 'Right, then, lads. Let's get this show on the road.'

Raven and Becca followed them to the house, but could only stand back and watch as the men went about their business. They knew it better than Raven, in any case. Much as he would have liked to be part of the action, he knew he would only get in the way and possibly jeopardise the entire operation if his bad leg gave way at a critical moment.

He watched as the team squared up, ready to execute their well-rehearsed manoeuvres.

The sergeant pounded a meaty fist on the front door. 'Police! Open up!'

There was no response from within.

He stepped aside for the officer carrying the big red battering ram. One sharp swing and the door splintered inwards.

'Police!' bellowed the sergeant again as they entered the house.

There was no rear access to the property, so Raven stayed out front, watching the windows in case Colin tried to bolt.

The windows remained firmly closed.

A shout rang out from upstairs. A few moments later, heavy steps descended the winding stairs. Colin Harris appeared in his dressing gown, flanked by two officers, hands cuffed behind his back, blinking in confusion.

'What the bloody hell is this?' demanded Colin. 'What are you doing in my house?'

'Take him to the car,' said Raven. 'We'll question him later.'

The search was now the priority.

With Colin in custody, Raven and Becca stepped inside. The house was just as they'd remembered – narrow, cramped and claustrophobic.

They moved through to the kitchen and unlocked the back door. The courtyard garden lay beyond, and in it, the shed. It was bigger than Raven remembered, half filling the small courtyard. A shiny new padlock secured the door.

'Get this open,' Raven ordered, and the officer with the ram produced bolt cutters. One quick snip and the padlock clattered to the ground.

Raven donned gloves and hauled on the door. It groaned in protest, but yielded with pressure, creaking loudly open.

Rusted garden tools lined one wall of the shed and coils of old rope lay tangled in the corner. The air was thick with the damp scent of mildew and engine oil, a sour, cloying smell that clung to the nostrils. A bare bulb dangled from the low ceiling. A battered workbench stood beneath the narrow window, cluttered with jars of screws, metal brackets and half-used candles. The window itself was too grimy to let in much light, but a single shaft of light from the open door illuminated a stained mattress lying at the far end of the shed.

Raven exhaled slowly. 'There's nobody here.'

He felt suddenly ridiculous. A garden shed. That's all it was. His theories had taken him down a rabbit hole.

'What now, sir?' asked the constable, standing at his shoulder. 'Shall we search the rest of the house for evidence?'

Raven gazed around the shed, taking in the various objects. What was he to say? Give the go ahead for the team to engage in what he now believed would be a fruitless search of the house? Seize Colin's computer and pass it on to cybercrime for examination? A search might uncover something... or it might waste precious hours.

A sharp beam cut through the gloom as Becca flicked on her torch. She swept the light slowly across the shelving. Tools gleamed gold and silver beneath its glare, their rusty edges catching the shine. The beam picked out the coils of rope, the stained mattress, a dented metal bucket in the corner.

Raven drew a sudden breath as the light revealed a narrow groove in the wooden floor.

'Wait, what's that? Go back a bit!'

Becca angled the torch down. The floorboards shimmered faintly with dust, and emerging from beneath the mattress were several narrow, straight grooves.

Raven crouched low. 'You see them? They run underneath.'

He grabbed the edge of the mattress and drew it back, revealing the unmistakeable outline of a trapdoor.

'Bloody hell!' muttered the constable. 'Want me to open it, sir?'

'I've got it.' Raven's fingers traced the grooves until they found a metal ring embedded in the floor. He lifted it, then pulled with all his strength, raising the heavy wooden hatch up and open.

A cold breath of air spilled out, heavy with damp, mildew, and the sharp sting of rot. Beneath the open hatch lay darkness, just the top rung of a wooden ladder visible.

'Raven?' Becca passed him the torch. 'Be careful.'

'I will.' He tested the first rung of the ladder with his foot. It creaked ominously but held. He rested his full weight on it, then took another step, groping blindly in the darkness with his foot.

He had the sense of descending into a much older structure. A coal cellar, perhaps. Or an abandoned basement from a part of the house long since fallen into ruin. Whatever this place was, it had long been abandoned by daylight.

His fingers found an old Bakelite switch on the wall, but it flicked uselessly. He continued in darkness, the beam from the torch sweeping around the walls, picking out cracked bricks and crumbling stone. Eventually his feet reached solid ground and he swept the beam around.

'What can you see?' called Becca from above.

'Not much.' The space was low and cramped, the walls stained green with moss and algae.

'I'm coming down,' called Becca and she descended the ladder carefully until she was standing next to him.

A sudden squeak came out of the darkness and Raven felt something warm and furry against his leg. He cried out as a rat rushed past, scurrying along the bare earth and disappearing into a black gap where the furthest wall was missing a stone.

Becca shrieked but quickly regained her composure.

'All right?' Raven asked. But her attention was fixed on the wall where the rat had gone.

'There's a door over there.' She moved towards it.

The door was metal, but so blackened it was almost invisible in the darkness. Raven trained the torch across it, picking out a handle.

'Careful,' he warned, but Becca already had her hand on the handle.

She turned and pulled.

Hinges squealed. The door gave way. Something heavy fell through the gap.

Becca let out a choked scream.

Raven closed the distance between them in an instant, his arms locking around her, steadying her before she could stumble. He could feel her shaking against him.

They gazed in horror at the body that had tumbled onto the floor.

A military-style frock coat over leather trousers. Hair black and gleaming. Skin as pale as death.

Becca's voice was barely audible. 'Oh my God. It's Mickey.'

Raven moved closer, eyes slowly adjusting to the dark. The torch beam picked out Mickey's face. Waxen skin, eyes like glass, fixed and staring.

He began to laugh.

'What?' asked Becca.

'This isn't Mickey. It's not even a body. It's a wax dummy.'

He turned the torch towards the black void behind the door – and nearly dropped it.

Four pairs of glass eyes stared back vacantly. The entire band, immortalised in wax. Robbie, Stu, Skye, Pete, dressed exactly as they had appeared on stage in their heyday. Their faces were frozen in time, their expressions hollow.

Colin Harris hadn't been holding anyone prisoner. He'd created his own personal wax museum. He was a fantasist, not a kidnapper or a killer.

'Come on,' said Raven, putting an arm around Becca's shoulder. 'Let's get out of here.'

*

The BMW drew to a gentle halt outside Becca's flat in Castle Terrace.

Raven had insisted on driving her, even though it was only a two-minute walk from Tollergate. 'Will you be all right?' he asked her, his voice quieter than usual.

His driving, too, had been subdued. None of the usual acceleration and braking and screeching around corners. If Becca didn't know him better, she'd have said the basement encounter had left him as shaken as her.

'I'll be fine, thanks,' she said, forcing a small smile.

She stepped out into the cold evening air, resisting the urge to invite him back for a coffee, a shared moment of reflection before returning to their separate worlds. It would be better for everyone if that didn't happen.

She watched his brake lights glow, then fade as he pulled away down the street.

Inside, the flat greeted her with silence, save for the hum of the fridge and an occasional sigh and rattle from the plumbing. Usually, the stillness was a comfort. Tonight, it felt empty and hollow.

She closed the curtains against the harbour's scattered lights – the shimmer of reflections on water, the garish glow of neon from the seafront amusement arcades – then sank into the sofa, allowing the tension in her shoulders to slacken for the first time all day.

The trembling in her hands hadn't completely stopped.

The dummy in Colin's cellar had rattled her more than she cared to admit. It had been too real – the clothes, the painted stare, the way it lurched towards her out of the darkness. For one terrifying moment, she had truly believed a corpse was falling on top of her.

She didn't usually scare easily. She must be more stressed than she'd realised.

Even that damn rodent had given her a fright, the way it rushed out of the darkness, as if it had been lying in wait for her. Maybe the unexpected confrontation with Felicity that morning had left her emotionally drained. Or perhaps it was a mistake to keep working when what she really needed was to take time off and be with her family.

She had set her phone to silent and she checked it now for messages. One missed call from her mum. Sue had phoned just as the uniformed officers were forcing the door of Colin's house.

No message.

She dialled back. Sue picked up immediately.

She could sense her mother's pain even before the words were out. 'Oh, Becca, love. I'm so sorry...' Sue's voice cracked, and the rest dissolved into sobs.

Becca didn't need to ask. Her grandmother was gone.

While she had been kicking in doors, chasing shadows underground, getting ambushed by wax dummies in a lunatic's basement, a chapter of her own life had quietly closed.

She had hoped to be there at the end, but her grandmother had passed away without her. That was the price she paid for doing her job, and she would have to live with that knowledge forever. But her job now was to be with her family. With her mum especially.

'I'm coming now,' she said softly.

Before leaving she sent a quick text to Raven.

Won't be in tomorrow. Need to be with my family

Then she took her coat from the hook, slipped it on, and stepped back into the night.

★

Becca's text arrived just as Raven was getting out of the car on Quay Street. He replied straightaway.

I'm very sorry. Take as much time as you need. R

He hit send, knowing there was nothing more he could say to make it better.

He shoved the phone back into his pocket and trudged towards the house, feeling the weight of everything pressing down. The investigation was falling apart. The latest suspect had turned out to be a delusional fantasist, and Mickey was either a ghost or the best hidden man in England.

And now Becca was out of action for the foreseeable future.

He unlocked the front door and stepped inside. At least his daughter and his dog were home. He'd missed them both. But when he walked into the sitting room, he found Hannah sprawled on the sofa with a phone in one hand and a glass of wine in the other. An open bottle – already half-drunk – stood on the coffee table. Quincey, lying on the rug, opened one eye but didn't get up to welcome him home.

The sight of the wine after the day he'd had was just the trigger Raven needed to snap.

'You need to stop drinking so much,' he said.

Hannah's eyes flicked up from her phone. 'You can't just walk in here and tell me what to do, like I'm five years old.'

Quincey rose, ears pinned back, tail low, sensing the argument before it had fully begun.

'I'm worried about you,' said Raven, seeking to avoid an outright confrontation.

'Well you don't need to be.' Hannah got to her feet now, a slight sway to her gait, her glass clinking down on the table a little too hard. 'And what about you?'

Raven frowned at the change of tack. 'What about me?'

'Sneaking home in the early hours of the morning. Skulking about with a guilty look on your face all the time. You're obviously seeing someone, but you haven't told me. Why? Is she married? Do you think I'm not old enough to understand? Did you think I wouldn't notice?'

The flood of accusations left him reeling.

He hadn't even realised he was hiding his relationship with Liz, and he hadn't done it deliberately. He hadn't mentioned it to Hannah because it didn't feel real. Or maybe because it was entwined so closely with the murders and felt tainted somehow.

Or maybe, just maybe, because a part of him knew it wouldn't last.

'She isn't married,' he tried to explain. 'It's just–'

'What?'

'I don't know. It's complicated.'

Yet, was it? Hadn't he been telling himself from the start how deliciously uncomplicated it was? He and Liz met for dinner and sex. He had never invited her back to his place and he hadn't been to hers. He didn't even know her home address. They were complete strangers in many ways.

When he framed it like that, it seemed... sordid.

'Well?' said Hannah. 'I'm waiting for an explanation.'

'There's nothing to explain. Her name is Liz Larkin. She's a TV presenter. I met her through work.'

But if he had hoped to placate Hannah, his words had the opposite effect. Her eyes widened. 'Liz Larkin? I've seen her on the news. She's half your age, Dad! What were you thinking?'

His rebuke was out before he knew it. 'Now who's acting like they're not old enough to understand?'

Hannah snatched her coat from the armchair and headed towards the door.

'Where are you going?' he asked, his voice sharp with worry.

'To see a friend.' She slung her bag over her shoulder. 'Someone who actually understands me.'

She pulled open the front door.

'Hannah–'

'And you know what? I'm thinking of leaving Scarborough and going back to London. There's nothing for me in this dead-end town. I'd be better off with Mum.'

The door slammed behind her.

Quincey let out a low whine.

Raven sat down heavily on the sofa, rubbing a hand over his face, exhaustion finally crashing over him like a dam bursting. What had he done? He should have told Hannah about Liz right from the outset. Instead, he had tried to keep her a secret. But he had fooled no one except himself.

Quincey padded over and laid his head quietly on Raven's knee. His big, mournful eyes looked up at him, as if to say: *I could have told you this would happen.*

'I know, Quince,' said Raven, scratching him behind the ear. 'I'm a bloody idiot.'

CHAPTER 33

The mood in the incident room was sombre. With Becca on compassionate leave, just Raven, Jess and Tony gathered around the briefing table for the morning meeting. Raven felt Becca's absence like a hollow in his chest, a dull, persistent ache he couldn't ignore. He missed her sharp instincts and calming presence, but more than that, he craved the strong reassurance she gave just by being there.

Despite his exhaustion the previous night, he'd spent hours lying awake, listening out for Hannah's return. When she was a child, he had always slept with one ear open, tuned to her fretful waking and occasional night terrors. Now he was the one with bad dreams and nightmares.

He'd cancelled his dinner date with Liz, giving pressure of work as his excuse. Guilt and a lingering sense of shame had kept him company instead.

Hannah had finally returned in the early hours, the front door pulling quietly shut behind her, the soft padding of Quincey's paws on the wooden flooring as he rose to greet her, her unsteady steps on the staircase as she made her way up to her room. Yet he had lain awake for a further hour after that, before snatching a few welcome hours of deep sleep before dawn. It would have to do.

He cleared his throat. 'Right. Where are we?'

He was acutely aware they were on the back foot, their best leads evaporated, the killer holding all the cards, pulling all the strings.

Jess spoke first. 'The cyber team have finished with Colin's computer, and they've found nothing linking him to *Frost and Fury*.'

'So he's just an obsessive fan,' said Raven, 'like we first thought.'

To be fair, Colin had taken his obsession into extreme territory, staging an abduction not only of Mickey, but of the entire band. His bizarre delusion had led him to a very dark place, but they'd had no option in the end other than to release him. Locking up waxwork dummies wasn't a crime.

'The toxicology report on Stu just came in,' said Tony. 'As we suspected, it's another case of poisoning. Nothing very difficult to get hold of this time, however. The beer glass was contaminated with traces of peanut oil. Apparently, Stu was severely allergic to nuts. After drinking from the glass he suffered anaphylactic shock. He would have been dead within minutes.'

Raven drew a sharp breath. 'That means the murderer must have known about Stu's allergy.'

'It would seem so, sir.'

Raven turned to the whiteboard, now crowded with names, dates, locations and photos. The list of murder victims numbered three. 'So let's walk through this. Robbie was poisoned by cyanide in his bottle of water. It must have been added by someone with backstage access to the concert. Pete was given an injection of heroin in his caravan, with no evidence of a struggle or a break-in. And now Stu has been killed by a person he agreed to meet for a drink. In each case, the murderer and victim must have known each other well.'

'That's got to be a very short list of suspects,' said Jess.

'We're still looking at vengeance as the primary motive,' continued Raven. 'Robbie, for the central role he played in Mickey's downfall; Pete, for giving him heroin; and Stu for walking away when Mickey most needed him. That's confirmed by the fact that the killer used those exact betrayals against the victims – Pete was injected with heroin before his caravan was set alight, and the emails sent to Stu played on the guilt he felt about failing to help Mickey. According to Chaz, the only people who know all that are Skye, Rupert and Chaz himself.'

'You're giving up on the idea that Mickey might still be alive?' said Jess.

'After Chaz's confession that he faked the letter and sightings, yes,' conceded Raven.

The computer-generated image showing Mickey as he might look if he were still alive was pinned to the whiteboard and Raven turned his attention to it now. The likeness of the young singer was still evident in the older face, especially in those haunted eyes, and Raven couldn't help wondering what had really happened to him all those years ago. In all probability, they would never know.

Tony tapped his notebook. 'I showed the impression of Mickey to the bouncers at the nightclub, and they were both certain that no one resembling him had been at the club the night Stu died.'

'That's conclusive, then,' said Raven. 'Whoever emailed Stu pretending to be Mickey, it wasn't really Mickey. It was just a ruse to lure him there. But it was someone Stu felt comfortable sitting down to have a drink with. Someone he knew and trusted.'

The truth felt close enough to touch, yet still tantalisingly out of reach. Raven scrawled the names of the three main suspects on the board.

Skye Kershaw

Chaz McDonald

Rupert Devizes

'It surely can't be Skye,' he said aloud. 'Why would she

have poisoned her own husband? Anyway, she's been under close supervision by PC Sharon Jarvis ever since Robbie's death.'

'Yet she gave Sharon the slip easily enough when she went to see Rupert,' Jess pointed out. 'And her connection to Mickey was the most personal.'

'True. But I still see Skye as a potential victim. Then there's Chaz. He lied about Mickey's disappearance, but faking a letter and paying an actor to pretend to be Mickey is a world away from acquiring poisons on the dark web and posting online using an untraceable account that the cyber team can't crack. He's not exactly tech-savvy.'

'He does have motive though, sir,' said Tony. 'If he found out that Robbie was going solo, he might have decided to immortalise Echoes of Mercury once and for all. It worked well with Mickey – why not a second time?'

Raven nodded, unable to find a hole in Tony's logic. He turned now to the photo of Rupert, taken before the brutal encounter with Chaz robbed him of his fine features and suave appearance. 'Rupert has the intelligence and cunning to be behind the plot. He sees everything and knows everyone. But what's his motive? Why kill Robbie after he had just signed a brand-new recording contract?'

'Maybe he had second thoughts about the deal,' suggested Jess. 'Robbie and Skye may have negotiated too large a share of the profits. Rupert might have decided that killing off Echoes of Mercury and watching their records shoot up the charts would be a better move, financially.'

'Still,' Raven said. 'Rupert may be ruthless and calculating, but that would make this whole thing just cold business. These murders feel personal.'

Jess hesitated, then said, 'There's one more name we haven't properly considered.'

Raven turned to her. 'Go on.'

Jess shrugged as if the answer were obvious. 'Taylor Reed, the band's social media manager. She was present behind the scenes at the spa, has inside information about the band and knew all the victims personally. Not only that, but she's a pro when it comes to working the internet.'

Raven stared at the whiteboard. Nearly all the pieces were there, he could feel it. But the picture was still maddeningly incomplete. Yet what Jess had said was true – Taylor was a perfect fit to the profile of the perpetrator.

'Come on then,' he said. 'Let's take a closer look at Taylor. Very close.'

★

Raven spotted Taylor in the far corner of the café, her face illuminated by the pale glow of her laptop screen. Around her, the café buzzed with low chatter and the hiss of steaming milk, the rich scent of roasted beans and cinnamon curling through the air. The place was cosy and full of life, but the table Taylor had chosen was tucked away and private.

She didn't look up as Raven and Jess approached, her fingers continuing to move over the keyboard, absorbed in her screen. A near-empty oat milk latte sat forgotten on the table, the foam collapsed into pale swirls.

'Thanks for seeing us,' said Raven, sliding into the seat opposite her.

'No probs.' She finally shut the laptop, flashing a brief smile.

Up close, Raven was struck again by how young she was. Younger than he remembered. Young enough to be Hannah.

His gut twisted at the thought of his daughter – her furious expression the last time he'd seen her, the way she'd turned her back on him before storming out. She'd been asleep when he left the house, and he hadn't wanted to message her an apology. Some things needed to be said in person. He recalled the closeness they'd enjoyed when she was a child, and he missed the girl who used to climb onto his shoulders, who laughed as they played together with her toys, until the world of phones and devices had intruded, building an impenetrable barrier between them, even before she had left home for university.

Taylor's voice pulled him back to the present. 'Do I have to stay in Scarborough now that Rupert's out of action? Only, I'd really like to get back to London.'

Out of action. That was one way of putting it. The last Raven had seen of Rupert Devizes, he was being helped into an ambulance, his nose a bloody mass of crushed bone and cartilage.

'You're free to go whenever you like,' said Raven. 'But first I need to ask you where you were at the time of the murders.'

Taylor's eyes widened, startled. 'Why are you asking *me* that?'

'We're asking everyone,' Raven replied evenly.

She swallowed and nodded, his words helping her regain her composure. 'Okay, well I was backstage when Robbie died. And then Pete... what day was that?'

'Monday evening,' said Jess.

'Yeah, right. I was at the hotel. I had dinner in the restaurant, then I spent the evening in my room, catching up with social media and email.'

'Can anyone vouch for you?' Raven asked.

'That TV presenter was in the restaurant. She might remember me.'

'Liz Larkin?' said Jess. She glanced sideways at Raven.

Raven didn't respond. If he hadn't been called away to Pete's caravan, he would have been in the restaurant with Liz himself. 'What about before dinner?'

Taylor shook her head. 'I was on my own. But you can check my socials. I was posting most of the day.'

'We'll look into that,' said Raven, and Jess made a note. 'What about Tuesday evening?'

Taylor hesitated before replying, a flicker of discomfort crossing her face. 'I went to a club.'

'Which one?'

'I don't remember the name. Somewhere on Ramshill Road, I think.'

'Did you go alone?'

She nodded. 'Didn't stay long. Clubbing solo is pretty bleak.'

'Did you see anyone you recognised?'

'No. And like I said, I didn't stay long. I left at about ten o'clock.'

Ten o'clock. That was shortly before Jess and Tony found Stu's body. Jess's pen moved quickly over her notepad.

'Last time we spoke,' Raven continued, 'you said that you got on all right with the band members, but you weren't particularly close to any of them... with the possible exception of Robbie.'

Taylor's expression gave nothing away. 'Robbie was nice, yeah. But I didn't have a problem with any of them.'

'Would you say you were a fan of their music?'

Taylor pulled a face. 'I mean... their fanbase skews older than me. But I understand the appeal.'

Raven nodded. He'd expected as much. Hannah also thought him a dinosaur when it came to his musical tastes. Becca probably did too. 'How much do you know about Mickey's disappearance?'

Taylor blinked. 'That was nine years before I was born.'

Christ. That was a sobering thought. 'But you must have heard the story?'

'Sure. The fans never stop talking about it. It's a key part of the band's DNA.'

'Did you speak to the other band members about it?'

'Not really. I sensed the subject was off limits.'

'Did any of them ever express remorse?'

Taylor looked puzzled. 'Why would they? It wasn't their fault that Mickey took his life. Mental health was taboo in the old days. People didn't talk openly about their feelings. Not like now.'

Raven guessed that was true. There had been a stigma attached to depression back then. People found it hard to open up, even to close friends and family. Raven still did.

Jess gestured at Taylor's laptop. 'You seem pretty comfortable with tech.'

'It's second nature,' said Taylor. 'Doesn't everyone know how to use this stuff now?'

'Let's say you wanted to post anonymously, how would you do it?' Jess asked.

'You could use a VPN,' said Taylor brightly. 'It masks your IP address and encrypts your data, although sites can still track you using cookies. If you wanted to totally vanish, you could use a browser like Tor.'

Raven tilted his head. 'Isn't that what people use to access the dark web?'

Taylor's expression darkened. 'That's one of its uses. But most users simply want to protect their privacy.'

'Do you use it yourself?'

'Sometimes.'

Raven leaned back. 'I'm going to have to ask you to hand over your laptop and phone.'

Taylor's face drained of colour. 'What?! Wait, I can't do my job without those. My whole life is online.'

'You'll get them back. We just need to examine them.'

Taylor hesitated, hugging her phone protectively to her chest. For a second, he thought she might refuse. But then, with a deep sigh, she handed it to him.

'And your laptop.'

She slid it across the table, looking utterly bereft.

Raven stowed them safely away. There were advantages to being old-school, to not living every second of your life through a screen. If someone took *his* phone away, all he'd lose was an endless stream of calls and messages. Calls he could quite happily do without.

'Please remain in Scarborough until we return these to you,' he said.

She gave him an angry glare in reply. 'How could I possibly go anywhere without them?'

CHAPTER 34

'We're missing something,' Raven told Jess as they stepped out of the café. 'Something important. I don't know what it is, but it's staring us in the face.'

Jess fell into step beside him, a cold drizzle beginning to speckle their coats. 'You don't think we'll find anything incriminating on Taylor's phone or laptop?'

'I don't know what we'll find, but something tells me Taylor's too young to be responsible for all this. She's sharp, sure, and tech-savvy. But like she said, she wasn't even born when Mickey vanished. And this' – he gestured behind them, back towards the café, towards the spa, where it had all started – 'goes deep. We need to turn the clock back. Mickey's story is at the heart of everything, I'm sure of it.'

'You could be right,' said Jess. 'It feels so personal. But if Taylor's off the hook, then we're left with Rupert, Chaz and Skye.'

'Maybe.' Raven drew his coat closer as a gust of wind swept down the street, the rain sharpening to fine needles. The sky was an iron grey, much like his mood. 'I want to speak to this taxi driver who reported seeing Mickey – he must be back soon.'

He reached into his coat pocket, retrieved his phone and dialled. 'Tony?' he said when the call connected. 'Any news on this taxi driver?'

'Yes, sir,' answered Tony. 'I was going to let you know. He's on a flight back from Málaga, due to land at Leeds Bradford at around noon. Shall I send you the flight details?'

Raven checked his watch. 10:07 am. A narrow window, but if he dropped off Jess with the laptop and phone and immediately hit the road, he could make it in time.

'Send me his details, Tony, and ask Border Force to intercept him upon arrival. I'll interview him at the terminal before he disappears again.'

'Will do, sir.'

Raven ended the call and handed the evidence bag to Jess. 'Get this over to the cyber team. Tell them to leave nothing unchecked. We're dealing with someone who knows how to cover their tracks and hide their data. I'll update you after I speak to the taxi driver.'

'Do you think he'll remember much after so many years have passed?'

'I don't know, but if he does, I want to know everything he can tell us about this man who was with Mickey that night.'

Without another word, Raven turned and headed for the car.

Twenty minutes later, he was pushing the BMW hard up the A64, wipers swiping rhythmically across the windscreen, the rain unrelenting. The miles ticked by, broken only by the low growl of the engine. His thoughts were racing. Time was against him, and what if this was just another dead end, yet another myth to add to the enigma that was Mickey Flint?

He pushed the accelerator a little harder.

Midday couldn't come soon enough.

★

Raven pulled the M6 into the drop-off zone at Leeds Bradford Airport and flashed his warrant card at a hi-vis-jacketed attendant.

'I need to leave my car here. Urgent police business.'

He didn't wait for a response. The attendant opened his mouth but closed it again as Raven turned on his heel and strode towards the gleaming glass and steel building.

Inside, the airport bustled with life. Not quite Heathrow, but busy enough. Business travellers glued to their phones hurried past holidaymakers escaping for a spot of winter sun before the year end.

Raven checked the arrivals board: the EasyJet flight from Málaga had touched down twenty minutes ago. If the man he was here to see was travelling light, he'd already be making his way through passport control, where he would be intercepted by UK Border Force and asked to wait. Not the most pleasant experience when returning from a family holiday, but Raven couldn't risk missing such an important witness.

He approached two West Yorkshire Police firearms officers patrolling the concourse and presented his warrant card again.

'I'm looking for Border Force.'

One of the officers nodded towards a set of double doors. 'Through there. Ask for Nev.'

'Thanks.'

He passed through the doors and into a side corridor where the background hum of passenger chatter and announcements gave way to something quieter and more professional.

Nev was waiting in a small office – stocky, red-cheeked, and visibly pleased to be involved in something out of the ordinary.

'DCI Raven,' he said, rising and offering a handshake that swallowed Raven's hand whole. 'We've apprehended the target. He's in a holding room.'

Raven sighed. 'Mr Williams isn't a suspect, Nev. Just a witness. Please don't treat him like a terrorist.'

Nev looked slightly deflated. 'Right, got it. Well, he's waiting for you. I'll take you to him now.'

The interview room was windowless and functional – an MDF table, four plastic chairs, and the faint hum of fluorescent lighting. Gordon Williams sat on the far side, fingers wrapped around a plastic cup of coffee. He started as Raven entered.

'What's going on?' he asked, his voice edged with concern. 'Am I under arrest?'

'Not at all,' said Raven. 'You're not in any trouble, Mr Williams.'

He nodded to Nev. 'Thanks for your help. I'll take it from here.'

Nev seemed disappointed he wasn't going to be sitting in on the interview. 'All right, then. Just let me know if you need assistance.'

Raven sat across from Williams and studied him. The taxi driver was in his late fifties, possibly early sixties, his bald head bronzed from his spell on the Costa del Sol. He was dressed in the crumpled attire of a man who had spent the last few hours crammed into an economy seat of a no-frills airline.

'Mr Williams, I'd like to ask you a few questions about a statement you gave to North Yorkshire Police in 1991.'

Williams frowned, then his expression shifted to one of understanding. 'This is about Mickey Flint's disappearance, isn't it? I saw summat on the telly in Málaga about the other band members dying.'

'That's right,' Raven confirmed. 'In your statement, you said you saw Mickey just before he disappeared. As far as we know, you may have been the last person to see him alive. I'd like you to tell me everything you recall about that night.

Williams sat back. 'I'll tell you what I can. But you have to understand it's been thirty-odd years. Some things blur, you know?'

'Of course. Just take your time.'

The man nodded. 'I was working that night. I've driven cabs my whole life. Never fancied office work. I like the people, you see – the personal contact. Plus I enjoy driving.'

Raven nodded his encouragement. 'So, how did you come to pick up Mickey?'

'Well,' said Williams, settling into his story. 'I was waiting for a fare when a call came in from the office. They wanted me to go to an address in town and collect a Mr Flint. He'd phoned to make a booking. This was just as it was getting dark – would have been around seven o'clock, I suppose. The thought crossed my mind that it might be Mickey Flint. It's an unusual surname, and I'd been to see the band in the early days, when they were still playing pubs and clubs. I've had famous people in the back of my cab a few times, you see. There was that time when I met–'

'If you could just stick to the night you picked up Mickey?' prompted Raven, not wanting to get sidetracked.

'Oh, yes, of course. Well, anyway, I went to the address I'd been given – it was on Belle Vue Parade, close to the railway station – and when I rang the doorbell, lo and behold, it's Mickey Flint!'

Raven was impressed by the amount of detail in the retelling. It seemed that there was little wrong with Mr Williams's memory.

'What impression did you have of him?'

Williams's expression took on a more serious air. 'Not a good one, to be honest. I said to him, 'Everything all right, Mickey?' But he didn't reply, just nodded. I got the impression he didn't want to talk. So I took his suitcase and put it in the boot–'

'He had a suitcase with him?'

'That's right. Not a big one. He looked like he might be heading off for a weekend or summat. So, when I asked where he wanted to go, he kind of sat and thought about it for a while, like he still hadn't decided. Then eventually he said "Broxa." I was a bit surprised, to be honest. It didn't sound like the sort of place a star like Mickey would go.'

'You knew where he meant?'

'Sure. It's the back of beyond. Hardly anything there, just a farm and a couple of scattered cottages. I asked if he was sure, and he said yes, his family lived there.'

Raven gave a slow nod. That matched what they knew.

'After that, he didn't say much. I can sense when a fare doesn't want to talk, so I left him in peace and drove him to Broxa. When we got there, he directed me down this narrow track to an old cottage. It didn't look promising, I can tell you – all dark, not a soul in sight. I told him I'd wait and see him safely inside, and I'm glad I did, because he didn't have a key. He rang the bell. Waited. No answer. I figured I'd be driving him back. But then someone came round the side of the cottage. Mickey must've known them because he turned and waved at me, like I could go. So I turned the car around and drove back to Scarborough.'

Raven was following intently. 'So, this is the man you reported seeing with Mickey?'

Williams shook his head. 'Man? No, I didn't see any man.'

Raven frowned in confusion. 'You just said Mickey met someone outside the cottage.'

'I did,' said Williams. 'But I never mentioned a man. No, this was a woman.'

'A woman? The police report said you saw Mickey with a man.'

Williams gave a shrug. 'No offence intended, but I don't think the police officer who took my statement was too fussed about accuracy. He didn't seem very interested in my story at all, to be honest.'

Raven pressed his fingers to his temples. The historic investigation had been hampered by sloppy policework from beginning to end, and this crucial lead had been misreported.

'What do you remember about the woman?'

'She wasn't very old. No older than Mickey. I can't give

you a detailed description, because it was so dark out there. But I'd say she was average height and slim build. With dark hair.'

'You've done remarkably well to recall so much,' Raven assured him. 'Thank you for your help, and I'm sorry that your statement wasn't recorded accurately in the first place.'

'Not to worry. I'm glad you're taking the time to listen to me now. It's weighed on my mind, all these years, knowing that I was one of the last people to see Mickey but never knowing what happened that night. Sometimes I wonder if I should've stayed. Called someone. Do you know if Mickey's really dead?'

'We can't be certain yet,' said Raven. 'But your information might help us find out.'

Raven rose to his feet and was already leaving as he pulled out his phone. His visit to the airport had borne fruit, but he needed to act on it quickly. There was only one woman the same age as Mickey who was linked with the band.

'Tony?' he said when his call was answered. 'We have a new lead.'

CHAPTER 35

Liz finished typing and hit the search button.

She could already feel it – the scoop of her career was within her grasp. She could taste it – sharp and electric like the scent of rain before a thunderstorm. One more lead. One more link. That was all it would take to crack this mystery wide open. She would finally be able to break away from stories of cats rescued from trees and families having fun on the beach and launch herself into the world of proper investigative journalism.

Her pulse quickened as she waited for the results to appear. The breakthrough was so close, she could already see the book deal, the true-crime Netflix docuseries.

And then there was Raven.

She pictured the expression on his face when she revealed the name of the murderer to him. He might not even realise he was in a race, but he would know it when she crossed the finishing line first.

Then her phone rang.

She glanced at the screen. Kevin.

Ugh. Her producer.

That idiot. She'd been letting his calls go to voicemail,

A Dying Echo

but she couldn't keep doing that forever. Not if she wanted to keep her current job.

She picked up and his voice exploded down the line. 'Liz! Where the hell have you been? I need you back at the studio!'

She forced her tone into something halfway civil. 'And a fine day to you too, Kevin.'

He barrelled on, tone acidic. 'You can't just bloody well go off grid when you feel like it. Who do you think you are? I can't spend licence-payers' money so you can swan around Scarborough playing detective. This story has run far enough.'

'But, Kevin, it's the story of the decade. A cult rock band, three mysterious deaths, a frontman who vanished without a trace.'

Kevin snorted. 'What? A bunch of washed-up rockers overdosing in seaside caravans. That's not headline news.'

Liz gritted her teeth, reminding herself that he didn't know what she knew. The official line was that the police were still treating the deaths as unexplained. Raven had kept the juiciest details under wraps.

But not for much longer.

'You're wrong,' she said, lowering her voice, letting the words come slow and deliberate. 'This is bigger than drugs and fading fame. There's something buried deep here. And I'm close. Trust me, Kevin. When I break it, it'll rock the music industry.' She sensed him pause on the other end of the line and didn't hesitate before delivering the killer blow. 'This is going to be a world exclusive, Kevin. *Your* world exclusive.'

'Fine,' he muttered. 'End of the week. I want your arse back in the office Monday morning. No excuses. And Liz?'

'Yes?'

'Don't make me regret this.'

She smiled. 'You won't.'

She ended the call and set the phone down, heart still racing. She turned back to her laptop. Her search results had finally finished loading.

She scanned the items in the list, her eyes darting over the names, scrolling down, down.

There.

She clicked the link. Read one line. Then another. Her lips parted into a slow, triumphant smile. This was it. She had found the missing piece – the person who could finally bridge the gap between Mickey's disappearance and the murders now gripping the town. This was the thread that would unravel the whole tangled mess.

She grabbed her coat and car keys and hurried towards the door.

The story was waiting.

*

Skye was waiting at the police station when Raven returned to Scarborough. He'd put his foot down the entire way, covering the distance from Leeds in record time. The moment he stepped into the interview room, PC Sharon Jarvis gave him a tight nod. She'd already made hot drinks, and the faint, bitter scent of coffee hung in the air.

Raven had now seen several different faces of Skye Kershaw. The grieving widow, eyes hollow with loss. The firebrand, slipping her police escort to confront Rupert over her stolen recording rights. And the potential target – kept under close protection in case the killer turned their sights on her next.

He wondered what aspect she would present this time.

She sat with one leg crossed over the other, her arms folded, her face impassive. Her features were drawn and pale, as if the past few days had drained the life from her.

Unless, of course, that was her usual cultivated goth aesthetic.

He sat down opposite her, settling slowly into his seat as he composed his thoughts. Throughout the drive back to Scarborough he'd turned the case over and over like a stone in his palm. Skye's motive was crystal clear now – to eliminate the other members of the band and use the tragedy to bully Rupert into returning the song rights to her. The elaborately constructed revenge scenario was nothing more than a red herring intended to misdirect the police. Skye had blown her own alibi by revealing how easily she was able to come and go unnoticed, even while under police supervision. The final step in building the case against her was to confirm her secret identity as *Frost and Fury* – and her laptop and phone were now with the cyber team.

Raven's only remaining question was what she had done to Mickey all those years ago. He decided to lead with that.

'New information has come to light. I've just spoken to a witness who saw Mickey the night he disappeared.'

Skye didn't react. No flicker of surprise, no widening of the eyes. Just that unreadable, porcelain mask she wore so well.

'A taxi driver took Mickey from his flat in Scarborough to his family home in Broxa. Did you ever visit the house yourself?'

'Yes,' said Skye. 'Mickey took me to meet his parents a couple of times. They were nice.'

'Did you go there that night?'

'No. I was at home, getting ready for the tour.'

'The taxi driver says Mickey met someone outside the house. Someone he knew. A woman.'

Skye gave an almost imperceptible shrug of her small shoulders. 'His mum, perhaps?'

'No. This was a younger woman. No older than Mickey. Was it you?'

'No.'

Damn her, she was a determined liar.

Raven leaned in, elbows on the table. 'Skye, we know your relationship with Mickey ended acrimoniously. Maybe you went there that night to talk to him privately before the band set off to tour the States. But things didn't work out. Mickey didn't react the way you'd hoped. Maybe he turned violent…'

He let the suggestion hang in the air, giving her a chance to react, to seize the opening he'd offered her. Invitation instead of accusation.

But she shook her head sadly. 'I wish I had gone to see Mickey that night. There were things I should have said to him. If only I'd understood what he was going through, I could've helped. But I didn't. I stayed away. And then it was too late.'

Raven leaned back, frustrated.

If Skye was lying, she was damn good at it.

'The taxi driver described seeing a woman of Mickey's age or younger. Average height, slim build, dark hair.' Raven gestured meaningfully at Skye's lustrous black hair, thick and untamed. 'If it wasn't you at the house, who might it have been?'

She hesitated, lips pressed together. 'Emily?'

Raven frowned, caught off-guard. He searched his memory for the name. 'Mickey's younger sister? She was just a kid.'

'She was seventeen. A young woman.'

That stopped him in his tracks. At the age of seventeen he'd joined the army and was learning how to fight. How to kill. He knew what seventeen could mean.

And yet Mickey's younger sister had barely registered in the investigation.

'How well did you know her?'

'Not very well. I saw her a couple of times, but she was shy. Very intense, the way only angst-ridden teenagers can be.'

'What colour was her hair?'

'Black, the same as Mickey. She wore it long and straight.'

Raven hesitated, not knowing what to believe. Was Skye spinning him a yarn to take the heat off herself? Or was this the final breakthrough he needed?

'What else can you tell me about Emily?' he asked. 'What happened to her after Mickey vanished?'

A sadness entered Skye's eyes. 'Emily took it badly. She

was always quiet and brooding. I never once saw her smile. A few weeks after Mickey disappeared, she tried to kill herself. Her parents were devastated, obviously. They'd already lost their son. But they got help for Emily, and she pulled through. I don't know what happened to her afterwards.'

Raven weighed up her explanation. It was a consistent story, he was willing to credit that. Tony had mentioned Mickey's younger sister – briefly. If Raven recalled correctly, she got married and moved away from the area after her parents died.

Still, he didn't know what to believe.

'All right,' he said eventually. 'Here's what we'll do. You can go home, but you'll remain under the supervision of PC Jarvis and another officer. The cyber team are still working through your laptop and phone. If they find incriminating evidence, you'll be charged with three counts of murder. In the meantime, we'll try to track down Emily Flint.'

He got to his feet, the chair scraping back with a shriek.

CHAPTER 36

Raven was back behind the wheel, this time with Jess in the passenger seat. The investigation was moving again. This time they were heading north along the A171, cutting across the bleak North York Moors as rain lashed the windscreen. Tony had traced Emily Flint, Mickey's forgotten sister, to an address in Whitby, where she was living under her married name.

Emily Sanderson.

She hadn't exactly left the area as they'd previously believed. Whitby was local enough – certainly within easy striking distance of Scarborough. Skye's testimony now pointed to Emily as the last person to see Mickey alive. And revenge – not greed – was back on the table as a possible motive. Though if Emily had played a part in her own brother's downfall, it was a twisted kind of revenge, to say the least.

Raven's mind was in turmoil, every thought chasing its own tail. The truth was as hard to pin down as it had ever been, but he sensed he was closing in on it. He pushed harder on the accelerator, desperate to get to the bottom of the mystery at last.

The satnav directed him to a development of new houses on the outskirts of Whitby, some of them still under construction. Those that were finished looked too pristine to be real homes, more like toy houses. Raven pulled the BMW onto the driveway of a detached house and stepped out into the rain.

A man answered the doorbell. Dark hair, a black polo-neck sweater, a face that betrayed the weathered lines of middle age.

'Mr Richard Sanderson?'

'Yes?'

Raven showed his ID. 'DCI Tom Raven. This is DC Jess Barraclough. North Yorkshire Police. Is your wife at home? We need to speak to her urgently.'

Sanderson's shoulders sank a little and he gave a resigned sigh. 'You'd better come in.'

Inside, the house smelled of paint and new carpets. Raven followed him through to the lounge, more spacious than the one in Quay Street, but rather lifeless, painted in safe neutral shades. The furniture was new and looked as if it had been ordered from a catalogue. In Raven's house, none of the walls or window frames were straight, and nothing quite matched, but everything had a story.

'Please take a seat,' said Sanderson. 'Would you like some tea or coffee?'

'No, thank you,' said Raven. 'Mr Sanderson, is your wife at home?'

'No. But you're the second lot to come here today asking about her.'

'The second?' The news took Raven aback. 'Who else was here?'

'A journalist from the BBC. Liz Larkin.'

Raven groaned inwardly. What on earth had Liz been doing here? There was only one possible explanation – that she had unearthed the identity of Emily herself. But she should have come to him if she'd found something out.

'I'll tell you what I told her,' said Sanderson. 'I've been separated from my wife for almost a year.'

'She doesn't live here?' asked Raven.

'No. I don't know where she is now. We only communicate through our solicitors.'

'I see. When did you last hear from her or have any kind of contact?'

'It's been over a month.'

'And did she say anything about her whereabouts?'

'No. Since we separated, she's responded to my questions with only the sparest of detail.'

Raven leaned back against the soft cushions, feeling deflated. To come so close, yet find that his quarry had slipped away yet again. Emily Sanderson had been a ghost from start to finish. Overlooked as Mickey's younger sister. Anonymous under her married name. And still invisible, her whereabouts unknown even to her husband.

'Mr Sanderson,' said Jess. 'Would you describe your wife as a creative person? Did she write poetry, for instance?'

He nodded. 'It was one of her hobbies. She was often jotting down lines that came to her. She painted too. It helped her to cope with her dark moods.'

'Dark moods?'

'She'd suffered from bipolar disorder since her teenage years. I did my best to help, but sometimes it wasn't enough. That's why we separated.' He turned away to look out of the window at the immaculate lawns, the neat and tidy gardens. The clean veneer that hid so much.

'And just to confirm,' said Raven, 'your wife, Emily, she's Mickey Flint's sister?'

A wry smile crossed Richard's lips. 'Her claim to fame, although she hated to talk about it. She and her brother fell out. She never told me why – it was an area of her life she didn't want to revisit. That's why she came to Whitby in the first place, for a clean break with the past. But the past has a way of creeping back.'

'What do you mean by that, exactly?' asked Raven.

'When she heard that Echoes of Mercury were getting back together, she took it very badly. It was as if an old wound had reopened. Everything she'd tried to forget suddenly came back into focus. Her brother's death' – he paused – 'her suicide attempt.'

'We know about that,' said Raven gently. 'Do you know exactly why she tried to take her own life?'

He shrugged. 'People with bipolar disorder don't necessarily need a reason. But I know that she blamed herself for what happened to Mickey. I told her it wasn't her fault, she was just a girl when he went missing, but she said there were things I didn't understand. I don't know what she meant by that.'

Raven rose to his feet, a fresh sense of urgency animating him. Everything that Richard Sanderson had told them confirmed they were on the right track.

'Thank you for your time, Mr Sanderson. One last thing – before we go, can I ask if you have a recent photograph of Emily that could help us locate her?'

'Certainly.' He reached across to a low table where a collection of family photos was gathered. 'This was taken about two years ago.'

He passed the photo to Jess, who gasped in astonishment. She handed it to Raven and recognition hit him like a thunderbolt.

He marvelled that he had never noticed the family resemblance to Mickey before. The sultry dark eyes, the sensual but downturned mouth. Her hair was a different colour now – blonde not black – but the essential features remained.

The ghost had finally revealed herself.

'You've seen her before?' asked Sanderson. 'Then I hope you find her soon, for her sake. She's tough, but she carries a darkness within her. It causes her pain, and she can hurt others too. But you should know that she doesn't go by the name Emily anymore. It carries too much emotional baggage. Since she left Scarborough, she's used her middle name – Francesca. Or Frankie for short.'

*

Liz drove back from Whitby, flushed with the knowledge that her hunch was right. Her investigative skills had tracked Mickey's sister to her estranged husband, and now she had unlocked the final link in the chain.

Emily Flint was Frankie Sanderson.

Mickey's sister had reinvented herself, shedding her past along with her name, and reinserting herself into the very heart of the story in the guise of a documentary filmmaker. What better way to watch, observe and manipulate the band members as they went about their daily lives?

But that didn't prove Frankie was the murderer.

For that, Liz needed more.

She made her way stealthily along the hotel corridor, stopping just before she reached Frankie's room to set her phone to record. Then she knocked on the door.

It swung open, and Frankie stood there, her dark eyes locked on Liz's, surveying her coolly.

Liz held her gaze, a soft smile fixed to her lips. 'Hello. Do you have time for another chat?'

'I expect you have more questions for me,' said Frankie. 'Come on in.'

Liz hesitated before crossing over the threshold, a note of caution sounding loud. Had Frankie guessed how much she knew? Perhaps Liz ought to have informed Raven about her plans before coming here. She had been too keen to get to the truth before him.

But she couldn't leave now. She was confident she could handle the situation. The murder victims had all been poisoned, and Liz wasn't stupid enough to allow Frankie to give her anything.

She stepped inside.

The room had a similar layout to Liz's own. Frankie motioned to a low, circular table and they took up seats facing each other. Liz positioned her phone on the table, well placed to capture everything that was said.

'How's the documentary coming along?' she asked. 'I

expect you're keen to get it edited now. After the deaths of the band members, I'm sure you'll have no problem securing a TV deal. Public interest in Echoes of Mercury has never been greater.'

'True,' agreed Frankie. 'You could say that I've landed a scoop, although I don't like the idea of making a profit from someone else's misfortune.' She smiled at Liz. 'You don't appear to have any such qualms.'

Liz narrowed her eyes, taken aback by Frankie's bluntness. 'I'm a TV reporter. It's my job to tell the public the truth.'

'I suppose somebody has to,' said Frankie. 'The truth matters, doesn't it?'

'Absolutely,' said Liz in earnest. If there was one thing that had always mattered to her, it was the truth.

Frankie tipped her head to one side as if weighing up possibilities. 'Would you like to hear my story? I expect you've already found out some of it yourself, but the rest you won't have guessed. Nobody knows the full story, not even my husband. You've met Richard, have you?'

So Frankie had guessed why she was here. 'I've just come from speaking to him.'

'I couldn't hide him forever. Not from someone as smart as you.'

Liz couldn't tell if Frankie was playing her. There was an honesty to her words, as if the time for playing games was over.

'So you know that I'm Mickey's sister. That's where the story began, but it's by no means the end.' Frankie rose to her feet. 'Would you like a drink?'

Liz couldn't resist smiling at the obviousness of the invitation. 'You surely don't expect me to fall for a trick like that.'

A glint caught Frankie's eye. Not malevolence. Amusement. 'You think I might poison it. I can hardly blame you. But I wouldn't insult your intelligence by doing that, Liz. Come on, we'll share a drink together.' She went to the minibar and lifted out two miniature bottles of gin and a can of tonic. 'Is it too early for a G&T?'

'Never too early for a G&T,' said Liz.

She watched carefully as Frankie unscrewed the bottles and pulled the ring on the can. She poured the drinks into two identical glasses and carried them back to the table.

'Choose whichever one you like,' said Frankie.

Liz hesitated, then picked the one on her left.

Frankie took the other one. 'Cheers.'

Liz had seen nothing to indicate that Frankie had tampered with the drinks. No sleight of hand or momentary misdirection. Yet still she held back.

Frankie raised her glass to her lips and swallowed a mouthful before setting it back on the table. 'You see? Completely harmless. Now where was I? Oh yes, my story.' She drew her chair closer and gestured at Liz's phone. 'I expect you're recording this. You won't want to miss a thing.'

It seemed that Frankie had guessed everything. Liz had to acknowledge that she was in the presence of a master. She'd thought she had beaten Raven to the finishing line, but Frankie had been waiting for them the whole time. Gingerly, she lifted the glass of gin and tonic to her nose. She gave it a good sniff and detected nothing out of the ordinary. And she had just seen Frankie drink from her own glass without coming to any harm… she took a careful sip.

Just G&T. Cold and refreshing as always.

Frankie didn't even seem to notice. She turned her gaze out of the window. The lights on the Esplanade were starting to come on as darkness crept across the headland. 'Once upon a time, there was a girl called Emily. She was a sad girl, always had been. Nobody knew why, not even Emily herself. In fact she wouldn't understand until she received a diagnosis years later. But she found peace in solitude, and especially in words. Poetry was her passion.'

Liz recognised the scenario well. She hadn't been a sad girl herself, but she had felt misunderstood by her parents and her friends. She had lost herself in classic works of fiction, and dabbled in writing too.

'The girl,' continued Frankie, 'was a prolific writer. She poured her heart and soul into her work. Nothing was off limits, for the expression of truth meant everything to Emily. That's why she kept her writing a secret, telling nobody, showing no one. She hid her poems at the bottom of a drawer and kept them there, a treasure never to be shared with anyone.'

Liz found herself spellbound, drawn into Frankie's tale. She would soon have a full confession – or repentance, or whatever this was – in the murderer's own words. She took another sip of gin and set the glass back carefully next to her phone. She was glad she'd had the foresight to record everything.

'The girl had a brother,' said Frankie, her words almost without intonation, as if reciting a fairy story. 'He wasn't much good with words. He was probably dyslexic. The condition – much like bipolar disorder – wasn't well understood back then. But he was creative in his own way. He had a gift for music and started a band with his mates. His singing voice was good, but he had no songs to sing. So he stole his sister's poems, set them to music, and passed them off as his own.'

'Mickey,' breathed Liz, taking another mouthful of gin and tonic.

There was no reaction from Frankie. It was almost as if she had entered a trance. 'When the girl found out what he'd done, she lashed out at her brother, but her parents punished her, accusing her of lies. After all, she had kept her poems a secret from the world. Who could believe that a young girl could write with such intensity? And so she was silenced, as if her very soul had been taken from her. She turned in on herself and found solace not in words but in pain.'

Frankie lifted her arms towards Liz, pulling back her sleeves to reveal faint traces of decades-old scars.

'Meanwhile, the brother's star continued to rise. The band signed a record deal. A tour of America was planned.

The music press hailed him as the next Lou Reed. A musical genius.'

'But he wasn't a genius,' whispered Liz. 'You were.' The room fell silent and all Liz could hear was the murmur of the hotel's heating and the thumping of her own heart.

'The night before the tour, Emily found her brother outside her house. He ought to have been happy, but instead he was feeling very sorry for himself. His girlfriend had left him, his mates in the band had betrayed him. Worst of all, he needed new songs but he couldn't write any lyrics himself. So he wanted to know if Emily had more poems he could use. He couldn't credit her, but at least this time he would pay her for them.'

The air in the room had grown warmer. A bead of sweat appeared on Liz's lips. She shrugged off her jacket and draped it over the back of the chair.

'But for Emily,' continued Frankie, 'it was never about the money. She just wanted to be acknowledged.' A tremor entered her voice as she finally gave vent to her anger. 'She had never even been asked! The words weren't her brother's to take. They belonged to her!' Her voice dropped to a whisper. 'And so it was right for him to be punished.'

'You murdered him,' said Liz. 'You hid his body somewhere.'

'The girl killed her brother as fair payment. He took her soul – she took his life. But still she found no peace. She tried to end it all but failed. She had to leave her past, leave her home, leave her own name behind before she could finally begin to breathe freely. And for a while, she found happiness. Then, many years later, the nightmare began again.'

Liz's throat ached. She reached for her drink but it slipped from her grasp as she tried to lift it. The glass was slick with condensation. Or was it sweat from her palms? She couldn't think. Her head felt like cotton wool. 'The drink...,' she murmured. 'It was spiked.'

'The band reformed without Mickey. But they kept his

songs. *Emily's* songs. Once again, Emily was condemned to a life in shadows. So she became a shadowy figure, hiding in plain sight, observing through the camera's lens, learning the band's secrets one by one and turning them against them. Emily needed vengeance, you see, not for her brother, but for herself.'

Liz's throat burned with fire, and her limbs felt as heavy as lead. It took all her strength to stand up. A wave of dizziness washed over her and the room tilted.

'Seems you weren't so clever after all,' said Frankie. 'I only took a tiny sip of my drink.'

Liz tried to lower herself back to the chair but missed and tumbled onto the floor. 'You've poisoned me,' she gasped, staring up at Frankie.

Frankie looked down at her, eyes cold and indifferent. 'Emily's story hasn't quite reached its conclusion. Her secrets aren't yet ready to share. But soon her vengeance will be complete. It's a shame you won't be around to witness it.'

She rose to her feet as the last of Liz's strength wilted and her vision turned black.

*

Raven pushed his foot down, the M6 picking up speed and pressing him back into his leather seat. The engine howled, drowning out the wind and rain as they left the neatly arranged houses behind, the open road beckoning.

'Boss,' said Jess, scrolling urgently through her phone.

'What is it?'

'Another poem just went online.'

'Title?'

Jess's face was pale in the darkness of the cockpit. '*I Am a Killer.*'

A tight knot formed in Raven's gut. 'Read it.'

She cleared her throat and read aloud:

In the darkest corners of our twisted minds,

We wrought our pact and made our fate.
You are the victim; I am the blade.
You know I approach; I know that you wait.

'There's more,' said Jess, but Raven had stopped listening at "I am the blade."

'Skye's the next victim,' he muttered. 'Call Sharon Jarvis. Let her know she's in danger.'

He floored the accelerator and the car shot forwards into the night.

CHAPTER 37

Raven screeched to a halt and ran from the car, Jess at his heels, their doors banging shut in unison. He didn't know how many speed cameras he'd tripped on the way back to Scarborough and didn't care. All that mattered now was time.

He'd called Sharon on the way, and she had assured him that Skye was safe and there was no sign of Frankie. He had stressed the importance of not letting Skye out of sight and then made straight for the hotel.

He strode to the front desk, flashing his warrant card at the startled receptionist. 'Frankie Sanderson. What room is she staying in?'

The young woman blinked at him in alarm. 'Uh, one moment, sir.'

He drummed his fingers restlessly on the counter as the receptionist tapped on her computer keyboard. Jess hovered beside him, jaw clenched, mirroring his tension.

'Room 326,' said the receptionist at last.

'I need room access,' said Raven. 'Now.'

Another staff member – a nervous-looking lad in a waistcoat – was summoned to lead them up with a master key. The lift crawled to the third floor, every second a hammer blow in Raven's chest. As soon as the doors parted, he was moving, fast.

He pounded on the door of 326 with the side of his fist. 'Police! Open the door!'

Silence.

'Key,' he barked.

The staff member swiped the card. The lock clicked.

'Wait outside,' Raven ordered, already stepping through.

He moved quickly, his eyes sweeping the entryway. Wardrobes and a minibar on one side. Bathroom on the other – empty. Then into the room proper.

He stopped cold.

A woman lay crumpled at the foot of the bed, her long gold hair fanning out across the carpet like spilled thread. A chair was overturned beside her.

Liz.

Raven dropped to his knees, heart in his throat, and pressed two fingers to her neck.

A weak pulse told him she was still alive.

'Call an ambulance,' he said.

He stood up and scanned the room. Where was Frankie now? There was only one place she might have gone.

He yanked out his phone and rang Sharon again.

Straight to voicemail.

Shit. Was he too late?

'Stay here,' he told Jess. 'Wait with Liz until the ambulance comes.'

'Where are you going, boss?'

He was already halfway to the door. 'To try to save a life.'

*

The house felt more like a prison than a home. Skye paced the small living room, the four walls pressing in, the air stifling. Two police officers were assigned to her now.

Sharon Jarvis and PC Grant Sadler, a great strapping bloke whose muscle-power far exceeded his communication skills. So far, all he'd said to her was "yes", "no", and "ta". Did she need him watching her every movement? Skye felt like she was the prisoner, punished for her brief flight of freedom.

She couldn't regret getting into trouble with Raven, however. It had been worth it to witness Rupert's nose being pulverised by Chaz.

She paced the hallway like a caged tiger. 'I'm going mad cooped up inside,' she moaned to Sharon. 'It's too crowded in here. I need fresh air.'

'You know I can't let you leave the house. It's not safe.'

Sharon was wearing her most serious face, the one she wore to boss people around with. But Skye had seen her chatting to her boyfriend, and knew she had a softer side. She just needed to be buttered up the right way.

'Look, I just want to go out to the studio and play for a while. I'll be safe there. It's only at the bottom of the garden.'

Sharon hesitated before agreeing. 'All right. But I'll come with you. Grant can stay here.'

Skye sighed. She really longed to go alone, but she knew why she was being treated like this. Sharon didn't trust her not to slip away again.

'Fine,' she said sulkily. 'You come with me. As long as you don't mind listening to a bit of bass.'

Grant settled himself into an armchair with a mug of tea and a book of sudoku puzzles while the two women stepped out of the back door.

Skye felt calmer the instant she drew fresh air into her lungs. Bad weather didn't bother her, and she walked down the concrete path, enjoying the sensation of raindrops splashing against her face. She had almost forgotten how it felt to be alive.

The garden was overgrown and neglected, and the little studio was tucked away at the far end. Skye hadn't been inside it for months, not since before the tour. She hadn't wanted to touch a guitar since the night of that final concert. At first it had been too painful even to think about playing again, but now she needed to feel an instrument in her hands. Music would be her therapy as she learned to live without Robbie at her side.

Robbie had always been the best guy in the band. Skye couldn't regret choosing him over Mickey, even though she had carried the burden of guilt for what then happened. She was certain Mickey was dead, and equally sure he had killed himself because of her, whatever some people said. Didn't they know how hurtful it was, always to be dredging up the past and stirring up doubts? If only Mickey's body had been found, it would have put all the uncertainty to bed. Instead, he had left nothing behind him but a trail of mystery.

She unlocked the studio door and groped inside for the light switch. A pang of nostalgia hit her as the warm glow flickered on. Instruments lined the walls – electric guitars in neon hues, a bouzouki from her and Robbie's travels through Greece. A keyboard stood in the middle of the room, where Robbie had composed the new tracks he planned to use for his solo career. The studio had been a sanctuary. Hers and his.

Memories rushed in now, unbidden – late nights, the two of them riffing together on their favourite melodies, bouncing lyrics back and forth, harmonising until their voices cracked.

Her throat tightened. Robbie would want her to keep playing.

It was quiet inside the studio, the soundproofed walls keeping the noise of the wind and rain at bay. Tentatively, she picked up her bass, plugged it into the amp, and struck a note. Sound reverberated through her chest, warm and familiar. She turned up the volume and played a chord. Soon her fingers were dancing across the strings, music rolling around the small room, bouncing off the walls.

Sharon grinned, clearly enjoying the free show.

She was well into her third song when the door clicked

open.

A cold gust swept in, carrying droplets of heavy rain. Skye's fingers froze mid-note.

Frankie. What was she doing here?

'Didn't know you were coming,' said Skye.

Frankie said nothing, but stepped inside, pulling the door shut behind her.

Skye regarded her, puzzled. Something felt off. The familiar documentary-maker, who had followed them throughout the tour, never without a video camera in her hands, now stood rigid in the doorway, her face an unreadable mask.

Sharon moved suddenly to interpose herself between the two women. 'Skye, move back. Stand against the wall.'

But Skye didn't move. 'Why? What's wrong?'

Sharon ignored her. 'How did you get here?' she asked Frankie. 'Grant should have stopped you.'

Frankie shrugged. 'The boy in blue? He doesn't know I'm here. I didn't come through the house. I climbed over the wall.'

A prickle of unease ran down Skye's spine. 'What do you want, Frankie?'

'Vengeance.'

Skye felt her blood turn cold. 'For Mickey?' she whispered.

'No. For myself. Don't you remember me, Skye? You knew me once as Emily.'

Mickey's sister?

'No,' said Skye. 'That's impossible.' Yet even as she spoke, she saw the resemblance staring back as if mocking her. Dark melancholy eyes. Full, lush lips. The dark roots of jet black hair dyed blonde.

Once, she had fallen head over heels for those same looks. But now it was the sister who wore them, not Mickey.

Frankie's hand reached inside her jacket and emerged holding a knife, its edge cold and cruel.

'Stand back!' warned Sharon, and this time Skye

obeyed, pressing herself into the furthest corner, putting as much distance as possible between herself and the intruder.

Fear gripped her and an animal cry of raw terror escaped her lips. Her greatest fear throughout these years had been that Mickey would one day step out of the shadows to accuse her. A revenant, come to lay the blame for everything at her feet. She had never once given a thought to his sister.

Emily Francesca Flint.

Yet it was the sister who had returned, her knife now raised to strike.

The blade flashed in Frankie's hand and Sharon let out a soft gasp.

She staggered backwards, both hands clutching her belly, blood oozing between the fingers and seeping into her clothes. 'Run,' she murmured to Skye.

But there was nowhere to go.

Skye screamed as Sharon dropped to her knees. Her phone fell to the floor.

It rang and Skye glimpsed DCI Raven's name on the screen just before Frankie kicked it spinning away.

Then she advanced towards Skye, the knife – now slick with blood – raised again.

*

Raven hammered on the front door, his fist unrelenting in its urgency. His heart was thudding like a drum. Still no answer from Sharon. Why wasn't she picking up her phone? He could only assume the worst.

The door swung open, revealing a broad-shouldered young constable, cheeks ruddy, eyes wide with surprise. Raven didn't know his name – didn't care.

'Where's Skye?'

'In the studio, sir. Everything's all right, Sharon is with her.'

'Has anyone been to the house?'

'No, sir.'

'Then why the hell isn't Sharon answering her phone?'

He didn't wait for an answer, but hurried past the officer, his boots thudding down the hall and out through the back door.

A single light glowed at the bottom of the garden. The studio.

He sprinted. The cold bit at his lungs, wet grass slick beneath his feet. The constable thundered behind him, but Raven barely registered his presence. His only thought: don't be too late.

He reached the studio and yanked the door open, taking in the scene inside at a glance.

Sharon Jarvis sat propped against one wall, her face ashen, her shirt drenched in blood. Her eyes were open but her breathing shallow. She blinked as Raven entered, but was too weak to speak.

Frankie stood at the centre of the room, pale and trembling, a bloodied knife clenched in one shaking hand. Her eyes were wild, her breaths ragged, an expression of pure hatred on her face.

Skye cowered in the far corner, a neon-green guitar clutched to her chest like a shield, her arms trembling.

Raven took a single step inside, hands raised, calm despite being unarmed. His voice came steady and low. 'Frankie. Or do you prefer Emily? Put the knife down. It's all over now.'

She didn't turn. 'No,' she spat. 'It's not over. Not quite.' She tightened her grip on the handle of the knife, her knuckles white.

Skye whimpered, hugging the guitar closer, her wide eyes pleading with Raven for help.

He edged forwards, slow and deliberate. 'I read your poems – *Frost and Fury's*. It was all there, wasn't it? Your reason for wanting revenge. "You took my words; you stole my dreams." Mickey stole your poems and used them as lyrics for his songs. Some fans thought that *Frost and Fury* was Mickey – the two voices were the same. But what the fans didn't know was that Mickey had never written those lyrics.'

Frankie's hand trembled. 'Mickey couldn't write a single line. His own attempts were useless. He could have come to me and asked for help, but instead he stole and lied to get what he wanted.'

'You were the true talent behind the band's success, Frankie. You had every right to be angry.'

'Mickey told me I was nothing,' she whispered, tears streaming now. 'A little girl with childish ideas. But he knew my words had fire. That's why he took them.'

Raven took another half step. 'Skye and the other members of the band didn't know what Mickey had done. It's not their fault.'

Her hand trembled, the blade shaking. 'Echoes of Mercury should have died along with Mickey! They should never have come back!'

'Skye's not to blame,' Raven said calmly. 'Now drop the knife.'

She faltered, her breath hitching.

Skye took her chance. She swung the guitar with a roar, knocking the knife clean out of Frankie's hand. Steel clattered to the hard floor.

Raven lunged, seizing Frankie's arms behind her back and snapping on a pair of handcuffs.

'Emily Francesca Sanderson, I am arresting you on suspicion of the murders of Mickey Flint, Robbie Kershaw, Pete Hollis and Stu Lomas, and the attempted murder of Liz Larkin and PC Sharon Jarvis. You do not have to say anything–'

The rest of the caution was drowned by the rising wail of sirens as police cars and an ambulance converged on the street.

CHAPTER 38

It was first light, and a steady rain was falling when Raven left the warmth of the BMW to head into the grounds of the old cottage. Not that rain seemed to trouble the team of police divers who were already on site in their black drysuits.

The building had long since surrendered to nature. Ivy scrambled across its stone walls, worming green tendrils through shattered windowpanes and creeping into the crumbling mortar. The garden, perhaps once neat and tended, was now choked with brambles and nettles that scratched at Raven's legs as he walked.

Emily Francesca Sanderson – Frankie – had inherited the property after her parents' deaths. She'd never returned to live there. Too many ghosts. Too much pain. But she'd kept it.

You couldn't sell a house if it was hiding a body.

Raven turned up his collar and approached the team leader, a grey-haired man with weathered features and a voice as flat as the sky overhead.

'We've completed the risk assessment,' the man said. 'No sewage or chemical hazards. Structure's holding.

We're ready to send someone down.'

Raven gave a curt nod and followed him further into the overgrown plot. The path was barely visible, half-hidden by the tangle of thorns. Then he saw it.

The old well.

It was circular, three feet in diameter, its stone wall slick with moss. A rotting canopy with a sagging roof leaned over it, and a rusted bucket still dangled from a chain strung across a wooden crossbeam.

Beside the well, a diver in full gear was adjusting his helmet light. His colleagues tightened his harness and ran final checks on the rigging. Eventually the team leader appeared satisfied and gave the signal to proceed.

The diver swung his legs over the lip of the well and descended slowly into darkness, the rope creaking under his weight.

Raven stood in silence, watching as the shadows swallowed the man.

This story hadn't started with a murder. It had started with a dream – a dream that Mickey Flint had chased with everything he had. Musical talent, charisma, and a voice that touched his fans' hearts. But the words? They weren't his. He had taken them from his sister – not mere lyrics, but the outpourings of a tormented soul. Mickey had stolen the most vital part of her.

And the world had cheered him for it.

But when the words ran dry and Mickey began to unravel, his closest friends turned against him. Skye, Pete, Stu – one by one they betrayed him, let him down or abandoned him. He found himself alone and vulnerable. And Emily had taken her revenge.

A sharp tug on the rope jolted Raven from his thoughts. The team moved quickly, hauling the diver up into the grey light.

As he emerged, he pulled off his face mask.

'I've found human remains.'

Raven exhaled, the tension in his shoulders ebbing. The myth of Mickey Flint could finally be laid to rest.

*

Once the last of Mickey's skeletal remains had been carefully retrieved from the well, Raven headed for the hospital. Strictly speaking, he hadn't been needed at the cottage, but he'd stayed long enough to watch the evidence team bag up the remains ready for transfer to the mortuary.

It seemed the least he could do. He'd never met Mickey, but the man had been an important presence in his life ever since those first tremulous vocals had reached out across the radio waves and touched him so deeply. But Mickey's story was over now.

Enough of the dead. It was time to concentrate on the living.

He arrived at the hospital carrying flowers in shades of yellow, pink and violet, and a box of chocolates tucked under one arm. The team at the station had done a whip-round and Raven had volunteered to deliver the card and gifts.

PC Sharon Jarvis was propped up in bed, pale but alert. Her face brightened at the sight of the flowers and chocolates. 'Are those all for me?'

'Just a little something to speed your recovery,' said Raven, setting them down on the bedside locker. 'How are you feeling?'

She gave a grimace. 'They stitched me up. No major damage done.'

Raven pulled up a chair. 'I wanted to thank you.'

She looked surprised. 'For what?'

'For what you did in the studio. You didn't hesitate. If you hadn't stepped in–' He left the rest unspoken. 'You saved a life. That took guts.'

'Just doing my job, sir.'

'Not every officer would've done the same. I'll be putting you forward for a commendation for bravery.'

'There's no need,' said Sharon, but there was a flicker of pride behind the modesty. 'What's the latest on the case?'

Raven gave her a brief summary of the morning's events as Sharon listened wide-eyed.

'So he's been at the bottom of the well all this time?'

Raven nodded. 'Since the night he vanished.'

He hesitated. 'I was a big fan of the band as a teenager. I always wondered what happened to Mickey. Now that I know... it leaves a strange sort of gap.'

She reached out and gave his hand a gentle squeeze. Then she nudged the box of chocolates towards him.

'Go on. You look like you need one more than me.'

Raven cracked a smile, took one, and leaned back. For the first time in days, he let himself stop. Just for a moment.

★

He arrived empty-handed for his next visit.

Liz was perched on the edge of the bed, checking her reflection in a compact mirror. She was dressed, hair freshly brushed, the faint sheen of lip gloss catching the morning light. It seemed that the gin and tonic Frankie had slipped her had contained nothing more potent than a fast-acting sedative. One night in hospital, and she was no worse for the experience.

But something in her eyes suggested she wasn't feeling quite so invincible.

She gave him a warm smile as he appeared in the doorway. 'DCI Raven. Have you come to take me home?'

He leaned against the doorframe, hands in his pockets, holding back from entering the room. 'No.'

Her smile wavered. A small crease formed between her brows, deepening as incomprehension turned slowly to annoyance. 'What then?'

She patted the empty space beside her on the bed, inviting him to sit.

Raven stayed where he was. 'You should have told me,' he said firmly.

'Told you what?'

'Don't play innocent. As soon as you discovered that Frankie was Mickey's sister, you should have called me. Instead, you went to talk to her alone. This wasn't a game, Liz, it was a murder investigation.'

Her lips pursed in a sulky protest. 'It was my investigation too. You're just upset because I got to the truth first.'

Heat flared in his chest and he fought to keep his anger in check. 'Your behaviour was stupid and reckless. Not only did you put yourself at risk, but your actions resulted in one of my officers being stabbed and almost led to the death of an innocent woman.'

He must have raised his voice more than he intended, because she flinched away, visibly shocked by his rebuke.

'I was doing my job,' she protested weakly. 'You, of all people, should understand that.'

'Your job?' His tone was quiet now, but the disappointment in it cut sharper than anger. 'You put your own career before anyone else. Before me. Before my team. You made your choice.'

She stared at him, eyes searching his face, as if trying to find a way back in. She must have realised there wasn't one.

'So, that's it?' she asked, her voice low. 'You're ending it?'

'There's nothing to end,' Raven said simply. 'Don't pretend that what we had was ever more than a passing convenience. And now, it's nothing.'

He turned and walked out of the room without looking back.

*

Raven bought more flowers on his way back from the hospital. Nothing extravagant – a simple arrangement of white and cream blooms threaded with pale green foliage. They were intended as a gesture of sympathy, but also as a peace offering.

At Castle Terrace, he rang the buzzer and waited.

Becca's voice crackled over the intercom. 'Hello?'

'It's me.'

She buzzed him in straightaway.

He climbed the stairwell, remembering the time he'd carried up box after box when she'd first moved into the top-floor flat. That had been a good day – a chance for fresh beginnings. This moment felt the same.

She met him on the top landing and he held out the flowers. 'I was sorry to hear about your grandmother.'

'Thank you,' she said, accepting the bouquet. 'Would you like to come in?'

He followed her inside, lingering near the entrance and pacing the wooden floor awkwardly as she unwrapped the flowers and found a vase.

'They're beautiful.' She carried the display of flowers to a coffee table. 'It was very thoughtful of you.'

'Becca–'

'Yes?'

'I'm sorry for everything. You were right all along. I should never have shared sensitive information with Liz Larkin. It was completely unprofessional.'

A faint smile played around her lips. 'Yes. It was. Is she… I mean, are you…'

'It's over. What can I say? I was a fool.'

He dipped his head, his neck flushing hot with embarrassment. It wasn't the first time he'd been an idiot when it came to women.

'No, you weren't,' said Becca, smiling at him properly now. 'You're a good detective. And… you're a good man, Raven.'

He wasn't sure he deserved that. 'The team's missed you,' he said, then corrected himself. 'I missed you.'

'I'm sorry I couldn't be more involved in the investigation,' she said. 'With everything going on, I felt like I was being pulled in two directions.'

'That's not what I meant.'

What had he meant? He wasn't sure.

He looked out of the window and saw his own house nestled far below at the foot of the castle hill. He had unfinished business there too.

'It'll be good to have you back,' he told Becca. 'I just wanted you to know there's no rush. Take all the time you need.'

She nodded. 'After the funeral, I'll be back. I promise.'

'Good,' said Raven. 'I need you beside me.'

*

It was a day for making amends. Heaven knows, he needed to.

He found Hannah in the house on Quay Street. She looked up from her phone as he entered, guarded but not hostile. Progress.

'Fancy a walk?' he asked. 'Take Quincey over to the North Bay?'

She hesitated for half a second, then gave a quiet nod. 'Sure.'

The morning's rain had cleared, leaving the air soft and still, heavy with the smell of damp earth. Patches of blue sky peeked out between thinning clouds, and the world felt as if it had been washed clean again.

They strolled to the sands in silence, Quincey tugging boisterously on his lead. When they reached the beach, Raven unclipped him and he bounded away, kicking up wet grit as he ran. The dog dashed down to the waterline, circled back, and stared up expectantly until Raven pulled a battered tennis ball from his coat and sent it flying.

Before bolting after it, Quincey paused, ears perked, eyes alert, casting a meaningful look between father and daughter. A nudge, if ever there was one. Then he tore away, all lean muscle and pounding limbs, a blur of motion receding into the distance.

As usual, it was Raven's turn to apologise.

He cleared his throat. 'I'm sorry I haven't been around

much lately. And I'm sorry I didn't tell you about Liz. Truth is, I think I knew it wouldn't last. It's over now.'

Hannah looped her arm through his. 'I'm sorry to hear that, Dad. I mean it. I didn't make things easy. And you were totally right about my drinking. I turned to Ellie because she was one of the few people I knew in Scarborough. She's been a good friend... but a bad influence.'

'Have you told her that?'

'I have. She seemed pretty shocked at first, but I think it struck a chord. She's going to get help.'

'I'm glad,' said Raven. 'And are you still friends?'

'I'm not sure,' said Hannah with a half-shrug. 'We'll see. But I've got more news for you.'

Raven's heart quickened. He wondered if this was the moment she would tell him what he most feared – that she had decided to return to London.

'What is it?' he asked, doing his best to mask his anxiety but bracing himself for the worst.

'I've quit my job at the bistro – it was only ever going to be a stopgap.'

'How did Keith react?'

'He wished me well. You see, Dad, I've finally decided what I want to be. I'd like to do legal aid work, helping people who get into trouble but can't afford a solicitor. I've found a firm here in Scarborough that's willing to take me on.'

He felt a surge of relief that she wasn't planning to leave, but it was tempered by doubt at the direction she had chosen. 'I thought you'd had enough of defending criminals?'

She shook her head fiercely, a spark of passion in her eyes. 'What I hated about the internship was that I was helping rich people use the law to get them off the hook. The clients were villains, but they could afford to hire the best lawyers. I want to work for people who have no money.'

'Some of them may be villains too,' Raven cautioned.

'I know that, Dad. I may be an idealist but I'm not totally naïve. But everyone deserves a chance, don't they?'

He stared at her, full of pride and something gentler he didn't know how to name. She looked so much like her mother when she was sure of something. He reached out his arms and hugged her tighter than he had in a long time. 'They do, darling. They certainly do.'

CHAPTER 39

Jess had made up her mind at last. Deciding what to do about a guy was harder than choosing a walking route, but she couldn't carry on ducking the difficult decisions. Not if she wanted to live her life to the full.

She'd found happiness once with Scott – until it had been snatched away. But she couldn't go on running – or hiding – forever.

Scott would have understood.

The hardest step in any walk was always the first. Jess had completed many journeys in her life and knew that to hold back would be a mistake. Gavin was still virtually a stranger to her, but every relationship had to start from nothing. She already knew they had some things in common, and she could tell he was into her.

Unless she wanted to spend the rest of her life alone, she was going to have to put herself out there, make herself vulnerable and risk heartbreak again.

She picked up her phone and brought up Gavin's number. Her thumb hovered over the call button.

Sure you're okay with this, Scott?

She knew how he'd have answered if he could. He'd

have told her to go for it.

And who knew – it might be fun.

She pressed the green button and waited for the call to connect.

*

It was the day after the funeral, and Becca was determined to make the most of her last few hours of freedom before returning to work.

She made her way up the steep incline of Castlegate and followed the road as it curved left onto a street called Paradise. To Becca, this really was a kind of paradise. The view through the gap in the tall brick wall was heavenly. From here, you could see right over the rooftops of the old town and across the bay to the spa nestled on the far shore.

Today, though, a sea fret was rolling in. The Grand Hotel was little more than a ghostly silhouette. The spa buildings themselves were almost totally obliterated by the mist. But Becca knew they were there, even if she couldn't see them. Just as her grandmother lived on in her heart and mind, offering her quiet wisdom, guiding her forwards.

She walked on up Church Lane past the solid and reassuring presence of St Mary's Church. To her right lay the old graveyard on the hill. A lone figure stood there, pale and ethereal in the cold mist, beside the grave of Anne Brontë.

Yet this was no ghost.

A long, turquoise coat belted neatly at the waist hugged the woman's slim frame, a cashmere scarf wrapped around her neck for warmth. Leather gloves, immaculately fitted, matched her heeled ankle boots. Her blonde hair, glossy and carefully styled, shimmered even in the flat light.

Becca felt a flicker of recognition.

The woman turned. It was Liz Larkin.

For a moment, neither of them spoke.

Liz looked different, somehow. Diminished. 'It's Becca, isn't it?'

'Hello, Liz.' Becca walked closer, joining her at the graveside.

The original inscription on the stone was nearly worn away. A newer plaque, laid by the Brontë Society in 2011, informed visitors that Anne Brontë had died at the age of twenty-nine. A year older than Becca. Far too young to die.

'I always visit Anne when I'm in Scarborough,' said Liz, her gaze fixed on the plaque. 'I admire her, you know. She tends to be overlooked by her more famous sisters, Charlotte and Emily, but she was quite the radical in her day.'

Becca didn't know what to say. 'Yes?'

Liz half-smiled. '*The Tenant of Wildfell Hall* is a truly feminist novel – one of the first. It's about a woman who leaves her abusive husband, taking her child with her, and sets up a new life on her own. It was shocking at the time. Women weren't supposed to leave their husbands, no matter what.'

'She was brave to write that,' said Becca.

'Yes,' said Liz. 'And I've come here to say goodbye to her.'

'Goodbye?'

Liz gave her a small, wistful smile. 'I'm leaving Scarborough and starting a new job in London. I won't be back.'

'I see,' said Becca. 'Well, I hope it works out for you.'

Liz gave a soft laugh, but there was something sad in it. 'You're lucky, you know.'

'Am I?'

Liz nodded, pulling her scarf tighter around her neck. 'Raven's a great detective. And he cares for you. Very much.'

Becca's chest tightened. 'He does?'

Liz smiled. 'Even when he was with me, he talked about you. I was just a diversion for him. Don't judge him too badly for it.'

Becca swallowed. 'I don't.'

Liz nodded, seemingly satisfied. 'Well, goodbye, Becca. Take good care of him.' And with that, she turned and walked away.

Becca stayed behind, watching until Liz turned the corner, her words still lingering in the damp air.

Then she looked back at Anne Brontë's grave.

Women who had left. Women who had started over.

The wind shifted, stirring the mist, and in the distance the familiar lines and colours of the town began to emerge once more.

★

Raven's phone rang. He almost didn't answer when he saw who was calling.

DI Derek Dinsdale.

But Raven was feeling magnanimous so he took the call. 'Derek, what can I do for you?'

A pause on the other end of the line. Then Dinsdale's voice. 'You remember you owe me a favour, Raven?'

Raven gritted his teeth. It was payback time. 'Go on,' he said, feeling suddenly weary.

'Not over the phone,' said Dinsdale. 'We need to meet. I'll explain it to you then.' He named a time and place, then hung up before Raven could object.

★

Becca turned back onto Castle Terrace, her thoughts a maelstrom. Had Liz meant what she said about Raven? She'd seemed sincere.

A figure was standing on the pavement outside her flat, his back to her, hands buried deep in the pockets of his dark coat.

Becca swallowed.

Raven.

But as soon as he turned, she saw that it wasn't him.

Oh my God. Sam.

She froze, her breath caught in her throat.

He smiled as she approached. 'Hi, Becca.' Beneath the woollen hat his hair was bleached blond by the Australian sun. His skin glowed with a healthy-looking tan.

She stopped a few feet from him, struggling to find her voice. 'Sam? What are you doing here?'

He gave a gentle shrug. 'Australia was good. I travelled around and saw loads of cool things, got some perspective. It was just what I needed to get my head straight. But after a while, I realised something was missing, so I've come home. Ellie told me you were living on your own. So I dropped by to see... if you'd missed me too.'

Becca stared at him, lingering over the hollows of his cheeks, the curve of his mouth, the twinkle in his eyes. She had loved that face more than any other, planned to spend the rest of her life gazing into those kind eyes.

When Sam had first gone away, she'd been full of regret, cursing her own stupidity for staying behind. She'd messaged him daily, asking for news and photos, sending him stories from home. But his replies, eager at first, had steadily petered out. She hadn't heard from him in months.

'I did miss you,' she said. 'I missed you for a long time.'

His smile faltered. 'And now?'

Her mouth felt dry, her tongue tied. She didn't know how to answer. He had flown halfway around the globe to see her. Just a few days ago she would have jumped at the chance to be with him again. But now – after her encounter with Liz?

'It's cold,' she murmured. 'You must be freezing out here.'

He nodded. 'Scarborough's a bit nippy after Adelaide.'

'I'll put the kettle on. Would you like some tea?'

His grin returned, like the sun emerging from behind a cloud. 'If it's proper Yorkshire, yeah.'

She unlocked the door and led him inside.

She still had no idea how she felt about him – or what she was going to say.

THE RAVEN'S CALL (TOM RAVEN #10)

The final reckoning has arrived.

When a Scarborough cocktail bar owner is gunned down during a winter light show, DCI Tom Raven is drawn into a web of intimidation, vengeance, and a chilling connection to his own past.

As a vicious crime family infiltrates Scarborough's businesses, evidence begins to mount, pointing at Raven himself. Suspended from duty and hunted by his own colleagues, he is forced underground to uncover the truth.

When his daughter Hannah is dragged into danger, the emotionally charged conclusion brings Raven full circle, forcing him to face the consequences of past choices. For Raven, this final case will cost everything – his reputation, his freedom, and possibly his life.

Set on the North Yorkshire coast, the Tom Raven series is perfect for fans of LJ Ross, JD Kirk, Simon McCleave, and British crime fiction.

THANK YOU FOR READING

We hope you enjoyed this book. If you did, then we would be very grateful if you would please take a moment to leave a review online. Thank you.

TOM RAVEN SERIES

Tom Raven® is a registered trademark of Landmark Internet Ltd.
The Landscape of Death (Tom Raven #1)
Beneath Cold Earth (Tom Raven #2)
The Dying of the Year (Tom Raven #3)
Deep into that Darkness (Tom Raven #4)
Days Like Shadows Pass (Tom Raven #5)
Vigil for the Dead (Tom Raven #6)
Stained with Blood (Tom Raven #7)
The Foaming Deep (Tom Raven #8)
A Dying Echo (Tom Raven #9)
The Raven's Call (Tom Raven #10)

BRIDGET HART SERIES

Bridget Hart® is a registered trademark of Landmark Internet Ltd.
Aspire to Die (Bridget Hart #1)
Killing by Numbers (Bridget Hart #2)
Do No Evil (Bridget Hart #3)
In Love and Murder (Bridget Hart #4)
A Darkly Shining Star (Bridget Hart #5)
Preface to Murder (Bridget Hart #6)
Toll for the Dead (Bridget Hart #7)

PSYCHOLOGICAL THRILLERS

The Red Room

ABOUT THE AUTHOR

M S Morris is the pseudonym for the writing partnership of Margarita and Steve Morris. They are married and live in Oxfordshire. They have two grown-up children.

Find out more at msmorrisbooks.com where you can join our mailing list, or follow us on Facebook at facebook.com/msmorrisbooks.

Made in United States
North Haven, CT
05 July 2025